D1379936

SCRAMASAX

Children's books by the same author

FICTION

The Arthur Trilogy:
The Seeing Stone
At the Crossing-Places
King of the Middle March

The Viking Sagas:
Bracelet of Bones
Scramasax

Gatty's Tale

Short!
Short Too!

Storm

Waterslain Angels

MYTH, LEGEND AND FOLK-TALE

Tales from the Old World

The Old Stories: Folk Tales from
East Anglia and the Fen Country

The Magic Lands: Folk Tales of Britain and Ireland

Outsiders

Viking! Myths of Gods and Monsters

PICTURE BOOKS

Beowolf
(illustrated by Charles Keeping)

The Ugly Duckling
(illustrated by Meilo So)

INFORMATION

King Arthur's World

THE VIKING SAGAS

SCRAMASAX

KEVIN
CROSSLEY-HOLLAND

Quercus

First published in Great Britain in 2012 by

Quercus
55 Baker Street
7th Floor, South Block
London
W1U 8EW

Text copyright © Kevin Crossley-Holland, 2012
Map copyright © Hemesh Alles, 2012

A CIP catalogue reference for this book is available
from the British Library

ISBN 978 1 84724 940 1

1 3 5 7 9 10 8 6 4 2

Printed and bound in Great Britain by Clays Ltd, St Ives plc.

for
Geoffrey Findlay
with gratitude

The Characters

Halfdan · *a farmer from Trondheimfjord, now a Varangian guard*

Solveig · *Halfdan's daughter, aged 15*

Harald Sigurdsson · *a Viking warrior and mercenary, later King of Norway*

Snorri · *a Varangian guard and storyteller*

Skarp · *a Varangian guard*

Priskin · *a Varangian guard*

Tamas · *a Varangian guard*

Grimizo · *a Varangian guard, German*

Zoe · *Byzantine Empress*

Michael · *Byzantine Emperor*

Maria · *daughter of Theodora and niece of the Empress, aged 16*

Leo · *a Byzantine nobleman, Maria's father*

Edwin · *an English diplomat*

Edith · *an Englishwoman*

Nicolaus (Nico)	*a Byzantine helmsman*
Vibrog	*a Viking cook*
Edla	*a Viking cook*
Georgios Maniakes	*commander-in-chief of the Byzantine fleet*
Abu Touati	*a Muslim traveller living in Sicily*
Silkisiv	*a Viking camp follower (or 'lioness')*
Lady Nameless	*a Byzantine noblewoman*
Kata	*Edith's baby*

And also

Market stallholders in Miklagard
Palace courtiers
Maria's servants
Byzantine bishops
Varangian guards (including Bolverk, Egil, Gissur, Gorm, Karly, Turgeis and Ulf)
Greek cooks
Saracen pirates
Townspeople in Sicily
Sicilian mountain men, women and children
Abu Touati's companions
Lady Nameless's servants

Gods and Goddesses, Giants and Spirits
(Norse unless otherwise indicated)

Ægir	*god of the sea*
Æolus	*(Greek) king of the winds*
Aigaion	*(Greek) a sea-giant*
Allah	*(Arabic) chief Muslim name for God*
Asgard	*world of the gods and goddesses*
Eir	*goddess of healing*
Freyja	*foremost Norse fertility goddess*
Hel	*realm of the dead. Also the name of its monster-ruler, a daughter of Loki*
Midgard Serpent	*terrifying serpent who lies in the ocean and encircles Middle Earth. Also known as Jormungand*
Njord	*god of winds*
Norns	*three goddesses of destiny*
Odin	*foremost of the Norse gods. Also known as Allfather and the High One. God of poetry, battle and death*

Ran	*wife of Ægir, god of the sea. She dragged down men with her net and drowned them*
Snotra	*wise and gentle goddess, the embodiment of self-discipline*
Thor	*god of the sky and thunder, and of law and order*
Valkyries	*beautiful young women who chose dead men on the battlefield and brought them back to Odin's hall, Valhalla*
Volund	*a supernatural smith. His English name is Wayland Smith*

ICELAND

ARCTIC OCEAN

STIKLESTA

FAROE ISLANDS

Trondheim

SHETLAND

NORWAY

ORKNEY

SIGUNA

PICTLAND

BAL

DUBLIN

YORK
RICCALL

DENMARK

IRELAND

ENGLAND

POLA

NORMANDY

R. DANUBE

Atlantic Ocean

Rome

SPAIN

SICILY

CORDOBA

G R

NORTH AFRICA

BALERM

ENNA

GIRGENTI

SIRACU

SICILY

IBL

—Hemesh·Alles—

SOLVEIG in MIKLAGARD and SICILY

0   200   400   MILES
0   300   600   KILOMETRES

o Islands

Finns

Lake Ladoga

R. NEVA

o Ladoga

R. VOLKHOV

o NOVGOROD

R. VOLGA

o BULGAR

LAKE ILMEN

R. LOVAT

GARTHAR

Kiev

R. DNIEPER

Pechenegs

UNGARY

Pechenegs

CATARACTS

ST GREGORY'S ISLAND

SLAVS

Black Sea

ARMENIA

MIKLAGARD

SEA OF MARMARA

BYZANTINE

EMPIRE

Caspian Sea

TURKS

thens

Chios

CRETE

CYPRUS

o DAMASCUS

HOLY LAND

o JERUSALEM

Baghdad
o

SEA

1

The man in the scarlet cloak planted himself in the middle of the aisle. He took not the least notice of the tide of people swarming all around him.

'Solva!' he bellowed. 'Solva! Where are you?'

The big man looked over his left shoulder. Over his right, into the smoky stall of the silversmith. He screwed up his eyes and opened them wide.

'Solva! Solveig!'

In their wicker cages, the long-tailed parakeets screamed; little children clung to their mothers' grubby skirts; old men, half deaf, hunched their shoulders and waited for the ground to open under them.

Then the man growled like a wild boar at bay. He whirled round, his scarlet cloak ballooned and the porter right behind him tripped and spilt his whole basket of oranges.

The traders closed ranks. Shoulder to shoulder, they jam-packed the narrow aisle. No way forward. No way back.

'Out of the way!' the big man yelled.

'You clumsy.'

'You pay.'

'Oaf!'

'Viking.'

All around him the man heard insults he did and did

not understand. He reached inside his cloak and grasped the gilded hilt of his sabre. He drew it.

'Let me pass,' he demanded. Then he stooped and picked up an orange, tossed it into the air, and with a flick of his curved blade sliced it in half.

The waters opened. The tide of traders and towns-people made way and, ignoring all the jeering in his wake, the Viking advanced, long-legged and limping. Peering into each of the stalls. Now and then he stopped and anxiously called, 'Solveig! Solveig!' Now and then he muttered, 'Enemies . . . enemies. You never know where enemies may be lurking.'

At the end of the aisle, the Viking glanced over his shoulder again, and then sheathed his sabre. And when he turned back, there she was! There was Solveig, steadfast, smiling, as if she had simply been waiting for him.

Solveig clicked her tongue, and around her there was a certain lightness and brightness.

'There you are!' she exclaimed.

'Where have you been?'

'I was just a few steps ahead of you.' Solveig opened her eyes wide, reached out and affectionately laid her right hand on her father's brow. She looked as if a pat of her cow Gerda's softest butter wouldn't have melted in her mouth. 'I'm all right.'

'You've no idea,' Halfdan told her. 'None. It's not enough to be sun-strong.'

'I am! That's what you named me.'

'I know that. But that's not enough, not here. You've been in Miklagard for less than a day. And the more days you're here, the more you'll understand. There's only one wolf chasing the sun, but in this market there are a thousand wolves, ready to chase a golden girl.'

Halfdan looked around him, and although they couldn't understand a word he was saying, at least a dozen dark-skinned young men nodded. Their white teeth flashed.

'I've heard of more than one young woman,' Halfdan told her, 'who entered this market and was never seen again.'

Solveig reached up and smoothed away her father's frown with her pink fingertips.

'Father,' she said gently, 'Father, the daughter standing in front of you now isn't the same child you left behind in Norway.'

Halfdan pursed his mouth at his daughter's words – not defiant, scarcely reproachful, so self-knowing.

'She isn't,' said Halfdan, 'but she is. I thought I'd lost you.'

'You never did lose me,' Solveig replied. 'I lost you and had to find you.'

Halfdan shook his head. 'The length of the grim Baltic,' he began, 'and Ladoga, Novgorod, the great rivers, the forests, the cataracts . . .'

'I haven't begun to tell you,' said Solveig, smiling.

'I want to know,' said Halfdan. 'My eyes can see you, my ears can hear you, but I scarcely believe you're here.'

'I am!' cried Solveig. 'Father, I am!'

Halfdan wrapped Solveig in his scarlet cloak. 'You're more at risk than you know,' he told her. 'Solva, to be wise is to be wary, to listen and learn, always to know how much you do not know.'

'This market is even bigger than the ones in Ladoga and Kiev,' Solveig said, 'so I did expect to get lost in it. But remember what you used to tell me. You have to get lost . . .'

'To be found,' her father said.

'To find yourself,' Solveig corrected him.

Then Halfdan turned round again, rather more circumspectly than before, and began to retrace his steps.

'I've seen this aisle already,' Solveig objected. 'Let's go down another one.' She tucked her hand through her father's right arm, but he resisted.

'A debt,' he said. 'I've got to settle a debt.'

When the angry stallholders saw the Viking limping towards them again, and the pretty young woman on his arm, they blocked the aisle.

Halfdan nodded and smiled, and when Solveig let go of his arm he spread both hands in a gesture of peace.

'Just a mistake,' he told the traders. 'I was clumsy.' He shook his head and nodded at his daughter. 'I thought I'd lost her.'

The man who had been carrying the basket of oranges threw one in the air and swiped at it with the blade of his hand.

'Just a joke,' said the Viking.

The stallholder spat into the dust right in front of Halfdan.

The Viking grimaced. He reached into an inner pocket and fished out a small silver coin and gave it to the stallholder.

'I sent him flying,' Halfdan told his daughter. 'Him and his oranges. You know me.'

'A clumsy great frost-giant,' Solveig said. 'I saw fruit like this on Saint Gregorios. A whole army of them bobbing in the harbour.'

Seeing Solveig's interest, the stallholder smiled and bowed and offered her a plump orange.

Solveig hesitated.

'Take it,' her father told her. 'What is freely offered is often best accepted.'

So Solveig took the orange. She thanked the

stallholder, and then felt his fingertips just brush the inside of her wrist. She lowered her eyes.

'Come on now,' said Halfdan. And as he and Solveig continued down the aisle, 'They're tricksters and charlatans, the lot of them. But Varangian guards don't get paid for stirring it. We're here to keep the peace.'

'And to guard Empress Zoe,' Solveig said.

'And Emperor Michael,' added her father in a dry voice. 'We mustn't forget him.'

'Boy-man,' said Solveig. 'That's what Mihran called him.'

'Shhh! Walls have ears. Even aisles can have ears.'

'And Harald's your leader?'

'He is,' said Halfdan. 'The gods be praised.'

'Man-man!' Solveig told him. 'That's what Mihran calls him.'

'Three hundred of us,' her father declared. 'Three hundred Vikings. The Varangians of the City. We garrison the city.'

'Garrison?' enquired Solveig.

'We guard the place and keep peace in Miklagard. And there are lots more of us Vikings, as many as five thousand, in the field.'

'What field?'

Halfdan spread his arms. 'All over the empire. The Byzantine Empire and west across the Great Sea. We have to protect the far borders. They're like old sleeves, always unravelling. Always needing to be sewn up.'

Solveig tugged at her father's left arm, and then she made claws of her fingers and screwed up her face like a savage troll.

'What?' Halfdan demanded.

'Is she . . . like they say she is?'

'I've warned you already,' growled her father. 'People

5

with secrets do well to sit behind closed doors, and speak in low voices.'

'You and your sayings,' said Solveig. Then she tugged at her father's arm again. 'Look! Those little plums.'

'Dates. Very sweet. This market is the largest on middle-earth. It's where all the empire's nations meet every other nation. Their products, their coinage, their language, their stories and sayings, their habits, their wit, their gods, their beliefs – they all meet here. Bulgarians and Slavs and Armenians and Arabs and Georgians and Serbians and Jews and—'

'Actually,' said Solveig, 'Red Ottar's boat was a kind of meeting place. We were Norwegians and Swedes, with one Icelander. Us and Edith too – she's English. Then Edwin came aboard – you met him.'

'Yes,' said Halfdan thoughtfully.

'And so did a Slav – he got an arrow through his left foot – and Mihran, our pilot, he's Armenian.'

'So what message was Edwin bringing to Empress Zoe?' Halfdan asked his daughter.

Solveig shook her head. 'He's very good at not saying.'

'Wordsmiths,' said Halfdan with no great liking. 'So, what about your carving?'

'I'll tell you about that,' Solveig replied. 'But first . . .'

Solveig and her father had walked right out of the market on to the Varangian quay reserved for foreign and other trading boats. White-tailed gulls swept around them in the warm south-west wind, mewing and shrieking. And there, right below them, like a shrimp among dolphins and water-dragons, was the tiny dugout in which Solveig had sailed all the way from Saint Gregorios to Miklagard with her companions.

For a moment the two of them stood there, looking down. Then Solveig slid over the edge into the boat and looked up at her father, smiling.

'What do you think?' she asked, smiling and bursting with pride.

'In this?'

'Yes!'

'This piddler! This piece of driftwood!'

Solveig nodded eagerly.

'Where from?'

'Saint Gregorios. You know, just before the River Dnieper flows into the Black Sea.'

'And you? You left home without telling Asta or the boys?'

'Father, I'll tell you everything!' Solveig cried. 'My journey, my carving, the shaman, the angel.'

'What angel?'

Standing there in the hot sunlight, Solveig shuddered. 'Everything. When there's time, I will. Then you'll understand.'

'Fathers sometimes admire their daughters, sometimes shake their heads, sometimes punish them,' Halfdan said, 'but I'm not sure they ever really understand.'

Solveig reached up with her right hand. 'Something's worrying you,' she said. 'Come down.'

Halfdan squatted on the quay, lifted himself on his hands and levered himself down.

'Four of us,' Solveig told him. 'Me and Mihran and Edwin and Edith. Well, five if you count her baby.'

'Much smaller than our coble,' said Halfdan, running a hand along the gunwale. 'And nothing like as well made. Just hacked out of a tree trunk.'

Solveig gazed at her father. 'In this boat . . .' she began. 'Oh! I can't explain. I felt so brave and so afraid, I laughed and cried, I thought my companions were my own lifeblood and yet I felt so lonely.'

Up on the quay traders shouted and dogs yelped and little children wailed, around them wavelets sucked and slapped, and the wind went on warbling. For a moment Solveig closed her eyes and they all sounded as if they came from miles and even years away.

'Sit down,' she told her father.

Then she swung her bag off her right shoulder and dropped it into the bottom of the dugout. She unloosed the tie and thrust her right hand down through a stew of bones, implements, filthy clothing, bits of rag, her rolled-up cloak, and closed her fingers round it.

'What is it?' asked Halfdan.

Solveig unfolded and opened a wad of grubby bog cotton. And there, shining in the sunlight of the Golden Horn, lay the glorious gold brooch Harald Sigurdsson had given to Halfdan more than five years before – the token of his lifelong friendship, the heirloom Halfdan had hidden inside Solveig's woollen pillow-sack before he left their farm.

Halfdan stared at the brooch: the little boat incised on it, with its single square sail hoisted, the two people sitting in it.

'I've looked at it and looked at it,' Solveig told him in a quiet voice, 'and I've wondered. The one in the bows, he's a man. A man or a god. But the one in the stern's smaller. Arms outstretched. Am I that one? Did you want me to follow you? Or did you . . . did you give it to me because . . .'

Halfdan didn't answer her. Not exactly. Not, anyhow, as Solveig really wanted.

He picked up the brooch between his thick fingers. He turned it over and stared at the runes scratched on the back of it.

'ᚻᛋ and ᚻᚠ' he pronounced. 'Harald Sigurdsson and Halfdan son of Asser. Harald cut these.'

'You told me.'

'I never thought I'd see this again.'

'Why not?' demanded Solveig.

'I mean . . .'

'Did you think I'd sell it?' Roses flared in Solveig's cheeks. 'Is that what you thought?'

Halfdan quietly shook his head and sighed. 'No, no.'

'You did.'

'Solveig,' said her father, 'I gave you my word that I would take you with me, but even as I did so, I felt the fates were turning against me.'

'I could see it in your eyes. Your heart and your eyes disagreed.'

'Sometimes people know things about us that we scarcely know ourselves,' Halfdan said.

'Especially daughters,' Solveig replied.

Halfdan replaced the brooch on the wad of bog cotton and closed his daughter's fingers around it. 'Keep it,' he said.

'No.'

'For the time being.'

'Why?'

Halfdan didn't reply.

'I don't understand,' Solveig said, frowning.

'It's better that way,' Halfdan told her. He drew her to him. 'We're in the same boat.'

So Solveig carefully wrapped the brooch again and pushed it down to the bottom of her heavy bag. She looked up at her father.

'Battle-ghosts,' she said. 'Life-songs.'

'What do you mean?'

'Father! There's so much to ask, so much to tell you. It will be Ragnarok before we've finished.'

Halfdan smiled. 'First,' he said, 'we must go back to our quarters. Harald will be off duty at noon.'

'Harald!' exclaimed Solveig. And then she stood up in

the dugout. 'Harald!' she bawled. Like a battle-cry.

'What are we going to do with you?' her father asked her. 'A young woman? A young Viking woman, here alone in Miklagard. Solva, my Solva! The question is whether you can stay here at all.'

2

Solveig could hear him braying.

She quickened her step down the long, candlelit corridor, and it was all that limping Halfdan could do to keep up with her.

When they reached the massive oak door, Solveig glanced over her shoulder. Halfdan drew his sabre. He rapped three times with his pommel, then swung the door open and stepped in. Solveig followed him.

The hall was spacious and airy, lit half by daylight flooding down from a cupola, half by its own inner lights: thousands of little pieces of glittering and shining gold mosaic covering the walls.

On the far side, Solveig saw three men, and the one wearing an ivory gown with a gold torque around his neck was a head taller than either of his companions.

'Harald!' she cried.

In her delight Solveig strode towards Harald Sigurdsson, arms outstretched, and only when she stood before him did she remember who he was and the respect due to him. She stopped and inclined her head.

'Look at me,' Harald boomed.

Solveig looked. She saw Harald's pale blue eyes, full of light and laughter. She saw his ropes of tousled straw-coloured hair, his long sideburns, and his bushy, thrusting moustache, gold and red-gold, and the way his left eyebrow was higher than the right.

Harald Sigurdsson stooped a little and took Solveig's hands between his own.

'Sister!' he declared. 'Almost-sister!'

And what he saw was not only the young woman stubborn enough to find her way from Trondheim to Miklagard but the ten-year-old girl with whom he had overwintered more than five years before.

'I recognised you,' Solveig told him.

'I should think so.'

Solveig shook her head. 'I mean, when I saw you yesterday. I was searching for my father, and the guards directed me—'

'My guards,' Harald corrected her.

'. . . your guards directed me up to the gallery.'

'Yes, and that fool of a baggy-trousered Bulgar challenged you. But yesterday you were bowed down by your sack. You were ragged and filthy and, frankly, stinking. Now, though . . .'

'Yes?' Solveig dared him, with a roguish smile.

But instead of replying, Harald took Solveig's and everyone else's breath away. He grasped her just above her hips, squeezed the bottom of her narrow rib-cage, and swept her off her feet. He held her at arm's length and whirled her round and round, round and round until her shift spread out behind her and she was flying.

When Harald set her down, Solveig reeled away, gasping. She put her hands to her eyes.

'Remember?' Harald demanded.

Solveig peeked at him through her splayed fingers. 'Oh! I'm seeing two of you. You did that on the last night before you left.'

'Very good,' said Harald.

'You were still wearing that strap,' Halfdan reminded him, 'to hold in your guts.'

12

'You swung me round until I was giddy, and do you know what you said?'

'What?'

'"Your father,"' Solveig told Harald, '"your hamstrung father, he's still worth double any other man."'

Harald Sigurdsson winked at Halfdan. 'I must have been ale-drunk,' he said.

'What I remember you saying,' Halfdan added, 'is that you might sail south to Miklagard, and join the Varangian guard. "But be sure of one thing, Halfdan," you told me, "I'll send for you. Yes, when the time's right, I'll send for you."'

'"And I will come,"' Harald Sigurdsson told Halfdan. 'That's what you replied.'

Halfdan nodded. He clamped his teeth together and avoided Solveig's eye.

'Well, now,' said Harald. He gazed thoughtfully at Solveig. 'I know a charm to blunt my enemy's blade. I know how to catch an arrow in flight between my hands.'

'But,' said Solveig helpfully.

'Exactly. What are we to do with you?' Harald Sigurdsson turned to his companions. 'Well, Snorri?'

Snorri was a quite small, stocky man. And he often kept people waiting for a reply. 'I know of no poem or story,' he said at length, 'not a single line about an army with a woman in it.'

'What about the Amazons?' Solveig demanded.

'Who?' asked her father.

'The Amazons. Mihran told me about them.'

'That's different,' said Snorri, and he shook his head and screwed up his face. 'A whole army of single-breasted women.'

'Yuch!' exclaimed another guard, whose name was Skarp. 'Unnatural!'

'Not a word about an army of men with a woman in it,' Snorri repeated.

'You can't trust them,' Skarp said. 'Always flying into a rage. Their hearts get in the way of their heads.'

Solveig said nothing. She just waited, but Halfdan could tell she was anxious because she kept twisting her left heel, as she'd always done since she was a little girl.

'Anyhow,' Skarp added, 'this one, she's more like a willow branch than a woman.'

Harald sniffed loudly. 'So, Solveig, you've heard what my polite companions have to say. The truth is, it would have been very much better if you hadn't come to Miklagard.'

Solveig looked Harald straight in the eye. But she felt as if her limbs were turning into cold stone.

'I'm sure your father has told you that. Better for us. Better for you.'

'No,' she replied in a quiet, flat voice.

'Understand me,' Harald went on. 'You have the heart of a bear. You've made a long and dangerous journey and no one can do that without purpose of mind and stamina, as well as good fortune. I well know it. But now you're here, what are we to do with you?'

'Sidles of snakes!' hissed Skarp. 'Twists of elvers!'

Harald frowned. 'Dear God!' he exclaimed. 'You do have a poor opinion of women.'

'And of men,' Snorri added. 'The only person good enough for Skarp is Skarp.'

'This is the problem,' Harald told Solveig. 'How are you to stay here in Miklagard safely? I know what you're thinking. But my guards have work to do, here and in the field. And anyhow –' he winked at Solveig – 'I mustn't expose my handsome young guards to you, must I?'

Solveig lowered her eyes.

'Well, Halfdan?' demanded Harald.

'I can become a guard,' said Solveig in a quiet voice. 'I can.'

Snorri and Skarp both guffawed.

'That you cannot,' said Harald in an icy voice.

'I can learn.'

'You cannot become a guard,' Harald told her. 'A woman is a woman. A man is a man.'

'Except for the eunuchs,' Skarp added.

'True enough,' Snorri agreed. 'They're women-men.'

Harald sighed. 'As I see it,' he said, 'these are your choices: you can marry a Byzantine lord—'

'Never,' said Halfdan gruffly.

'No,' said Harald slowly. 'Or you can become one of the boy-man's concubines.'

'What's that?' asked Solveig.

'Mistresses.'

'Out of the question!' exclaimed Halfdan angrily. 'As you well know, Harald.'

'Your third choice,' continued Harald in a calculating voice, 'is to become a novice.'

'A what?'

'A novice in a monastery. A young nun.'

'No! I can't. I'm not a Christian.'

'No,' said Harald. 'Not a guard. Not a wife. Not a concubine. Not a novice. And so I say again: what are we to do with you, here and now? And when we go away?'

'Away?' cried Solveig.

Now it was plain to all of them how anxious Solveig was. She tossed her long fair hair and stamped her right foot like a colt, and then she almost moaned.

'Away,' Harald repeated very deliberately.

'Where?'

'Sicily.'

'What's that?'

'An island. An island rife with Arabs and enemies of the Empress.'

Solveig rounded on her father. 'You're not going?' she exclaimed. 'Are you going too?'

Halfdan stared at her, and he looked quite stricken.

'You are! How long for?'

Halfdan shook his head.

'A year,' replied Harald. 'I don't know. Maybe longer. Until we've cleaned the place up.'

'When?' demanded Solveig. 'When are you going?'

Solveig cried out. In her desperation, she reached up above her head and smacked her hands.

The hall heard her. It echoed her. Her cry and her hand-clap. Then, without warning, a piece of the high cornice – a lump of plaster as big as a human head – fell from the ceiling. It smashed on to the marble floor beside them. A thousand shards and splinters skidded across the shining tiles.

For a moment no one said anything.

Harald sucked his cheeks and glared at the cornice accusingly.

'It's an omen,' Snorri said. 'A sign of some kind.'

Solveig turned to her father. 'You're not,' she said, and her voice broke. 'You're not leaving me again.' Several times she swallowed. And then, in a low voice, 'I summoned all my strength to find you. For month after month I've crossed the mountains and sailed the seas and followed the rivers to find you. To be with you.'

For a while no one said a word.

Harald Sigurdsson sat down in the massive dark chair, the only chair in the room. Snorri and Skarp made their way to the centre of the hall, now and then glancing suspiciously at the ceiling, the cornices, and her father slowly padded along the length of the room.

'So, fair one!' Harald called across to Solveig. 'Come over here.'

As Solveig walked up to him, she saw that even when he was sitting down Harald was almost as tall as his companions.

'What's the real reason?' Harald asked her. 'Why have you made this journey to Miklagard?'

'I asked myself that many times on my way here.'

'What was your answer?'

'When my father left home, he took away my grounding. I didn't belong any more. Not to my stepmother, my stepbrothers, not even to the fjord and the mountains. My home was no longer my home.'

'Go on,' said Harald.

'Then I began to imagine my father's journey, and the more I imagined it, the more I wanted to follow him. I grew curious. Out-eager!'

'That's how we Norwegians are,' declared Harald. 'Out-eager.'

'We want to find out,' Solveig agreed.

'Not like your two brothers, then,' remarked Harald. 'Two lumps, if I remember them rightly.'

'Blubba's all right,' said Solveig.

'It's better to live, isn't it?' Harald demanded. He opened his arms wide and looked round at Snorri and Skarp. 'Better to live than lie at home, stiff as a corpse. Well, Solveig, your answers are good ones. Very good. You're your father's daughter.' Harald turned to Halfdan and nodded.

'I know,' said Halfdan, and he sighed.

'Don't be so rueful, man. Problems need answers. And there's no problem that doesn't have an answer.'

'If you let me come with you,' Solveig said, 'you'll be glad of it.'

Harald Sigurdsson shook his head. 'What are we

going to do with you? Here and now, today?'

'Tomorrow,' Snorri declared, 'today is yesterday.'

'What kind of consolation is that?' Harald barked.

'Piss!' exclaimed Skarp. 'The piss of giantesses.'

'No,' said Snorri, unperturbed, 'that's what comes out of your mouth, Skarp.'

'Get things wrong today and we wreck tomorrow,' Harald continued. 'I know that. Well, I do have one idea.'

Solveig looked at Harald with a mixture of trepidation and longing.

'Our beloved Empress,' Harald explained, 'has a sister. Theodora. These two women hate each other.'

'Why?' asked Solveig.

Harald held up his right hand. 'I'll do the talking. All you need to know for now is that Empress Zoe has exiled Theodora to a nunnery . . .'

'I don't want to be a nun,' Solveig said fiercely.

'. . . a nunnery,' Harald continued, 'but she allows Maria, Theodora's daughter, to live here in the palace.'

Halfdan gave his friend a thoughtful look and narrowed his eyes.

'Maria,' said Harald with a half-smile. He paused, and pushed himself against the back of the oak chair. 'She's as sallow-skinned as you're fair. As plump as you are willowy. Your eyes are grey and violet, hers are cinnamon.' Harald gave a rather mirthless laugh, remembering something.

'How old is she?' asked Solveig.

'One year older than you. Sixteen.'

'Can she speak Norwegian?'

'As a matter of fact, she can,' Harald said. 'As much as she needs to.'

'Harald taught her,' Snorri told Solveig.

'And that's not all he taught her,' added Skarp.

'What about her father?' Solveig asked. 'Where's he?'

18

Harald rubbed his beard. 'A nobleman,' he said. 'A dying man.'

'Solveig,' her father warned her, 'Miklagard's full of shadows, whispers, rumours, things better not known.'

'Maria lives in spacious quarters,' Harald continued. 'She has her own courtyard with several rooms around it, and a fleet of servants. Now, I think I may be able to prevail on the Empress—'

'Prevail on the Empress!' jeered Skarp. 'All Empress Zoe wants is to prevail on Harald Sigurdsson. Isn't that right, Harald?'

'Why do I put up with you?' Harald snapped.

'And take him to bed with her,' the guard added.

'Skarp!' said Harald very sharply.

'Each of us needs someone to tell us the truth,' Skarp retorted.

Harald turned back to Solveig and her father. 'You're only the daughter of one of my guards,' he said, 'but the Empress might be prepared to allow you a room next to Maria's quarters.'

'You could persuade her of anything, you could,' said Skarp. 'Though if she ever saw you with Maria, your hungry eyes . . .'

Harald Sigurdsson stood up.

'. . . she'd have you blinded.'

Harald took a swipe at Skarp with his open hand and Skarp wasn't quick enough to avoid it. It stung his left cheek.

'What do you say, Halfdan?' Harald asked.

'Solveig would be safe inside this palace,' her father replied. 'And she'd have company.'

'Maria would welcome that too,' Harald agreed. 'She's a prisoner. This court, it's full of *cans* and *can'ts* and manners and modes and bowing and scraping.'

'Mmm!' agreed Snorri. He looked at Solveig and his

eyes glimmered. 'It's blazing gold, and hellish black. You'll see.'

'Yes,' said Harald thoughtfully. 'The Empress will want to . . . appraise you. Before she decides.'

Solveig shivered. 'If you let me come with you,' she repeated, 'you'll be glad of it. I'll make myself useful.'

Harald Sigurdsson ignored her. 'I have an audience with the Empress late this afternoon, and I'll discuss this with her then. Yes, she'll want to see you. A young woman who has travelled here, from Norway, alone.'

'And unscathed,' said Halfdan. 'King Yaroslav gave Solveig an audience.'

'He did?' exclaimed Harald. 'I want to hear about that.'

Solveig shook her head. 'I belong on a farm,' she said, 'or a boat. I don't belong here.'

'Nothing lasts for ever,' her father told her.

'In the fields . . .'

'Solveig!' Harald warned her in a stern voice.

All at once, Solveig could see herself sitting in the little dairy, milking their two cows. She could hear her stepbrothers chopping wood outside. She could even smell the thick, pasty, comfortable odour of new dung.

Solveig pressed her left hand against her palpitating heart and gave a single, dry sob.

3

'What is it?' exclaimed Solveig.

She trailed her pink fingers along the flat marble rim. She stared at the steeple of water rising from the brimming basin, four feet, five feet, almost as tall as she was, rising and falling back, plashing and bubbling.

'A fountain,' Snorri told her.

Solveig's face shone. 'I've never seen one before. Not indoors. Does a spring rise right under this hall, then?'

Snorri closed his eyes, as if he'd never met anyone who knew so little. 'Of course not. The builder used machines. A contraption.'

'How?'

'At great expense, I'd say. Our Empress has more wealth than she knows what to do with.'

'It looks like a water-tree,' Solveig said, 'and it sounds like a water-harp.'

'I'm the wordsmith,' said Snorri. 'Near our farm . . .'

'Where?'

'In Iceland.'

'You come from Iceland?'

'I just said so. Near our farm, there's a boiling fountain as high as the dome of Hagia Sophia. Well, half as high. A geyser, we call it.'

'Geyser. Is that made with machines and contraptions too?'

21

Snorri gave a scornful laugh. 'It's a wonder that was made when the nine worlds were made. Like the bluestone mountains that divide us from the world of the giants. Like the flaming rainbow bridge between middle-earth and the world of the gods.'

'I wish I could see it,' Solveig said.

'Maybe you will, girl.' Snorri dug into a pocket and pulled out a coin. 'Here! Throw this into the water and make that wish.'

'What? Throw away a coin?'

'Much that happens begins with a wish,' Snorri told her, 'and this is a wishing fountain. If you throw a coin into it, it will help your wish to come true.'

Solveig tossed the coin into the dancing water, then she dipped in her hands, and for a moment they looked as though they had been severed at the wrists and were floating free. Solveig wriggled her fingers.

'It's strange,' she said, 'when you know things are not as they look.'

'Like everything in this Christian . . . this godforsaken court,' Snorri replied. 'Ugh!' The guard sucked his cheeks, and then spat into the fountain.

As if to prove the truth of Snorri's words, the heavy door between them and an inner hall was thrown open so violently that it thudded against the marble wall.

Three men burst into the room, dragging a fourth behind them. This wretch was bound in chains, but that didn't stop him from kicking his captors, headbutting them and howling.

Solveig backed away from the coping of the fountain.

Then the poor man snarled. He thrust his neck forward and seized the thumb of one of his captors between his teeth.

'Vermin!' yelled one of the guards.

And that was all Solveig and Snorri saw before the

22

three men manhandled the wretch through the other door.

Solveig looked wildly at Snorri. 'Who were they?'

'How should I know?'

'What had he done?' she demanded, and her breath was jerky.

Snorri shook his head. 'The names of this palace are Rumour and Fear and Suspicion. You don't have to do anything to be punished. It's enough for someone to point a finger.'

'But that's wrong,' Solveig protested. 'It's rough justice.'

'It's not justice at all,' Snorri said.

'What will they do to him?'

Snorri gave her a stony look.

'I've seen worse than you know.'

'If they don't behead him, they'll dig a hole and put him in it, right up to his neck, and then they'll stone him. If they don't stone him, they'll strangle him.'

Solveig lifted her hands to her pretty neck.

'Or else they'll blind him, or else . . . the shears.'

'What?'

'They'll cut out his tongue.'

Solveig screwed up her face.

Snorri nodded. 'The Empress and the Emperor, they hold court and they're the judges.'

'I've heard terrible things about her,' confided Solveig in a low voice. 'Edwin told me. The Englishman.'

'You, Solveig,' said Snorri with a reassuring smile, 'you're Harald Sigurdsson's almost-sister. Your father is a Varangian guard. You have nothing to fear.'

And yet I am afraid, thought Solveig. I never felt like this in the seven cataracts. No, not when I came between Edith and the Angel of Death. Not on my whole journey.

A young boy appeared at the door. He was wearing crocus yellow, baggy silk trousers.

He gave a little squeak, like someone learning to play a reed-pipe, and beckoned them. Then he turned on his heel, and Solveig and Snorri followed him through three connected halls.

'When the Empress receives us,' Snorri instructed Solveig, 'keep a careful eye on me. Do what I do.'

I did meet King Yaroslav, Solveig told herself. I did. I should be all right.

'Flattery,' Snorri said. 'That's what they want. They gorge themselves on it.' He pulled up his hood.

'What are you doing?'

'What does it look like? Come on, pull yours up too. No man and no woman is allowed to be bareheaded before the Empress and the Emperor.'

The pageboy led the two Vikings into an enormous golden hall, full of echoes, whispers, little knots of people.

Solveig looked all around her, and up at the high arched roof, and back over her shoulders. Then, right ahead of her, she saw something astonishing.

An almost bald elderly woman and a young man were sitting side by side in two high-backed seats on a stone dais. And as Solveig approached them, their seats very slowly began to ascend. On stout marble columns they rose until they were twice as high as the steepling fountain, well above Solveig's head.

Snorri got down on to his knees, and folded into himself.

Solveig did likewise.

Then Snorri pressed his forehead against the cold marble floor, and Solveig copied him.

'Long lives to our Empress and our Emperor,' Snorri called out. 'May God multiply your years.'

24

'Long lives to our Empress and our Emperor,' repeated Solveig. 'May God multiply your years.'

But the Empress is an old woman, she thought. How old did Edwin say she was? Fifty-four! She's got one foot in the grave. So what kind of prayer is that? She doesn't want to live for hundreds of years.

'Stand up!' said Snorri under his breath. 'Do as I do.'

Solveig scrambled to her feet. She stood with her head bowed.

'Girl,' intoned the Empress, 'you may look at me.'

Solveig looked. Empress Zoe was swaddled and swathed in purple silk, up to her neck and down to her heels, and Solveig found it impossible to tell how tall she was, and whether she was fleshy or frail. But she could see her face was rather grey and unpleasantly wrinkled. Her eyes, though: they were dark, dangerous, not to be deceived.

Black, thought Solveig. Black yet burning.

She was aware of the boy-man sitting beside Empress Zoe, and she wanted to look at him too. But it was as if the Empress had Solveig under a spell, and she could do nothing but return her gaze.

'Girl,' she said loftily, and in Norwegian, 'Solveig. That's your name.'

Solveig was taken aback by how mild her voice was. Not at all like the Angel of Death, she thought.

'Well, is it or isn't it?' asked Empress Zoe.

'Oh!' said Solveig. 'Empress, Holy Mother—'

'What did you call me?'

'Holy Mother!'

Empress Zoe gave a chilly little laugh. 'Holy Mother!' she repeated. Then she looked down her nose at Solveig. 'Whatever I am, I'm not the Virgin Mary,' she said. 'Holy Mother!'

'Forgive her, Empress,' interrupted Snorri.

Empress Zoe raised her right hand a little, and Solveig saw at once that her fingers were clenched and misshapen.

'Before I see you again,' she told Solveig, 'have Harald Sigurdsson instruct you on how to address me.'

Solveig swallowed loudly.

'For now, call me Princess . . . Princess of Peace.'

'Princess of Peace,' repeated Solveig.

Kneeling beside her, Snorri didn't make a sound. But Solveig could tell it was all he could do to stop himself from snorting.

'Solveig,' resumed the Empress, 'Sun-Strong. You're lucky to be alive.'

Solveig bowed her head.

'Look at me, girl! Where you come from, many a baby girl is left out on the ice. Until her blood curdles and freezes. Until the wolves get her. Isn't that right?'

Solveig nodded. 'Princess,' she whispered.

'Of Peace,' the Empress corrected her, slowly and precisely. 'Yes. Savages, that's what you Vikings are. Savages! We're Christians here. We don't murder little girls.' The Empress paused. 'And after your mother died . . .'

Solveig drew in her breath sharply.

'. . . after she died, didn't your grandmother counsel your father to leave you out on the ice? Didn't she, Solveig? Didn't she say that if he kept you, the day would come when you failed him?'

Solveig began to tremble. She tucked her head on to her chest.

'How do I know such things?' the Empress asked. 'That's what you're thinking.' She leaned forward a little. 'My business is to know. The business of my guards is to tell me. Everything.'

Solveig sniffed.

'And those who don't . . . That man! You saw him?'

'Yes,' whispered Solveig.

'He didn't tell me,' the Empress said, and now her voice was much more clipped. 'He chose to bite on his tongue. So I decided he had no further need of it.'

Solveig shuddered. Her voice. How can I have thought it was mild or gentle? It's bitter. Ferocious.

'Now then,' continued Empress Zoe, 'when you were in Kiev, King Yaroslav granted you an audience?'

'Yes,' replied Solveig. 'Princess.'

'Of Peace.'

'Of Peace.'

'So Edwin told me. And what did the King of the Rus say to you?'

'He said . . . he knew my father had saved Harald Sigurdsson's life.'

'Of course he did! Why else would he have granted you an audience?'

'Loyal and honourable. That's what the king called him.'

'What else?'

'He told me he'd given my father a sabre made by one of his own smiths.'

'Yes,' said the Empress. 'I allow your father to wear it. What else?'

'He warned Red Ottar – he was our skipper – that the Pechenegs were massing on the banks of the Dnieper, north of the Snake Ramparts. He said he'd have to fight the greatest battle in the eighteen years he had sat on the throne.'

Empress Zoe and Emperor Michael were both listening intently.

'King Yaroslav told Red Ottar he needed to send a messenger to Miklagard as a matter of urgency.'

'To Miklagard?' the Empress repeated.

27

'Yes.'

'Not to me?'

'To you, yes. That's what he meant. He praised you, Princess. Princess of Peace.'

'He did, did he?' said the Empress in an expressionless voice.

'And then he gave us cranberry juice. It tasted so sour.'

'Solveig,' said Empress Zoe, 'can you remember King Yaroslav's exact words? About the messenger?'

Solveig frowned. '"I'm asking you to carry my messenger to Miklagard as quickly as you can." I think that's what he said. "For me – my family, my followers, my kingdom – I believe it's now or never."'

Empress Zoe nodded. 'You heard that?' she asked.

'I did,' said the Emperor Michael, and at last Solveig allowed herself to look at him. He was tall, though not as tall as her father, let alone Harald, and he had short, prickly black hair. So far as she could see, his eyes were dark and he was just starting to grow a moustache and beard.

'The Englishman Edwin, he was King Yaroslav's messenger,' Solveig volunteered.

'I'm aware of that,' replied the Empress.

'And he told me he was coming to see you,' Solveig added, sounding puzzled.

Empress Zoe waved a hand and a servant stepped forward carrying a tray with a jug and two small glasses on it.

'Sour, was it?' said the Empress. 'The cranberry juice. Try this wine instead.'

It did just cross Solveig's mind that the Empress might be giving her poison but, following Snorri's example, she took a glass and tossed it back.

Solveig coughed and the Empress pursed her cracked lips into a kind of smile.

'Well?' she asked.

'Fire,' croaked Solveig. 'And . . . I don't know.' She coughed again. 'Resin, I think. Pine resin.'

Empress Zoe nodded. 'It is.'

'Something dark too. Like pitch for caulking boats.'

The Empress lost interest in Solveig's attempts to describe the wine.

It's disgusting, thought Solveig. Worse than bilge water. But I'd better drink it anyhow.

Emperor Michael caught Solveig's eye, and she could see he was grinning. Then he threw back his head and laughed out loud.

'Well, now,' said the Empress. 'Harald Sigurdsson's request.' She pinched her nose. And then with both hands she smoothed back her wrinkles. 'You're . . . what are you? A farmer's daughter. The daughter of one of my guards. Still! You've found your way alone across half the world . . .' The Empress hesitated, as if she were still making up her mind.

'Not alone,' said Solveig, 'Princess of Peace.'

Empress Zoe raised her right hand to silence Solveig. 'I summoned you here without your father because I didn't want him to speak for you, as fathers often do. I didn't want you to hide behind him. I wanted to see you for who you are.'

Solveig gazed up at the Empress, unblinking.

'You've got your wits about you,' Empress Zoe continued. 'You've got a tongue! Yes . . . yes. I require much of Harald, and expect more. I see no reason not to grant his request.'

Solveig frowned.

'I mean, girl, that I grant you rooms here in this palace. The servants who wait on my niece, Maria, can wait on you too.'

'Thank her,' whispered Snorri out of the corner of his mouth. 'Praise her.'

'Princess of Peace,' Solveig began in a measured voice, 'I'm most grateful to you. I won't stay long.'

Empress Zoe arched one plucked eyebrow. 'Evidently,' she replied, 'you know more than I do.'

'I mean, I'm resolved to sail with my father to Sicily.'

'Pff!' spat the Empress.

'I must.'

'Must? Must? No one speaks to me like that.'

Solveig lowered her eyes.

'Secure your hood!'

Solveig pulled her hood forward and downward.

'Sail to Sicily?' hissed Empress Zoe. 'Certainly not. It's out of the question. I shall tell Harald so.'

'But . . .'

'Girl,' said the Empress, 'I'm aware you've travelled here because of your father, and you're stubborn as a mule, I can see that.'

'How long?' asked Solveig. 'I mean . . . when will . . . ?'

'How should I know? One year. Two. But in the meantime Maria will teach you court manners. And no doubt she'll tell you all about her . . . scheming mother, and her wretched, sickly father.'

Solveig felt herself beginning to shake.

'And she will teach you some Greek,' added the Empress, and she leaned forward and pointed at Solveig with her hooked right forefinger. 'Harald would never dare to defy me. He owes his position and all he is . . . he owes his whole self to me. He does as I say. And so will you.'

Empress Zoe snapped her right finger and thumb. She beckoned, and at once a young woman detached herself from a small group of courtiers and glided forward.

Solveig could see that she was quite short, quite plump,

and had a great wave of luxuriant, almost luscious dark hair.

The girl just glanced at Solveig and then bowed to the Empress and Emperor.

'Maria,' said Empress Zoe, 'you speak some Norwegian.'

'Harald is a good teacher,' Maria replied.

'This is Solveig, Halfdan's daughter. 'Teach her court manners. And instruct your servants to wait on her.'

'Gladly,' said Maria, and Solveig could hear that she meant it.

Then the Empress raised both hands from her lap to signal that the audience was over.

'Do as I do,' Snorri said hoarsely.

The Viking guard bowed until his forehead touched the ground, and Solveig copied him. Then they both stood up and backed away, so that not for one moment were their backs turned on the Empress and Emperor.

Snorri hadn't even passed through the next hall before he began to growl.

'Shhhhh!' Solveig cautioned him.

'The ghastly hag! The old tombstone!'

'Shhhhh!'

'The miserable burnt-out lump of coal!'

'Snorri!'

'"Harald does as I say . . . he owes me his position . . . all he is . . . he owes his whole self to me." Just wait until I tell him what she said!'

As they walked through the next hall into the one with the fountain, Snorri went on spluttering to himself. 'Princess of Peace! Tongue-slicer! Ghastly!'

I've got no choice, Solveig thought miserably. None. How can I change her mind? How can I?

My father. It's the same for him. He doesn't want to leave me. I know that.

31

Solveig bit her lower lip. Her brow was furrowed.

I keep thinking of our brooch. The two of us, one in the bows, one in the stern. Both in one boat, under one sail. What am I to do?

4

Servants kept circling round Solveig's spacious quarters, removing imaginary specks of dust, plumping up cushions, smoothing silken carpets, bringing sherbet for Solveig and Maria to sip, and then fanning them until Maria dismissed them.

I don't belong here, thought Solveig. I never will. This place is too grand for me. And I don't like the way Maria's servants keep buzzing and hovering around me.

Then a beardless man who might have been thirty or fifty or even seventy was admitted with a message for Maria, but after this the two girls were left on their own for a while.

Or so Solveig supposed.

Maria widened her cinnamon eyes, dark and shining.

'Behind tapestries,' she warned Solveig. 'At keyholes. Always eyes, always ears.' Except that the way Maria pronounced the word sounded more like 'yezz'.

'Always speak in a low voice,' Maria murmured.

I wish I had a voice like yours, thought Solveig. Like summer bees in a meadow.

'Your father,' said Maria. 'You come because of him?'

Solveig nodded. 'I had to,' she replied. 'I was so lonely. I missed him.'

Maria nodded, and Solveig noticed how, when she did so, the muscles in her graceful neck twitched.

Maria waited for Solveig to say more and, for just a moment, Solveig found herself wondering whether Maria herself could be a spy, working for the Empress and waiting for Solveig to incriminate herself. But then she felt guilty at having such a thought. It's only because of all the suspicion and fear in this palace, she told herself. It's the place's fault.

'I miss the same,' Maria said sadly.

'What do you mean?'

'My father.'

'Your father?'

'He is ill, he is weak. I am his daughter.' Maria's voice was still low and controlled but Solveig could hear her strength of feeling. 'I should look after him.'

'I don't understand,' said Solveig. 'Why can't you?'

Maria took a deep breath and then let it all out again in hot, jagged spurts. 'I cannot say.'

Solveig bit her upper lip.

'Do not ask,' Maria told her. 'Not now.'

'And my father, he's going away again.'

'Your father,' repeated Maria slowly, 'and Harald.' Her voice lifted, as if she had just glimpsed the Morning Star. She pushed out her puffy lower lip. 'He told me how your father saved his life.'

Solveig nodded. 'At Stiklestad.'

'And how he hid in your farm until his wounds healed. And you're his almost-sister.'

'I know. But he's the son of a queen, and the half-brother of King Olaf. Me . . . I'm just Solveig. A farmer's daughter.'

'Sun-Strong,' said Maria.

Solveig gave a start. 'Who told you that?'

'Harald. He said our names can show us who we are.'

Solveig narrowed her eyes. 'When did you talk like this?'

'Last year,' Maria replied. 'The Empress allowed my mother and me to make a pilgrimage.'

'What's that?'

'A pilgrimage!'

Solveig shook her head.

'It's a journey to a holy place. Sometimes a long journey. The greatest one of all is to the Holy Land. Jerusalem.'

'Is that where you went?'

Maria nodded. 'Harald Sigurdsson escorted us. From here across the Great Sea, as far as Antioch. And from Antioch overland through Syria and Palestine. We were away from Miklagard for more than three months. Harald taught me Norwegian . . .' Maria paused, recalling something, and gave a wistful smile. '. . . and other things.'

'Did he tell you about his name?'

Maria shook her head.

'It means a great army and it means power.'

'He's so ambitious,' said Maria, wide-eyed. 'So single-minded. His heart batters his chest.'

'When he was only three, he thumped the chest of King Olaf, his half-brother, and pulled his moustache. I'll tell you some time.'

'And so tall,' added Maria dreamily.

Solveig looked puzzled. 'But your mother, why can't she . . .'

'You heard,' Maria replied in a low voice. 'You heard Empress Zoe. Her hatred. She and my mother argued, they screamed.'

'What about?'

'And then the Empress exiled her to a nunnery.'

'But . . . your father. Her own husband. Didn't he . . .'

Maria lowered her eyes. 'Not her husband,' she said. 'My mother has no husband.'

'Ohh!' exclaimed Solveig, and she slowly nodded.

'I told you,' Maria went on, her voice throbbing. 'He is ill, but I cannot look after him, or bring him food and medicine. One time each week! That's all.'

'Is he here? In this palace?'

Maria shook her head. Her whole body shook.

'In Miklagard?'

'In a damp stone house. It kills him.'

'Oh, Maria!' said Solveig gently, and she boldly took the princess's warm, plump hands between her own.

'She is a monster,' Maria whispered.

Solveig squeezed her hands. 'I'll help you.'

Maria shook her head.

'I can,' said Solveig at once, even though she didn't know how.

'No one can.' Maria's eyes flooded with tears.

At this moment another beardless man entered the chamber. He bowed to the two young women and then he asked Maria to tell Solveig that her father Halfdan wished to speak to her and was waiting for her in the guardroom.

'Go!' Maria told her. 'He needs you and you need him. You must keep him company while you still can.'

Halfdan was alone, and Solveig clung to him.

'It's not what I want and not what you want,' he told her. And then he thrust out his elbows as if he were trying to escape from an armlock. 'But neither of us can do a thing about it.'

Solveig took a step back. 'I asked the Empress,' she said. 'I told her I wanted to go to Sicily.'

Halfdan snorted. 'And she got down on one knee and granted your wish.'

36

'No,' Solveig replied, 'but she said she understood. And she said how stubborn I was.'

'You are.'

'I think she meant she liked how I spoke up for myself – and for you.'

'Solva,' her father said, 'first your audience with the Empress. Then your meeting with sweet Maria . . .'

'She is,' agreed Solveig.

Halfdan grinned. 'I know! There isn't one guard who wouldn't like to . . .'

'The Empress would have them strangled,' protested Solveig.

Halfdan nodded. 'I want to hear everything, beginning at the beginning. Come on!'

Halfdan led the way, limping out of the airy room and along the dark, candlelit corridor.

'Where are we going?' Solveig asked her father as they left the palace precincts.

'The Column of Serpents . . . You'll see.'

Then she and her father began to talk as they had not done since they had stood on the battlefield at Stiklestad almost a year before. They talked and talked, and for the most part, Halfdan asked the questions.

'King Yaroslav was right,' he said, 'when he told you he'd never known the like of it. Travelling on your own from Trondheim to Miklagard! There must have been times when you felt afraid.'

'Oh yes!' replied Solveig. 'Many.' She paused. 'But never more than the night before I left.'

'How did you face that?'

'I went down to the graveyard. They kept me company, all the grandparents and great-grandparents I've never known. I knelt beside my mother's grave and told her I'd never been so afraid, but also never so sure of what I had to do.'

Halfdan nodded. 'Asta didn't suspect you?'

'Not until it was too late. I could hear her calling. I still can.'

'There are some things,' observed her father, 'some sights, some scents even, that we carry with us all our lives.'

'The sweet scent of pinewood, that's one. The tables and chairs and doors and everything here are so dark and grubby, but pinewood is so light and bright and clean.'

'Nothing better,' her father agreed.

'Yes,' said Solveig, 'I was afraid. Several times. Those cataracts.'

'Dreadful!' exclaimed Halfdan.

'I was attacked by hounds . . . and I fell asleep in the fjord and was carried far beyond Trondheim . . . and Bulgar merchants tried to buy me as a slave . . . and little Brita – when we were portaging she tripped and fell right under the keel of our boat . . .' Solveig shuddered.

'Each question has many answers,' Halfdan told her. 'And each answer leads us to more questions. However well a traveller is prepared, he still needs hospitality and good fortune.'

'That's true.'

'So, Solva, who was hospitable to you?'

'Many people. In Trondheim an old couple welcomed me to their hearth. Well, Bera did. She led me to the Swedish traders, and unless they'd taken me with them . . .'

'What did you offer them in return?'

'My carving,' said Solva. 'I paid my passage all the way here with my carvings.'

'Did you ever carve that shoulder blade?' her father asked her. 'The one you found at Stiklestad.'

38

Solveig shook her head. 'Not yet. I've carried it all the way here, and sometimes it sings to me.'

Halfdan smiled.

'Turpin, he was the Swedish fur trader . . . I reminded him of his dead daughter. He thought I was asleep but I heard him saying, "What father can bear the loss of his daughter? Part of him is lost with her, and as long as he lives he goes on searching for her."'

Halfdan murmured in agreement.

'But I haven't even told you yet,' said Solveig, 'and I've been longing to. The helmsman on Red Ottar's boat remembered you. "Big man. Clumsy. He had a limp." The moment Torsten said that, my breath grew jerky, my eyeballs burned.'

'Torsten!' exclaimed Halfdan. 'Bright blue eyes.'

'He said you told him all about my mother, and Asta, and our farm, and Harald Sigurdsson. How we sheltered him, and how you were sailing to join him.'

'I did, yes,' said Halfdan. 'We were holed up in Ladoga for two days. Plenty of time to talk.'

'And you told him how . . . most of all . . .' Solveig faltered.

'How, most of all, I was missing you,' declared Halfdan. 'I did. And I was.'

Solveig gazed at him and nodded seriously. 'Torsten was like my ship-father,' she said. 'On Red Ottar's boat, he watched over me. He counselled me.'

'I'm glad to hear it, replied Halfdan. 'When a girl is fatherless, many other men are ready to half-father her.'

'Or take advantage of her,' said Solveig with a cheerful smile.

Halfdan gave his daughter an examining stare.

'No,' Solveig reassured him, 'they didn't! Many people were generous and expected nothing in return. Oleg, the master-carver, in Ladoga, he gave me this.'

Solveig tugged at the piece of cord around her neck and held up the glass bead suspended from it.

'The same colours as your eyes.'

'My third eye. That's what Oleg called it.'

'And he gave it to you?'

'Twice!' exclaimed Solveig. 'I'll explain why some time.'

'Solva,' said Halfdan, 'is there anything you were ashamed of?'

'Oh yes!' Solveig replied at once. 'Not giving anything to the lepers in the leper-boat. After they had gone, nightmares galloped through me.' Solveig clutched herself. 'Yes, and I never honoured my deal with Red Ottar. Not really. And not telling poor Vigot my true feelings when we had to leave him behind in Kiev. And . . .'

'And, and, and . . .' said Halfdan, smiling. 'So what are you proud of?'

'That's easy,' Solveig replied. She stared at her father with a stony face. 'Bergdis was the Angel of Death, and after Red Ottar died she was going to cut Edith's throat and lay her alongside him on the funeral pyre. Because Edith was his slave-girl. No one spoke up for her because they were all so afraid of Bergdis.'

'And you did?'

'She was wearing a bracelet of bones,' Solveig went on. 'And she commanded all my companions to gag me. All the men. I rounded on them. "Edith's innocent," I told them. "And she's carrying Red Ottar's child. What matters to the gods is the good and bad he did in his life. How can Edith's death help Red Ottar? How can it?"'

Solveig realised she was talking more and more loudly, but Halfdan didn't try to stop her. 'Bergdis was going to strangle her, and cut her throat and . . .'

Halfdan laid a firm hand on Solveig's arm.

40

'She was!' Solveig looked wildly at her father. 'Edwin! Edwin stopped her.'

Halfdan took Solveig into his arms, and there and then, in the open concourse, he embraced her. He did not let her go until she had stopped shaking.

'So, girl,' said Halfdan, 'your journey's over. The first part, anyhow. But . . . there's still an open wound?'

'You know there is,' Solveig said huskily. 'You're going away again.'

Halfdan nodded. 'I will come back. I will.'

'A whole year,' said Solveig. 'Two years . . .'

'You were right,' Halfdan said, 'when you said that the young woman standing in front of me wasn't the same as the girl I left behind in Norway.'

'She isn't but she is,' Solveig replied.

'There is much more to say,' Halfdan replied. 'What made you heartsick? What was your greatest surprise? Your greatest wonder? Who would you be most glad to meet again? But I won't ask you now.'

'My greatest treasure,' Solveig told him, 'is what I found inside my own head and heart.'

'What was that?'

'Little children believe that their fathers and mothers are gods. They obey their commands. They worship them. They know their parents know everything.'

Halfdan pursed his chapped lips.

Solveig took her father's arm. 'I found my treasure by asking questions. In Hagia Sophia, at the end of my journey, I questioned myself. I questioned my love for you.'

Halfdan frowned.

'And my head and heart answered me. Little children worship their parents blindly. They are born of the same blood, and they cleave to them, but they do not love them. Standing there, in the gallery, gazing at you, I

41

questioned why I loved you. Yes, I'm your daughter, I'm born of your blood, but why . . . why should I love you?'

Halfdan stared at his daughter, unblinking.

'Because you're a man,' Solveig told him. 'You're strong and yet weak. You're weak but very strong. Not a god but a man. You've taken right turnings and wrong turnings. You told King Yaroslav you had one grief you would regret all your life . . . Leaving me behind.'

Halfdan swallowed and nodded.

'But that wrong turning . . . that only made me love you all the more,' cried Solveig. And then she leaned into her father, put an arm round his bulky waist and gave a loud sigh.

For some while the two of them stood in the shadow of a huge column made of three bronze serpents with their bodies twined around each other.

'Look!' said Halfdan. 'Can you see how their heads are splaying in three directions? They're spewing venom at anyone who attacks Miklagard.'

Solveig tilted back her head and screwed up her eyes. 'The light's so bright here,' she said.

'This column's Greek and it's more than one thousand years old,' her father explained. 'Snorri told me it was shipped here by Constantine.'

'Who?'

'Constantine. He founded this city – and he built the palace where your quarters are. Solveig, at least you'll be safe there. And Maria, she'll be a good companion.'

'She's so unhappy,' Solveig said.

'You must thank Harald, you know.'

'Maria . . .' Solveig half-smiled. 'I think she's taking aim at him.'

'Ah!' Halfdan exclaimed. 'Here he is! Your almost-brother.'

'Oh!' exclaimed Solveig. She swept back her hair and smoothed it. Then she moistened her lips.

Harald Sigurdsson stalked towards them.

'I know that look,' said Halfdan. 'Beware!'

'Halfdan!' bawled Harald. 'You! Solveig!'

Solveig and Halfdan stepped towards him.

Harald Sigurdsson scowled at them. He bared his teeth, then he roared like a lion.

Passers-by swerved out of the way. Everyone sitting on the stone steps, gossiping or simply dozing, turned their head to see what was happening.

'I've been looking for you,' growled Harald. 'Snorri's just told me what the Empress said to him.'

Halfdan frowned. 'What? What did she say?'

'"Harald would never dare to defy me. He owes his position and all he is . . . he owes his whole self to me."'

Harald Sigurdsson rounded on Solveig. 'Is that right?' he demanded. 'Is that what she said?'

Solveig nodded.

'"He owes his whole self to me,"' Harald repeated, mocking the clipped way in which the Empress spoke. '"He does as I say."'

Again he glared at Solveig, and again Solveig nodded.

'Is that what she thinks?' demanded Harald in a cold, biting voice. And, for a second time, he roared to heaven. Then he jerked back his head and horse-laughed.

Harald slapped Halfdan on his right shoulder. 'I know who my friends are,' he asserted. 'And I know when to repay them. Loyalty breeds loyalty.'

Then Harald gazed at Solveig and his pale blue eyes glittered. 'The Empress can hang herself,' he proclaimed. 'You're coming with us. Yes, Solveig, when your father and I set sail for Sicily, you're coming too!'

5

Solveig hastened back to the guardroom between Harald Sigurdsson and her limping father, and there Harald told his two most trusty companions, Snorri and Skarp, of his decision.

'Keep it to yourselves,' he warned them. 'No one else needs to know yet.'

The two guards yelped and smacked each other's hands when they heard of their leader's defiance.

'She'll take it out on her courtiers,' asserted Snorri.

'For what they didn't do,' said Skarp.

'And never knew.'

But their grim satisfaction soon gave way to talk about what Solveig could do, and couldn't do, alongside the Varangians.

'Women,' said Skarp. 'Good for bed and for bearing our whelps.'

'Some women have second sight,' observed Snorri.

Skarp wrapped his arms around himself, and stared at Solveig.

'We only admire them,' Snorri added, 'if they behave like men.'

'Not that we expect them to fight in battle,' Harald interrupted. 'It may come to that. Solveig may have to fight, but I hope not.'

Snorri raised his right hand. 'Blood splattered her

mail-coat,' he declared, 'and a sun-ray shone from her spear.'

'I know that poem,' Harald told him. 'But it's about a Valkyrie, not a woman.'

'Valkyries are women,' Solveig objected.

'More than women,' stated Harald. 'You can help the cooks, Solveig. You can pluck and skin and gut and chop. You can groom the horses, and muck out the stables . . .'

'I'll find out,' Solveig asserted. 'I'll find out what I can do.'

Harald looked as if he'd tasted something sour, but his pale blue eyes were shining. 'And be so good as to inform me,' he told her.

'How far is it to Sicily?' asked Solveig.

Harald shook his head. 'You'll have to ask one of the helmsmen.'

'I can fish,' she volunteered. 'I can ice-fish too!'

Everyone laughed.

'Good idea!' said Skarp. 'Where will you find the ice?'

'When winter comes.'

'No,' said her father. 'Not this far south. There's no ice.'

'And it never snows,' Skarp added. 'Except when pretty Viking maidens show us their—'

'Skarp!' Harald warned him.

'Never snows!' exclaimed Solveig. 'But we need frost and ice and snow . . . to scour the year.'

'And chill our blood,' Harald agreed.

'We do,' said Solveig. 'Before the world grows green again. I can mend sails.'

Harald nodded. 'Talk to one of our boatmen.'

'And weapons. I think I could.'

Skarp leered at Solveig. 'You can mend mine,' he told her. 'It's a bit rusty.'

'Oh, Harald!' cried Solveig, and she flung her arms wide. 'I'm so glad. So glad.'

'Hmm!' grunted Harald. 'Sing me the same song in a year's time.'

'If I had to stay in this palace,' Solveig told him, 'I'd be imprisoned, like a songbird in a golden cage.'

'Pretty words,' said Harald. 'But now, Solveig, you must prove your worth.'

'I will.'

Harald wagged his right forefinger. 'When you go back to your quarters . . . you mustn't breathe a word of this to Maria.'

'Of course not.'

'Not even in your manner.'

'Sometimes,' observed Snorri, 'what we do not say tells no less than what we do say.'

'When will we sail?' Solveig asked Harald.

Harald Sigurdsson shrugged. 'Soon. Very soon.'

Solveig looked at him warmly and expectantly.

'Before an army sets sail . . .' Harald said, and he spread his big hands. 'All the clothing, the weapons, all the provisions, all the horses.'

Solveig nodded.

'And then we'll have to wait until the Empress, the divine Empress, gives us permission.'

'And asks her bishops to bless us,' Snorri added in a cutting voice.

'There's nothing wrong with that,' argued Halfdan. 'Better to have more gods on our side than too few.'

'Wait until I send you word,' Harald told Solveig. 'And when I do, you must come at once.'

'At once,' repeated Solveig.

'In the meantime, arouse no suspicion. None. Understand, Solveig, if anyone finds out, not only will it endanger your life, it might endanger mine.'

No sooner had Solveig returned to her quarters than Maria came to see her.

'What's happened?' asked Solveig.

Maria quickened across the receiving room, smiling, and embraced Solveig.

'What is it?'

'I have permission to take you with me to see my father.'

'Me?' Solveig stiffened. 'When?'

'You do not want?'

'Yes, yes, of course I do. But . . .'

Maria looked at Solveig, perplexed. 'What has changed?' she asked.

Solveig shook her head and gave Maria a wooden smile. 'Nothing,' she protested. 'When do we go?'

'Tomorrow. We must be back before sundown.'

I'll be glad to be out of this palace, thought Solveig. I'm a farm girl, not a princess. And I know Maria's servants are watching me.

As they left the palace together, Maria said, 'First we go to the almond-seller. My father likes fresh almonds. Almonds and oranges. Oranges make him stronger in his blood.'

In the Hippodrome, the girls met seven Varangian guards running towards the palace, scarlet cloaks flying, and seeing them in such a hurry made Solveig nervous that the fleet might be about to set sail.

No, she thought. That's impossible. Not already.

'Men,' said Maria gaily. 'Varangians are men. Harald is the most man.'

'And my father,' Solveig declared.

Is it possible, she wondered, that Maria and Harald could make a marriage? After all, she's the niece of the Empress, and Harald's the half-brother of King Olaf. She worships him, but Harald . . . What about him? What are his feelings?

I can't ask Maria. Not yet. She wouldn't open all her heart. But before I sail for Sicily, I'll try to find out.

In the same market where Solveig's father grew so anxious that he had lost his daughter, the two girls bought almonds and oranges, and Solveig told Maria how her father had to repay a porter for sending him and his whole basket of oranges spinning.

'And he made the porter even more angry by throwing one orange into the air, and slicing it in half with his sabre,' Solveig exclaimed.

'Harald's the best swordsman in the whole of the Varangian guard,' Maria said.

'Is there anything at all that Harald cannot do?' Solveig demanded, laughing.

Maria lowered her eyes, and her eyelashes flickered. 'Come on now,' she purred. 'Before my father, we go to see silk-weavers.'

Maria guided Solveig through the bustling market to an aisle selling nothing but leather – boots, belts, purses, trousers, straps, bridles, bits, saddles, shoulder bags. Then she dived between two stalls and led Solveig into a much quieter, wider aisle, decorated with banners – scarlet and orange, saffron and lime and grass-green, dusky pink and indigo – hanging from the supports of each of the stalls.

'Silks,' Maria told Solveig in the most silken of voices. 'Nothing but silks.'

Solveig stared up the aisle and down the aisle.

'The Jews are not Christian,' Maria said with a little frown. 'Sometimes dark flies buzz in their heads and fly out of their mouths, but . . . they weave silk like angels. Better than anyone in the world.'

As soon as the two girls began to walk along the

spacious aisle, now and then pausing to finger a silk, this one so gauzy it almost floated, that one thick and heavy, Solveig realised Maria must be a regular and welcome visitor to the silk stalls. Many of the merchants stood up from their stools to greet her, and smoothed their long black beards between their fingers.

Then one merchant held up two goblets, smiling and inviting the girls to drink with him, and Maria replied to him in his own language.

'What were you saying?' asked Solveig. 'I didn't know you could speak . . . speak . . .'

'Hebrew,' Maria told her. 'I can't. Not much. But I learned some in the Holy Land. I was saying part of a poem about drinking old wine among myrrh and lilies.'

'What's myrrh?'

'In the orchard of pomegranates,' Maria went on, 'and palms and vines, full of scented flowers and tamarisks . . .'

'What?'

But now Maria was in full flood. '. . . to the hum of fountains . . .'

'I've seen one of those. The fountain in the palace!'

'. . . and the throb of lutes. There we shall drink, drink out of goblets!'

By now, quite a group of merchants had gathered round, delighting not only in Maria's spirited recitation but in the girls themselves – the one sallow, the other so fair. Haltingly, Maria explained that today she didn't want to buy anything, but only to show her friend 'this silken paradise'.

One merchant shook out a panel of glistening silk, and held it up in front of Solveig, and it kept changing colour. It was woad and ice-blue and bluebell; it was the light in the north on the longest summer day that never darkened, not even at midnight.

Solveig gazed at it, astonished.

'Not today,' Maria repeated. 'But we'll come back soon. It suits you, Solveig.'

'I could never wear anything like that,' Solveig protested when they had emerged from the aisle. 'It's much too grand for me. Anyhow, I have no money.'

'None?' exclaimed Maria, surprised.

Solveig shook her head.

'I'll give you some,' Maria said. 'I've no freedom,' she added fiercely, 'and a mother in a nunnery and an ill father, but money . . .' She shrugged and spread her hands.

They walked out of the market and down a sun-baked street, and Solveig slipped a hand through Maria's arm. 'I'll carve something for you,' she said.

'The Jews are richer than anyone else in Miklagard,' Maria informed her. 'They lend money to lots of people.'

Solveig looked puzzled. 'What happens if you can't pay them back?'

'The worse for you,' Maria replied. 'If you borrow three *nomismata*—'

'What's that?'

'Gold coins. After twelve months you have to pay back four. And if you can't, the Jews will have the furniture out of your house and the clothes off your back.'

'No!'

'Or else, they'll take it in meat.'

Solveig crossed her hands across her chest. 'What do you mean?'

'They'll slaughter your lambs and calves. To the value of four *nomismata*. Or else they'll complain to the city justices, and have you thrown into prison.'

'Prison,' repeated Solveig. 'Like the nunnery where your mother is.'

'Yes,' said Maria. 'That's like a prison.' She indignantly tossed her luxuriant dark hair. 'The Empress only allows me to visit her once in each season.'

'Why?'

'She thinks we might start plotting. Or that I'll be carrying messages for her. And she won't allow my mother to see my father at all, even though he's so ill. I don't think he can live much longer.'

'Surely Empress Zoe knows that,' Solveig said.

'She knows everything,' Maria replied. 'I told you, she hates my mother.'

The street in which Maria's father lived was very narrow – people living on opposite sides could almost have stretched out from the upper windows and touched fingertips. Little sunlight ever touched the damp walls of the houses, and Solveig noticed that some were stained with dark, angry patches.

It's as if Maria has brought me to another city, she thought.

Maria stopped at a big wooden door with a smaller door cut out of it.

'My father knows you're coming,' she told Solveig, 'and he will be pleased. His name is Leo.'

Maria had to knock on the door four times before a stooping servant opened it. The hinges groaned.

'They need olive oil,' said Maria with an apologetic smile. 'So does his servant.'

The servant shuffled down a short passage and led the girls up twisting stone steps. In the bedroom facing the top of the staircase, Maria's father was waiting for them, lying on a kind of raised divan, propped up with cushions and pillows.

Solveig saw at once how handsome he was or, rather, had once been. His brow was broad, his nose aquiline, he had a generous mouth and a sweeping wave of grey

51

hair. But he looks like a spirit or a ghost, she thought. I can almost see through him.

First, Maria embraced her father, and then Solveig stood before this noble man. She courteously cupped her hands and inclined her head, and Maria's father, who spoke no Norwegian, indicated that she should sit on one side of the divan, and his daughter on the other.

Maria said something to her father. 'I tell him,' she explained, 'how you followed your father. How you travel all the way from Norway to Miklagard.'

Leo murmured a few words and gently nodded.

'My father says,' translated Maria, 'you are your father's true daughter as well as a daughter of the gods.'

Solveig wasn't entirely sure what Maria's father meant, but she understood it to be some kind of compliment and smiled prettily at him.

During the following months, Solveig thought quite often of her meeting with this man, reduced to such a sorry shell, and she remembered not only his bearing and dignity but also his flashes of wit, and how readily they had talked about fathers and daughters, about trust and friendship.

'I believe,' Leo told Solveig, 'that you can be a true friend to Maria.'

But I'm not, thought Solveig. I know I haven't betrayed her but I haven't told her about Sicily.

'A Varangian guard told me an old saying of yours,' Leo went on. '"When I was young, I walked alone and so I soon lost my way. But when I found friends I felt rich. Each of us needs and delights in others."'

Solveig gave Leo a tight smile. 'I will be as true to Maria as I can be,' she said.

After this, Leo talked with his daughter for a while.

To begin with, Solveig listened to the music of their words, but she soon began to grow nervous about how long she had been away from the palace, and whether Harald might have summoned her during her absence.

Little escaped Leo, and he could see Solveig was anxious.

'Life is long but time is short!' he exclaimed, and Maria translated his words. 'That's what people say when they have much to do, or much on their minds. But for me . . .' Leo said, 'for me it's the other way round. Life is short but time hangs heavy.'

Solveig understood. She knew Leo meant he had only a little time left to live, and time dragged heavy between the one day each week when his daughter was allowed to come and see him.

Solveig's visit was brought to an unexpected end. Leo had just noticed her third eye and was asking her about it when he began to whiffle and wheeze and belch.

Then he coughed up green phlegm. He coughed up blood.

If he goes on like this, thought Solveig, he'll cough up his guts.

But when it seemed Leo might be about to cough himself to death, he spluttered into silence and, by way of apology, feebly waved his pale hands around like giant moths.

Solveig stood up to leave, and Leo snuffled and murmured something about Solveig coming to see him for a second time. Then Solveig asked Maria to tell her father how she hoped he would soon make a full recovery, but she knew she would never see him again.

When Solveig returned to her own quarters in the palace, one of the servants immediately tried to tell her something, but she spoke very little Norwegian and Solveig spoke no Greek at all.

'Wait!' Solveig said. 'No! Follow me! We must find Maria!'

'A visitor,' Maria translated. 'You have had a visitor.'

'Oh!' yelped Solveig.

'Why are you making a face at me?' asked Solveig. 'I don't understand.'

The servant stretched his mouth and tapped his teeth.

'Why is he doing that, Maria?'

Maria spoke to the servant. 'He says the man has big teeth and came very soon after we left the palace.'

'Oh, no!'

'What's wrong? Who were you expecting?'

'No one.'

Maria looked reproachfully at Solveig.

'Did he leave a message?' asked Solveig.

The servant pulled a face. 'He is still here.'

'Here!'

'All afternoon, my servant says, she has given him wine and little cakes, and fruit for the lady . . .'

'What lady?'

'English,' the servant said.

'English!'

'The man and the lady, both English.'

Solveig cried out in joy and relief. 'It's Edwin,' she explained. 'He's the man who came here with me from Kiev. He came with a message from King Yaroslav for Empress Zoe. And Edith, she was Red Ottar's slave. She's carrying his baby.'

When the servant ushered Edwin and Edith into her

receiving room, Solveig cried out for a second time. She half-ran towards them and gathered them both into one long, warm, laughing embrace.

'What's happened?' she asked, quite breathless. 'When we met at the water-pool . . .'

'The cistern,' said Edwin.

'You told me you were about to have your audience with the Empress.'

'That's right.'

'And would be leaving again for Kiev immediately after.'

'Many's the plan,' said Edwin, shaking his head.

'Mihran found us a pilot,' Edith explained, 'but when we went down to the water-steps to meet him, he wasn't there. We looked for him everywhere; we waited all afternoon.'

'We couldn't find Mihran either,' Edwin said.

'Anyhow,' Edith said brightly, 'we've found another pilot. Well, Edwin has. And this one's trustworthy.'

'Thin ice can look trustworthy,' Solveig warned her with a smile. 'That's what my father says. His mouth is full of sayings.'

'Oh, Solveig!' said Edith. 'You look so . . . bright-eyed!'

The two of them embraced again, as best they could with the bump of the baby between them.

'I've got the ring,' whispered Edith, 'and when my daughter cuts her teeth on it . . .'

'Daughter!' exclaimed Solveig. 'How do you know?'

'I just do!'

'How?'

'It's not so strange, is it? After all, she's living with me day and night, and I'm living with her.'

'Oh, Edith!'

'I won't know what to call her until I see her.'

56

'You told me that before,' Solveig said.

'Not long now. Kata, maybe.'

'Kata,' repeated Solveig slowly. 'Kata. I don't know that name.'

'And when she cuts her teeth . . . I'll think of you.'

Solveig took a deep breath. 'But I'll never see her. You'll have gone back to England.'

'Oh, Solveig!' cried Edith, and the two of them clutched each other.

'I'll never see her, and I'll never see you again.'

'You can't know that,' said Edwin.

'It's our fate,' Solveig replied.

'Fate . . .' said Edwin. 'As I've told you before, fate moves in the mind of God.'

'Did you meet the Empress?' Solveig asked him.

'And the Emperor.'

'She gave me an audience too.'

Each of them met the other's eye but neither said a word. But then Solveig screwed up her face as if she'd sucked a sloe or a lemon, and Edwin laughed so that his buck teeth stuck right out of his mouth.

'The Empress asked me exactly what King Yaroslav had said to me,' Solveig told them, 'and when I explained the king wanted to send a messenger to Miklagard as a matter of great urgency, she challenged me.'

'Oh?'

'"To Miklagard", she repeated. '"To Miklagard, not to me?"'

Edwin was listening intently, chafing the tip of his tongue against the back of his teeth.

'I told her the message was for her. I said I was sure King Yaroslav meant that. And I told the Empress how the king had praised her.'

Edwin smiled. 'You could be an emissary,' he said. He nodded and linked his fingers over his paunch.

'A what?'

'A go-between.'

Solveig shook her head. Wordsmiths, she thought. Isn't that what go-betweens are? Pushers and pullers and twisters?

Edith read her thoughts and shook her head. 'Red Ottar didn't like wordsmiths,' she observed.

'Neither does my father,' Solveig replied. 'He says they're dark magicians. They shape-change meanings.'

Edwin smiled. 'You credit us with more power than we really have,' he told them.

'King Yaroslav's message,' Solveig pressed him, 'it was for the Empress, wasn't it?'

'And the Emperor.'

'I mean . . .'

'I know what you mean, Solveig. My mission was from King Yaroslav to the Empress Zoe and Emperor Michael.'

Solveig narrowed her eyes at him.

Edith laughed. 'Trying to get Edwin to say something when he doesn't want to is like squeezing a stone for water.'

'I know,' agreed Solveig, 'or trying to shove our cows when they dig in their hooves.'

'What I will say,' Edwin volunteered, 'is that it would be a strange messenger who travelled for many weeks with only one song in his mouth.'

'You mean,' Solveig said, 'a go-between can sing out of both sides of his mouth.'

Edwin raised an eyebrow.

'So was your other message for . . .'

Edwin raised his right hand and gently pushed it against Solveig's mouth.

'It was,' said Solveig in a muffled voice. 'I know it was.'

'This won't be my last journey here,' the Englishman told her.

'You're coming back?'

'Very possibly.'

Solveig's heart lifted. 'Then I'll see you again. I will, won't I?'

Edwin smiled. 'If you're here,' he replied.

Before they left the receiving room, Edith and Edwin stared for a while at a mosaic of two children riding on a strange beast with two humps on its back.

'A camel,' Edwin told them. 'They only need to drink once each week, and even then they prefer muddy water.'

Edith shook her head. 'I feel thirsty the whole time. It's so hot in Miklagard.'

'And they live for more than one hundred years,' added Edwin.

'Even older than the Empress,' Solveig said with a smile.

'And the females fight in battle. They're very brave.'

Females in battle, thought Solveig. I'm telling Harald.

'Look how long their legs are,' observed Edith, fingering the mosaic's tiny, glittering tiles. 'Not like our pony.'

'In Riccall, you mean?' asked Solveig.

Edith nodded.

'Can Emma and Wulf . . .'

'Oh, yes! They ride her. Along the riverbank. Oh, Solveig!' Edith sighed.

'Tell me,' Solveig said gently.

'All the water lilies.' Edith gulped and swallowed. 'I wish you could see them.'

'It's a bumpy ride,' said Edwin, 'on a camel.'

'Have you ridden one?' Solveig asked him.

'In Africa,' the Englishman told her.

'I wish I could.'

'Yes,' said Edwin. 'And the three of us, we had a bumpy ride on our way here. A very rough ride. We shared hardship. And that makes this leave-taking all the more painful.' Then he began to sing-and-say:

'On middle-earth there's no one so assured
that he harbours no fears about seafaring
and what the Lord will ordain for him.
He thinks not of the harp nor of receiving rings
nor of rapture in a woman nor of worldly joy,
nor of any thing but the rolling of the waves . . .'

Edwin gave a gentle groan, almost a hum. 'So, then, may the Lord ordain our return journey is a calm one.'

'Sineus is waiting for us on Saint Gregorios,' Edith reminded them.

'Oh!' said Solveig. 'I hope his foot has healed well.'

Edwin gave her a wry smile. 'I hope he's got two legs!'

'Do you remember telling me about that English poem?' Solveig asked Edith. 'The one that begins "I saw a wonder".'

'That's right,' said Edith. 'When Edwin pointed out the red-breasted geese and water-mint and bald ibis and tamarisks. And I said it's how you see. I said that if you're sharp-eyed, anything and everything becomes a wonder.'

'Oh, Edie!' exclaimed Solveig. 'I hope your life's always like that.'

'What about yours?' Edith said, slipping her arms around Solveig's neck. 'It's so roomy here. So grand.'

'Too grand,' said Solveig. 'I don't belong here. I don't like it.' She gazed at Edwin over Edith's shoulder.

'Harald Sigurdsson,' said Edwin, 'he's sailing to Sicily.'

Solveig nodded.

'With your father, no doubt.'

She nodded again.

'Yes,' said Edwin in a quiet voice. 'Well, Solveig, maybe there are camels in Sicily.' Then he puckered his mouth, just like a camel, and winked at her.

Solveig's eyes shone.

7

'Wait until I send you word,' Harald had told her. But three whole days had passed and neither he nor Solveig's father had been in contact with her at all. Not unless the servants she shared with Maria had turned them away.

What if they suspect me? Solveig thought. What if my servants have been instructed not to allow me any more visitors? My father and Harald could sail out of the Horn and halfway across the Great Sea without my knowing anything about it.

'If anyone finds out, not only will it endanger your life, it might endanger mine.' That's what Harald had said.

But no one's found out anything. Not from me. It's me who needs to find out.

So on the morning of the fourth day, Solveig worked her way back through the warren of the palace to the Varangian guardroom.

This palace, she thought, it's like that grim labyrinth Mihran told me about, and the Empress Zoe is the Minotaur. She eats seven young men and seven young women each year.

Snorri and Skarp and at least a dozen other men were in the spacious guardroom, some standing, some lounging against the walls, some flat on their backs, but

Solveig noticed that none of them, not even Skarp, made so bold as to sit in Harald's high-backed chair.

Snorri greeted Solveig and spread his arms. 'Your father and Harald are down at the harbour,' he told her. 'It's been like this for days. To and fro, to and fro, readying everything.'

'When are you leaving?'

'Soon, I'd say, very soon. What do you think, Skarp?'

'I don't know. Tomorrow?'

'Ask Harald,' Snorri advised Solveig. 'He'll be back before long.'

'Birth pangs!' said Skarp. 'They're always painful. All the gathering and counting, carting and carrying on board, all the stowing and storing. You've no idea, girl.'

'You're forgetting,' Snorri told him, 'Solveig has sailed from Sigtuna to Ladoga, and Ladoga to Kiev, and Kiev . . .'

Skarp ignored him. 'Friends!' he called out. 'Solveig here is missing her father. She's in need of company.'

Shuffling and grinning, half a dozen guards gathered round Solveig.

'Not as much as what we are,' lamented one man. 'Company.' His eyes were blackberry-bright and his cheeks hollow, and Solveig thought he would be more at ease in a monk's habit and cowl than chain mail and a scarlet cloak.

The guard reached out and took Solveig's hands between his own, and Solveig saw how bony they were.

'Priskin,' he said.

'Priskin,' repeated Solveig.

Then another guard offered himself to Solveig. His long, acorn hair was completely tangled, and somehow his expression was eager and hopeful, as if the world had not yet disappointed him, and maybe never would.

'Tamas,' he told Solveig, and he gathered her hands between his own and lightly pressed them.

'Tamas,' she repeated. Her heart skipped.

One by one the guards got to their feet and ranged themselves round Solveig, seeing in her every other Viking girl with pale skin and golden hair, and remembering how far away they were from their own families, the fjords where they fished, their farms.

One by one, Solveig listened to a whole litany of names, the shoulder-companions of Snorri and Skarp: not only Tamas and Priskin, but Karly and Ulf and Gissur and Gorm and Bolverk and Egil and Turgeis . . .

Rough, gruff music in Solveig's ears.

'Grimizo,' said the last guard. He was clean-shaven, and his chin was square as a spade.

Solveig frowned.

'He's German,' Snorri told her. 'Now and then the Empress admits a foreigner to the ranks of the Varangians.'

Solveig smiled at the guard, but Grimizo didn't smile back. He just . . . regarded her.

'But the Empress has other foreign guards, hasn't she?' asked Solveig.

'Oh, yes!' Snorri said. 'Bulgars, Georgians, Serbians . . .'

'Southerners,' added Skarp. 'Soft!'

'Not the ones dragging out that chained man,' protested Solveig. 'What happened to him?'

Snorri clamped his jaw.

'He got trimmed,' Skarp told her. 'That's what I heard. Topped and tailed, you might say.'

Solveig screwed up her eyes.

Skarp winked at Solveig. 'You'll be all right. Here with Maria.'

You know I'm coming with you, thought Solveig,

and Snorri knows. But no one else does. Not Tamas . . .
When they hear about it, what will they say?

'Yes,' Snorri said thoughtfully. 'Our beloved Empress
will look after you. She won't do anything to upset
Harald.'

'Her darling,' declared Skarp in a scornful voice.

'He's not!' exclaimed Solveig.

'She wishes he was!' Skarp retorted.

Many of the guards laughed.

'Instead of Michael, you mean?' Solveig demanded.

Snorri shook his head. 'As well as Michael,' he said
slowly.

'Blazing fires need feeding,' added Skarp.

'Harald would never agree to that,' said Solveig.

'And neither would Michael,' Snorri replied. 'He may
look as fresh as a flower and blush like a young girl, but
he's not as soft as he seems.' He gave Solveig a steely
look.

'Shall we tell her, lads?' asked Skarp.

For a moment no one replied. But then Priskin began.
'Last year, the old Emperor Romanus died. But not before
he had challenged the boy-man. He accused Michael of
bedding the Empress, but Michael denied it. He denied
it on the bones of saints.' The hollows of Priskin's cheeks
were flaming.

'Sometimes the gods madden Michael,' Skarp
interrupted. 'He hurls himself to the ground, and
writhes around, and rolls his eyes. He keeps banging his
head . . .'

'Last year, the Emperor Romanus died,' Priskin began
again. 'But he did not choose to die.'

'Few people do,' Snorri said in a dry voice.

'What people believe,' Priskin continued, 'is that he
was . . . helped.'

'You mean . . .' Solveig began.

'I do,' said Priskin calmly. 'He lost his appetite. He couldn't sleep. He'd always been quick to laugh, that's what people said, always friendly, but he became peevish and irritable.'

'Was it a charm?' asked Solveig. 'Was a spell put on him?'

'His face became swollen,' Priskin intoned. 'I saw him myself and his colour had changed. Grey. Grey-green. He looked like a man who'd been dead for three days.'

'And his hair fell out,' added Skarp.

'What some people say,' Priskin went on, 'is that his own wife, Zoe, and the boy-man were poisoning the Emperor. One morning, Romanus went to the palace baths with some of his servants . . .' The guard paused and swilled saliva around his mouth. Then, using both his hands, Priskin pretended to push the old Emperor Romanus down, right down. 'Several servants held his head under the water for a long time,' he told Solveig, 'and then they ran away. After a while the Emperor's body rose to the surface – that was because of the air inside it – and he floated like a cork. Another servant put his arms around him, and pulled him out, and laid him on a bench. Romanus gave a long, long . . . first a moan, then a growl. His breathing quickened. Faster and faster. He gaped like a great fish. And out of his mouth there seeped thick . . . dark . . . goo . . .'

Solveig took a deep breath and swallowed loudly.

'Whatever the truth of all this,' Priskin continued in his measured way, 'there's no argument about what happened next. On the same day her husband had died, our beloved Empress married the boy-man.'

'Fresh as a flower and blushing like a young girl,' said Snorri.

'The same day! I was there. I was one of the guards!

And there and then,' Priskin completed his ghastly account, 'Michael was crowned Emperor.'

Solveig was so shocked she didn't say anything.

'You must keep your eyes skinned,' Priskin warned her. 'And keep yourself to yourself.'

'Yes, Solveig, you must,' Tamas repeated, eager and concerned.

'No one's safe in this snake-pit,' Priskin went on. 'Not you. No one. Not even the poor old Emperor.'

'Honour,' said Tamas in a firm voice. He pursed his lips and shook his head. 'Truth-telling. Loyalty . . .'

'Life is much too easy in Miklagard,' observed Skarp. 'Sunlight, sherbet, silks, spices.'

'And what's easily won is easily thrown away,' Snorri agreed.

'Maria,' said Priskin, 'she may mean well, but the Empress can bend or break her. Be wary what you tell her.'

'You will, won't you, Solveig?' Tamas asked her earnestly.

Solveig gave him a gentle smile and nodded.

Now there was a hammering at the door. A eunuch walked in. He crossed the hall to Solveig and informed her that she was to return to her quarters.

'Why?' asked Solveig.

'Empress Zoe has summoned you and Maria to Hagia Sophia,' the eunuch told her.

'So you can help her and the Emperor,' Snorri added.

'Help them?' said Solveig, looking alarmed. 'How?'

'And all the oily priests. So you and the whole court can pray for us and bless us before we set sail.'

Maria instructed her servants to dress Solveig in one of her own gowns. It was made of heavy silk, misty grey-blue.

'It matches your eyes,' Maria told her. 'Almost.'

But Solveig shook her head. 'It's so stiff. Was it woven by those Jews in the market?'

'No, I brought it back from Antioch.'

Solveig looked puzzled.

'Across the Great Sea. The weaver said, "He wraps Himself in a cloak of morning light."'

'Who does?'

'God, of course. And he told me that when I wore his gown, I too would be wrapping myself in morning light.'

Solveig gazed at Maria. 'You should see the early light north from our farm. I wish you could.'

'Let my servants dress you,' Maria told her. 'At least this gown will cover what's beneath. Nothing but rags and tatters.'

'My sealskin boots are all right,' Solveig replied. 'In fact they're better now than when I left home. They fit like gloves.'

'Webbed ones,' said Maria, and both girls laughed.

As soon as one of her servants had combed Solveig's golden hair and secured her hood, three rosy-cheeked eunuchs conducted the girls to Hagia Sophia, and on their way they passed through several halls Solveig hadn't seen before.

Maria read her thoughts. 'In my Father's house are many mansions,' she intoned. 'Many mansions . . . the Gospel according to Saint John. But in my aunt's palace are many halls – that's what I always think.'

In one hall there was a forest of slender columns, each a slightly different colour: trunks of ash, hornbeam, maple, beech.

At once Solveig was back in the forest that horseshoed round her farm, back with Blubba and Kalf, crouching, panting, knowing the least snap of a twig might give her hiding-place away.

'Jasper,' Maria told her, 'rock crystal, porphyry. Speckled marble from Phrygia, white marble from Prokonessos – that's quite near here – and this purple one, it's from Egypt.'

Solveig shook her head, but before she could ask any questions, the eunuchs had led the girls through the stone forest into another hall. And there, waiting for them, right in the middle of the room, stood a glorious golden lion.

Solveig broke her step and then shuffled forward; her thick silk gown rasped and rustled. She edged round the beast so she could look right up at its wild mane, its blood-orange eyes . . .

And at that moment, the golden lion opened his jaws and he roared. One stupendous, terrifying roar. A roar that ricocheted around the room and rose to heaven.

Solveig jumped back. She tripped on the hem of her cloak, stumbled and cracked her head against the tiles.

The golden lion snapped his jaws shut.

Solveig looked up at the beast, amazed, and the three eunuchs helped her to her feet. Maria laughed.

'How . . . I mean . . . Is there a man inside?'

Maria shook her head.

'How then?'

'I can't explain exactly. It's a machine. This palace is full of machines.'

I want to find out, thought Solveig. I want to understand. I know some people can make magic with spells and charms, but some can with machines!

Hagia Sophia was just as gloomy and chilly as when Solveig had first entered it, searching for her father. But now the entrance hall was packed with Varangian guards, courtiers and townsfolk, as many women as men. The eunuchs had to use their sharp tongues and sharp elbows to force a way through to the concourse below the great dome – the dome that Solveig had thought was floating halfway between earth and heaven when she first saw it.

The concourse was packed too, and everyone was talking, shouting, pointing, laughing. When the eunuchs had led the girls to their places, Solveig gazed all around her, trying to accustom her eyes to the shining gloom, incense-thick and incense-sweet, lit by candles and oil lamps.

Then she saw someone in the middle of the throng. Waving. Waving at her and calling, 'Solveig! Solveig!'

But although Solveig stared and stared, and could see one pink hand waving, she wasn't at all certain who it was.

It could be, she thought. I mean, it might be! Solveig smiled a little secret smile. Well, it won't be Grimizo, anyhow!

Now there was a flourish of trumpets from the trumpeters stationed high up in a gallery.

The great crowd below began to draw back, even to jam themselves against the people behind them, until there was just room enough for a stream of priests to flow between them, carrying silver crosses and caskets and chalices, swinging their censers, singing-and-saying prayers.

Very last in this long gold-and-silver procession came the Empress and Emperor themselves and, as they passed, many people in the milling crowd tried to get to their knees but were unable to do so, let alone press their foreheads against the cold, shining tiles.

'That purple!' whispered Solveig. 'That purple they're wearing. I've never seen such a colour.'

Empress Zoe and Emperor Michael stepped up on to a white marble plinth. They sat down on two golden chairs and surveyed the vast crowd.

Then Empress Zoe raised her right hand and at once a man stepped forward. A very tall man.

'Harald!' said Solveig in a husky voice.

Harald Sigurdsson strode up to the plinth and prostrated himself.

He has to do that? Even Harald, thought Solveig.

'Shhh!' whispered Maria, as if she could hear the thoughts inside Solveig's head.

Now everyone in the concourse fell silent, many with heads cocked or half-turned, straining to hear what the Empress had to say.

'Harald Sigurdsson, this is what we require of you. You are to lead my Varangian guard across the Sea of Marmara, across the Great Sea to the island of Sicily. You are to clean the whole island of filth. All the filthy Saracens who've swarmed in from north Africa. Drive them out. Better yet, put them to death.'

Ferocious as the Empress's instructions were, she uttered them in a soft voice that made them seem all the more terrible.

Harald Sigurdsson, still on his knees, gave a curt nod.

'You will fight alongside Georgios – my commander-in-chief,' Empress Zoe continued. 'I've sent out messengers to find him, wherever the man is, and instruct him to set sail for Sicily. Be sure you're even-handed in your dealings with each other. Misfortune always follows on the heels of greed.'

This time, Harald jerked his chin upward and, watching him closely, Solveig thought it almost looked like a gesture of contempt.

'If you meet Saracen pirates on your way,' the Empress went on, 'and board their dung-pits . . .'

'Dhows,' volunteered Harald.

'I know what they're called,' replied the Empress in a cold voice. 'I require one hundred marks for each . . .

71

dhow. If there's a surplus, you and your men may divide it between you.'

'My men,' said Harald in a strong voice, 'and my women.'

At once Solveig stiffened. Her neck. Her shoulders. Her arms. Every muscle in her body.

'Women?' demanded the Empress.

He's not going to tell her, Solveig thought. Surely he's not.

'The stable girls,' Harald said, 'the women working in our kitchens, washerwomen . . . aren't they entitled to anything?'

Empress Zoe sighed. 'You Varangians, you Vikings, you treat your women differently to us. You give them greater freedom. You embolden them.'

Solveig took a deep breath and blew it all out again.

Now the Empress surveyed the guards massed in front of her. Her eyes glittered; the corners of her thin lips tightened and twitched.

'Not all of you will come back to Miklagard,' she announced, though only the front few rows of guards could hear her. 'This is how life is – how death is. Sometimes speedy, sometimes slow. But all of you, you're bearing shields, you're swinging your axes in a just cause. The cause of Christendom! The glory of Byzantium!'

Then Empress Zoe spoke directly to Harald again.

'I expect you,' she said, 'to punish wrongdoers in your own ranks. You Varangians are subject to my laws.'

'Empress,' replied Harald, 'my men know very well how I punish them without fear or favour.'

'If you regain Sicily,' the Empress told him, 'each man who returns will be well rewarded, over and above his pickings in the field. As for you, Harald . . .' her voice softened, 'I will give you my treasures . . . and grant you favours . . .' The Empress tailed off and bestowed a smile on Harald Sigurdsson. Her withered face crinkled, and Harald lowered his eyes.

'Errch!' moaned Maria.

'Shh . . . shh . . . shhhhh!' Solveig whispered, soft as a summer wave spreading out along the shoreline.

The Empress turned to the Emperor. 'Won't we, Michael?' she asked in a cutting voice.

Emperor Michael inclined his head.

'I trust you, Harald,' the Empress continued. 'And I have a gift for you.' She raised her right arm and two eunuchs stepped forward side by side, bearing a pole between them.

Empress Zoe closed and opened the claw of her hand.

'Open it!' she instructed them. 'Fly it!'

Then the hairless eunuchs stood one end of the pole on the tiled floor, and they loosed and displayed the square silk banner attached to it. It was copper. It was saffron crocus, woven with little crimson dots and crosses.

'This banner,' the Empress told Harald, 'was made by witches fifteen generations ago. Prayers are sewn into it, spells are stitched into it. For as long as it flies before you, you'll come to no harm in battle.'

Harald Sigurdsson got to his feet. He glared at the banner. He grasped it and swirled it.

'Land-Ravager!' he shouted at the top of his voice. 'Land-Ravager!'

Everyone held their breath and looked at the Empress Zoe. But the Empress, she simply nodded.

'My best men,' Harald Sigurdsson declared, 'Snorri and Skarp and Halfdan, they'll fly it before me. Land-Ravager! I'll lay siege to the towns of Sicily, and sail your island back to you!'

As if guided by the unseen hand of God, an unseen choir of men and eunuchs massed behind the high altar began to chant a hymn of praise. They sang in four-part harmony and Solveig listened, astonished and entranced.

Are they light-spirits? she wondered. Or angels? What are they?

No sooner had the choir fallen silent than away up in the gallery the trumpeters blew dozens of short, sharp bursts. Their instruments blazed in the sunlight shafting through all the strip windows.

Solveig's heart pounded. To her ears, they were spurring troops into battle. And no sooner had the trumpets, and the echoes of their echoes, wound into the dark than Empress Zoe and Emperor Michael rose from their seats. First they showed the great crowd their open hands, then they both reached up, as if they were grasping for the edge of heaven.

The Varangian guards shouted, more than one thousand of them. One explosive, fierce, barbaric shout.

The old walls of Hagia Sophia shuddered. Its doors rattled on their hinges and the high windows shook in their frames.

At once the priests began to disperse through the huge crowd, brandishing their silver crosses like swords and axes, sprinkling water from their pyxes, singing-and-saying blessings.

A few guards reached out to touch their white garments, a few murmured, 'Amen! Amen! Amen.' But most simply ignored the priests.

They're Vikings, thought Solveig. They'd rather say one prayer to Odin than one hundred prayers to Christ. How can Christ help them – the God who tells us to forgive and turn the other cheek? That's what they're thinking.

At that moment Solveig caught sight of Halfdan for the very first time: there he was in the middle of the throng, unstooping, enduring; one man in a thousand;

her own father. Solveig half-waved to him, then quickly remembered where she was.

Maria turned to Solveig, and her dark eyes were glowing, her sallow cheeks flushed.

'What is it?' Solveig asked her.

'Harald!' she breathed. 'Was there ever such a man?'

8

'Who is it?'

Whoever it was, whoever they were, said nothing.

Solveig struggled to sit upright in her feather bed. 'Who is it?'

Now the oil lamp advanced towards her.

'Who?' Solveig tried to sound strong, but the walls could hear, the palace night could hear, the whoever-it-was could hear how anxious she was.

The lamp was lifted, and Solveig could see eyes. Dark searchlights. She scrambled to her feet.

'Who are you?' she demanded.

'It is!' said a familiar, husky voice in broad Norwegian. 'It's Solveig.'

Then the man held his oil lamp right up and danced the dark away.

'Father!' cried Solveig, and she threw herself into his arms.

'And me,' said the other man. 'Snorri.'

'Oh!' exclaimed Solveig. 'You've taken my breath away.'

'Come on!' Halfdan told her. 'You'll never win fame by lying on a feather bed.'

'I'd rather have my straw mattress,' Solveig protested.

'Get some clothes on.'

'Why didn't you answer? When I asked who you were.'

'We wanted to be certain,' her father replied. 'We thought this might be Maria's chamber.'

'You can never be too careful,' Snorri told her.

Solveig kept shaking her head, and yawning, and screwing up her eyes. Part of me is still asleep, she thought. My head, not my limbs.

'Come on!' Halfdan said impatiently. 'First your own clothes, then these.' He stooped and picked up something: a scarlet cloak and helmet.

'Me? Those?'

'Until we're out of the palace.'

'Oh! My servants. Where are they? They always sleep outside my door.'

'You'll see,' said Snorri. He harrumphed.

'Which is more than they can do,' added her father.

'No!' gasped Solveig. 'You haven't . . .'

'For the third time, Solveig, hurry up! First your own clothes, then this cloak, and then whatever you're bringing with you.'

Solveig rubbed her eyes. 'My bone-bag, yes, and the bog cotton in it and . . . you know.'

'I know,' Halfdan said curtly.

'There's only one thing you don't want in a bag,' observed Snorri.

Neither Solveig nor her father asked him what it was, but Snorri told them anyhow. 'A hole,' he said. 'A hole in your bucket, your pocket, your bag, and they're no more use than a hobbled nag.'

'What else?' asked Halfdan. 'Come on, Solva!'

'My files . . . my saw . . . my carving knife . . .' rehearsed Solveig, speaking more to herself than the two men. 'My third eye . . . oh! my grindstone . . . and the fish-hooks Vigot gave me, I'll need those . . . my linen shift, the spare one . . . my felt cloak, my reindeer skin . . . oh! my leggings, and my soft shoes—'

'In the name of the Norns,' complained Halfdan, 'what else? If you bring much more, you'll need your own boat.'

'Father!' Solveig reproached him.

'When you set out on a journey, the best thing you can bring weighs the least,' pronounced Halfdan.

'Your wits,' replied Solveig, and she gave the most enormous yawn. 'Well, they'll have to just follow me.'

As soon as Solveig had gathered her few possessions, her father swung the Varangian cloak round her shoulders and secured the handsome silver clasp.

'It's too long,' complained Solveig.

'Grow taller!' Snorri growled.

'Now your helmet,' said Halfdan, grinning. He handed the lamp to Snorri and told Solveig, 'Hold back your hair. Bunch it up as high as you can.'

Then Solveig's father lowered the conical iron helmet over the crown of his daughter's head until the nosepiece was resting on her nose, gently squashing it.

Snorri held up the oil lamp and both men chuckled.

'A man-woman,' Halfdan declared. 'A boy-girl.'

Snorri shook his head. 'More like a light-elf, I'd say. A light-elf from Asgard.'

'I'm not!' said Solveig.

'Or a wood nymph.'

'Except,' said Halfdan, 'she hasn't got a cow's tail. Not that I know of. Now, Solva!'

'I'm ready!'

'Come on! Follow me.'

In the passage outside Solveig's bedchamber, another oil lamp was sitting on a stone shelf, and by its light Solveig saw her two servants, but neither of them could see her. They were both blindfolded with strips of rag.

Their arms and legs were trussed with rope so that they couldn't even roll over, and they were both gagged – their mouths stuffed with wodges of linen so they were unable to call for help but could only give the most piteous little cheeps and squeaks.

'They won't come to harm,' Snorri said. 'Poor chicks!'

'Just a feather or two,' agreed Halfdan. 'Right, my daughter, you've left nothing behind you – nothing but dust.'

No, that's not true, thought Solveig. I'm leaving Maria, and her friendship, and all her hopes and fears. 'Maria!' she exclaimed. 'I must tell her!'

'Come on!' Halfdan growled.

'I must.'

Solveig's father rounded on her. 'Are you mad?'

'I can't just leave her.'

'Solveig!' barked Halfdan. 'Once Maria knows, everyone will know. Come on! Down to the Golden Horn before anyone can do a thing about it.'

The sickle and the beehive and the lion's tail, the whale, the sail and the keel, sparkling and dim, large and small, the astonishing stars seemed to rain down on Solveig as she struggled to keep up with her father and Snorri. As she struggled and began to weep.

Solveig didn't know why she was weeping. Because she wasn't losing her father for a second time. Because Harald had honoured his word. Because it was all too sudden, this arriving in Miklagard and double leave-taking of Edith and Edwin, this first making of a friendship with Maria only to break it, this rough waking from deep sleep before dawn and rushing down to the Golden Horn.

'What is it, girl?' Halfdan asked.

Solveig didn't answer.

'Come on! Out with it!'

'Nothing,' gulped Solveig. 'Everything. All the stars showering down on me.'

The three of them hurried through the deserted Hippodrome and up the rise past the huge dark hulk of Hagia Sophia.

'Not all of them, I hope,' Snorri observed. 'The stars.'

Solveig sniffed.

'We'll be needing them as soon as we set sail.'

'Quite right,' agreed Halfdan. 'The full moon won't get you far, but you can navigate by the smallest star.'

'I've never heard that one before,' Snorri said.

'Saracen,' Halfdan told him.

The cool of the night chilled Solveig's damp cheeks. She blinked away her tears, then hoicked up her scarlet cloak and rubbed her face against it.

'I'll tell Tamas,' Snorri gently teased her. 'I will.'

'What?' Solveig sniffed again.

'You've been weeping into his cloak,' her father explained.

Snorri guffawed. 'He doesn't know we, er, borrowed it. He'll be hunting for it all over the place.'

'Oh!' exclaimed Solveig.

'He doesn't even know you're coming,' Halfdan said. 'No one does.'

Cool as the night air was, it smelt rancid too and in one narrow street much worse than that. The stink made Solveig cough.

'Follow in my footsteps,' her father told her. 'You too, Snorri.'

'They're even worse during the day,' said Solveig, 'some streets are. All the dead rats and the dung and droppings. When Maria took me to meet her father, one street was . . . slobbering.'

As soon as the three of them had crested the hill, they could hear a hubbub rising from the dark below them. Clanking and banging and bawling and neighing. They could see a network of criss-crossing lights. But already, in the east, the velvet curtain of light was beginning to lift.

Some way down the track in front of them, a man began to sing:

> 'We'll ride our kicking sea-steeds
> west over the whale's road . . .'

'Grimizo,' said Snorri at once. 'A voice fit for the gods.'

'The strongest in the guard,' Halfdan agreed.

'Strange, that. Mulish man, matchless voice.'

> 'We'll sniff our way below the stars
> through restless saltwaters.
>
> We'll gallop our land-steeds
> over hills and furrowed fields.
>
> Pounding hooves, pounding blood!
> Come scorch of sun, come shine of flood,
>
> We'll torch the forts of Sicily.
> Syracuse will spurt crimson.'

'Syracuse?' asked Solveig.

'The main town in Sicily,' Halfdan told her. 'So Harald says.'

'Grimizo!' Snorri called out.

The German didn't answer him. Not one word. It was as if night had swallowed him whole.

'I told you,' said Snorri. 'A mule of a man.'

81

'Not one,' observed Halfdan, 'as you'd choose to meet on a dark night.'

Two minutes more and Solveig and the men had descended to the Varangian quay and at once they were swept into a muscling throng.

Grimizo's words are singing them all to life, Solveig thought. The sea-steeds and the land-steeds and the guards and oarsmen. Some words can do that. They can make things happen.

By lamplight and quickening daylight, Solveig soon saw how purposeful all the Vikings were. Carrying heavy chain mail, padded leather jerkins and armfuls of shining weapons, they hurried to and fro, their scarlet cloaks swirling.

In contrast, the Byzantine harbour-men, stablemen, horses all seemed to be getting in each other's way, but Halfdan and Snorri knew where they were heading. They bumped and bruised their way through the crowd, and led Solveig up a shuddering gangplank.

Solveig saw Harald Sigurdsson at once, standing in the stern in his ivory cloak, towering over a group of his guards.

'Ah!' he boomed. And as Solveig stepped up to him, 'The first shapely sight I've seen all night.'

Solveig bit her lower lip. She smiled.

'Look at this mess!' he complained, waving at the confusion down on the quay. 'Sawyers, caulkers, sailmakers, rope-makers, oarsmen and porters, cooks, grooms . . .'

'When are we leaving?' asked Solveig.

Harald growled. 'We should've set sail already. To leave you in the palace until the last moment, and to sail before dawn. Those were my orders. '

'No one saw us,' Halfdan assured Harald. 'Not even Solveig's servants.'

Harald inspected Solveig. 'Now! You're not the only woman aboard, but you're the only one who's young, and not a drudge or a camp follower.'

Solveig wasn't sure she knew what drudges or camp followers were. 'I'll find out what I can do,' she assured Harald in a measured voice.

'You'll do what I tell you to do,' he retorted. And then he hawked and spat the phlegm overboard.

Solveig drew herself up, but the top of her helmet was still only a little higher than Harald Sigurdsson's shoulders. 'I'm not a Valkyrie,' she began with a bright smile.

'Well,' said Harald, grating his teeth, 'I suppose we should be grateful for that.'

'And not a one-breasted Amazon.'

One of the guards sniggered.

'But I can carve bone and wood and stone. I helped Bruni.'

Harald sniffed.

'Red Ottar's smith,' explained Solveig. 'Bruni Blacktooth. I know how to put an edge on a weapon.'

Before Solveig realised what he was doing, Harald Sigurdsson reached inside his cloak, snatched a blade from the back of his belt and roared.

Solveig gasped and swayed back.

Harald held the blade up right in front of her nose. It gleamed in the half-light.

'Know what this is?' he asked in a threatening voice.

'Yes. Yes, I do. Bruni forged them.'

'Scramasax,' hissed Harald. He stared at Solveig. 'Sharper than a sword. Deadlier than an axe.'

Solveig swallowed, and then nodded.

'It's yours!' Harald announced.

'Mine?' yelped Solveig.

'Just in case . . .'

Solveig took the scramasax. She grasped the handle and gazed at the blade, the way in which both the edge and the back curved towards the tip. It was almost one foot long. Then Harald closed his fist over hers. She felt his great strength, she felt her own fear. In her head. Her bloodstream. In all her limbs.

'I'll be brave,' she said. 'I'll try to be.'

'Being brave,' Harald told her, 'doesn't mean you're not afraid. Not at all. Being brave is when you take action despite your fear.'

Harald opened his fist, flexed his fingers and pushed his right thumb against the tip of the scramasax. 'Just in case . . .' he told Solveig again. 'Anyhow, it'll come in handy. For skewering meat, and shearing your golden hair. For fending off young Vikings!'

Solveig looked up at Harald under her eyelashes. 'If it weren't for you . . .' she began, but then she hesitated and shook her head.

Harald pursed his mouth. 'So long as you know it,' he told her.

9

Shoulder to shoulder, Solveig and her father stood at the starboard gunwale, looking forward, looking aft, while the Greek oarsmen eased their galley out of the Golden Horn, followed by a fleet of twenty-three ships.

Halfdan sighed. A long, noisy sigh.

'What?'

'Oh! . . . Herring. Goat's cheese – so sweet. Tender-skinned blueberries, small as a baby's fingernails.'

'Home, you mean.'

'Up the fjord, fishing. Just you and me.'

Solveig leaned into her father, and smiled.

'I'm sick of grilled meat and more grilled meat and horse-piss wine and—'

'Father!'

'You will be too.'

'Nothing could have stopped me from sailing to Miklagard, but there were many days when I longed for home,' Solveig admitted.

'Like father, like daughter,' Halfdan replied.

For a while the two of them were silent, but then Solveig began, 'That palace . . .'

Halfdan waited.

Solveig moved away from him and crooked her arms and pulled back her shoulders. 'I didn't realise. That palace is a prison. I was bound with hoops of wire. But now I'm free. Free!'

'A boat can be a prison too,' her father told her.

'I know,' said Solveig, remembering her long journey through the forests of Garthar.

'Being on a galley with a hundred men,' Halfdan continued. 'Come on. Let's talk to Nico.'

'Who?'

'The helmsman. Nicolaus.'

Solveig frowned.

'Greek or Latin or something,' Halfdan said. 'He's the saint Christian sailors pray to. Anyhow, he speaks decent Norwegian.'

'Why haven't we got a Varangian helmsman?' Solveig asked.

'Because this galley belongs to Empress Zoe,' her father told her. 'She's part of the Imperial Fleet. Nico will tell you about her.'

Nicolaus was as upright and thin as a broom handle. His hair was so sparse that it seemed to consist of single strands, and he had high cheekbones and a pointed chin.

'Yes, twenty-three ships,' Nico informed Solveig – and her father was right, he did speak good Norwegian. 'Twenty-four including us, but two are transporters, carrying our siege engines, and twenty are tubs. Not fit for fighting-men. Tubs for traders!'

Solveig shook her head.

Nico thrust out his lower lip. 'Empire,' he told Solveig. 'Byzantine Empire is like tub.'

'What do you mean?'

Nico jabbed towards the deck with his chapped right forefinger. 'Leak!' he explained. 'Plug it. Moss. Tar.'

'I know,' Solveig said. 'Wool. Resin. Fat. Anything.'

'Anything,' agreed Nico, and he jabbed towards the deck again, this time with his chapped left forefinger. 'Next day, new leak. New place. Empire like tub.'

'Nico's right,' Halfdan said. 'Empress Zoe is fighting on too many fronts. Her empire's not watertight. But it's the same at home, isn't it? How can one man ever rule for long over all of Norway and Denmark?'

'And England too,' added Solveig.

'Even Harald,' said Halfdan with a sly smile.

'Could he?' cried Solveig. 'I mean . . .' Her eyes shone.

'No man knows what lies in store for him,' her father replied. 'But the wish, what's the saying, the wish is father to the son.'

'Mother to the daughter,' Nico corrected him. 'Fathers don't bear children.'

Solveig laughed. 'No,' she said, 'daughters bear their fathers.'

The helmsman looked perplexed.

'What's this galley called?' Solveig asked him. 'I mean, I know she's not a karv, or a knar or a skute, so what is she?'

'A dromon. Every warship's a dromon. This kind is *ousiai.*'

'Ooze-ee-eye,' Solveig repeated slowly.

'She's light,' Nico told her. 'She's fast. One hundred oarsmen.'

'Ooh!' exclaimed Solveig. 'That many? There were only six on Red Ottar's boat. I rowed a half-shift.'

'You won't be rowing on this one,' Halfdan told her.

'I will if Harald tells me to,' replied Solveig, and she slipped her father a cheeky smile. Then she turned to Nico again. 'Ooze-ee-eye. *Ousiai!* I like that word. How far is it to Sicily?'

The helmsman held out his hands and balanced them. 'Seven days. First, Sea of Marmara. Here, in front of us.'

'And then?'

'Very soon the Great Sea.' Nico opened his arms and puffed out his cheeks like a statue of a sea-god, but Solveig still thought he looked more like the skeleton of a bream or a mackerel. 'Sudden winds,' added Nico. 'Sudden squalls. Near Chios.'

'Where?'

'The island of Chios. Then we sail south-west and west, five more days to Sicily.'

'Unless . . .' said Halfdan, but he didn't complete the sentence.

The helmsman shrugged. 'Always unless,' he agreed.

'Tell Solveig about the ram.'

'Ah!' exclaimed Nico, and his dark eyes glittered.

But at this moment Skarp came bounding along the deck between the upper banks of oarsmen.

'There you are!' he exclaimed. 'Still wearing Tamas's cloak, I see.'

'Oh! Has he asked for it?'

Skarp guffawed. 'He doesn't even know, does he?'

'What do you mean?'

'He's not on this boat. Not as far as I know.'

'Oh!' Solveig lowered her eyes to hide her disappointment – and so she didn't see Skarp winking at her father.

'Hmm!' grunted Halfdan. 'Well, let's hope we haven't left him behind. It's a long swim from Miklagard to Sicily.'

'Pfff!' exclaimed Skarp. 'He doesn't even know how to swim!'

When it came, it was so sudden.

One moment Solveig was standing at a long wooden table in the stuffy hold, chopping up hunks of mutton alongside muscular Vibrog and lanky Edla and the three Greek cooks, all of them twice her age or older, and the next moment the galley was lurching as if Ægir had grasped it and was giving it a good shaking. The Greek women were bawling, and all the mutton slid off the slimy counter into the soupy water swilling around in the bottom of the galley.

It was so sudden, and yet Solveig had already sensed it.

Sometimes, she thought, I'm like . . . more like a gull or a wild goose, like a goat or a cow. They know when to take wing, and when to huddle and herd and keep their heads down. My earlobes tingle. My feet sweat. Sometimes my back teeth ache. Yes, my body tells me when a storm is coming.

At dusk, the wind from the north sprang up and smacked the galley.

'Etesian! Etesian!' wailed the Greek women. Ai-ee! Ai-ee! That's how the wind sounded.

And then a wind from the north-west added its voice to the storm: violent, thudding, hissing.

Solveig and the five women tried to hold on to the counter and they could not. They threw down their meat-knives for fear of cutting themselves or stabbing each other. Trying to stay on their feet, they slipped and staggered on the spot. Then all six of them lost their footing at the same time, they whacked their ribs and knees against the galley's ribs and knees, they tore their fingernails on the galley's rough tree-nails, and they howled.

The three Greek women repeated the same word over and over again. 'Aigaion! Aigaion! Aigaion!' they cried out.

Then Solveig thought she could hear her own name. She heard someone above her yelling, bawling her name.

'Solveig! Solveig!'

Solveig tried to get to her feet and at once she was

thrown sideways again. She gasped, gulped and spat out a mouthful of the foul soup swirling around her feet.

'Solveig!' the voice roared, and it wasn't a sea-god.

Solveig got to her bruised knees. She grabbed the edge of the counter.

'Reach!' the voice insisted. 'My hands! Reach!'

Solveig dared, she let go of the counter, she reached, and at once she was lifted, light as thistledown, out of the hellhole, out and into the squall. In the muzz and the murk, she stared up at Harald Sigurdsson, white-faced.

'To the stalls!' he bellowed. 'Now!'

Solveig choked and spat out more soup.

'Now!' Harald insisted. 'Lose our horses and we're lost ourselves!'

'Yes,' gasped Solveig.

'Lift them!'

'Lift?'

'Strap them!'

'How?'

'Over the beams! Understand?'

'I don't know. Where is everyone?'

Harald growled and bared his teeth. 'Some are down there. Go on, girl! I'll send more.'

Solveig's breath was jerky. Her whole body was shaking.

'Go on!' Harald urged her hoarsely.

Sweat. Foam. Sopping leather. Sloppy dung.

Just for a moment Solveig flinched. Then she slapped her right haunch, as if she were a mare herself, got on to her knees and reached down with her feet for the ladder.

It wasn't there.

It's been uprooted, she thought. Everything has. My teeth are aching. It's a wonder we're still afloat.

Then Solveig lowered herself over the edge, took a deep breath and dropped into the horse-stalls.

At once she could hear what the roar-and-bluster had silenced for as long as she had been up on deck: neighing, whinnying, squealing, screaming and a strange pounding and grinding.

All the oil lamps hanging from the beams had swung themselves into darkness, but halfway across the stalls, in the middle of a storm of wild horses frothing and skidding, lashing with their back hooves, a single lamp bracketed to a beam-stanchion was still guttering.

Where is everyone? thought Solveig. Only those three men down at the far end . . . We need far more than that.

Solveig saw that while some horses were swinging from side to side as the galley rolled because they were half suspended by leather straps hanging from the stout beams, others weren't well secured at all. Their own slipping and sliding maddened them. They rammed against each other, they blew and bellowed, they thumped their proud heads against beam-stanchions – that was the hollow pounding Solveig had heard – and they groaned, they whinnied, they tried to jam their hooves into the deck – that was the grinding – and in terror, they screamed.

Not on my own, Solveig thought. I can't. Lift them! Strap them! Where is everyone?

As Solveig tried to pick her way towards the shuddering lamp without being kicked or crushed or trampled, she felt for a moment as if she were a little girl again. She was shuffling out into the waves, shin-deep, knee-deep, and the water was rushing at her from ahead, from her left, her right, and then it was swishing up behind her. She was completely at sea and yet safe; she was crying out not in terror but sheer exhilaration.

Solveig tossed her head, and her golden hair sparked in the lamplight. There was a man standing right in front of her. His back was turned and he was shoulder to shoulder with one of the horses, his brow pressed against the horse's brow, right between its wide eyes.

The man's fingers were linked under the horse's muzzle, and Solveig watched as he gently raised its heavy head until he could breathe right into its nostrils.

The warhorse snorted. It pulled away a little. But the man stepped forward and again pressed his forehead against the horse's brow.

Then he whispered something, Solveig couldn't hear what, and gently rubbed the horse's neck.

The Horseman's Word, thought Solveig. I'm sure it is, though I don't know what the words are. Who is he, anyhow?

Solveig couldn't help herself – the stench of the horse-stalls caught her by the throat, and she choked and then coughed.

Quite calmly and slowly, so as not to disturb his horse, the man turned round. His acorn hair all tangled, his face pink and open and eager.

'Tamas!' exclaimed Solveig.

Tamas opened his eyes wide, and gave Solveig an incredulous smile. 'Solveig!' he breathed.

'Harald changed his mind. He said I could come.'

Tamas put a filthy finger to his lips, but he couldn't stop smiling.

'Skarp told me you weren't even on this boat.'

'The trickster!'

'Horse-whispering. Is that what you were doing?'

'You heard?'

'Not the words.'

'They're between me and him.'

Solveig nodded. 'Like a charm.' She pointed to something sticking out of Tamas's sleeve. 'What's that?'

'Oh! A bone.'

'What of?'

'Not now, Solveig.'

Solveig spread her arms wide. 'It's terrible,' she said.

Once more Tamas turned to his horse and laid his forehead against the horse's brow and rubbed his neck, and Solveig ran her fingers through his silky mane.

'Is he . . . ?' she hesitated.

'An Arab,' Tamas told her. 'All our horses are Arabs.'

'What's his name?'

'Alnath.'

'What?'

'One of the stars.'

'What does it mean?'

'The butting one!'

'It sounds like a mixture of Norwegian and Saracen.'

'There!' said Tamas. 'I've settled him now.'

'Harald told me to hoist them. Lift them and strap them.'

'On your own!'

'He said he'd send more men down.'

'That horse,' said Tamas, pointing to one whose ears were flat back and who was baring his teeth. 'Mizer. He's terrified.'

Then Solveig and Tamas took hold of the broad strap under Mizer's girth and, pulling together, they were able to tighten it until he was swinging free, still showing the whites of his eyes but no longer pounding the deck with his hooves.

Solveig puffed out her cheeks and noisily blew out her breath.

'Tough work,' agreed Tamas.

'We need help.'

'Much more.'

'Harald said he'd send men down.'

'I'm here to go and get them. There are twenty-four horses here. All this . . . rumpus! This havoc! Before long, the other horses will upset Alnath again.'

'I'll come with you,' Solveig said.

Tamas led the way to the deck-hatch.

'I had to jump down,' Solveig told him.

'Me too. I don't know where the ladder's gone. Stand on my shoulders.'

Oh! Despite the stench and the squalor and the suffering horses, Solveig was feeling so light-hearted.

'Skarp said you weren't even on this boat,' she told Tamas for a second time, 'and my father said he hoped we hadn't left you behind.'

'Left me!'

'Searching.'

'What for?'

Solveig drew back a little. Her eyes were dancing. 'Don't you know?' she teased him, and with both hands she grasped the lapels of her cloak.

'Ohh!' exclaimed Tamas.

'My father and Snorri found it in the guardroom. They wrapped me in it, and put a helmet on my head so they could . . . spirit me out of the palace.'

'We'll have to cut it in half,' Tamas told her.

At once Solveig started to unbuckle the cloak, but Tamas covered her fingers with his own warm hands.

Solveig's heart skipped, just as it had done in the guardroom in the palace.

'I think I saw you,' she said.

Tamas opened his eyes enquiringly.

Acorn, she thought. The same as his hair.

'In Hagia Sophia.'

Tamas smiled. 'I saw you. I waved.'

Up on deck, day had almost darkened into night, but Solveig could see that most of the Greek oarsmen were slumped over their oars and many of the Varangian guards were grasping the gunwales, spewing into the water.

'No wonder they didn't come down,' said Tamas grimly.

'They need strapping and lifting themselves,' Solveig agreed.

'Come and gone!' a man shouted from the stern. 'All over!'

'That's Nico,' Solveig told Tamas. 'He's the helmsman.'

It was true, the squall had already spent itself. The *ousiai* was battered, rigging was draped over the lateen sail like giant cobwebs, guards and oarsmen were moaning and retching, while below deck the cooks were clinging to each other and the warhorses were swinging, unable to win a firm footing; but the worst of the storm was already on its way elsewhere.

'What about the others?' Solveig asked Nico. 'The other boats, I mean.'

'Tubs.'

'Will they be all right?'

'Only morning will tell,' Nico shrugged. 'As long as our siege engines are safe.'

Through the gloom, Solveig made out two men leaning against the sternpost, involved in earnest conversation. Their backs were turned and she took a step towards them.

'But you! What would you do?'

'Me? It's your choice.'

'I know it is, man!'

Although it was difficult to hear everything, Solveig still recognised their voices.

'. . . could ask Nico.'

'I'm asking you, not Nico! Head for port? Onward?'

'That depends, you know it does . . . the damage . . . the other boats . . .'

The two voices belonged to Halfdan and Harald Sigurdsson, and Solveig swelled with pride that Harald was asking her father for his advice.

10

Solveig drowsed and woke and drowsed, dreaming of Harald's fleet of twenty-three boats, manned by more than one thousand Vikings. In one of her dreams they were sailing along the seabed, and in another they had already reached Sicily and were scattered across a beach of bones, feasting and singing and grinding their axes.

In the dark, Solveig sat bolt upright.

'The Vikings grind their axes, and they whet their scramasaxes,' she said out loud. 'The sea grinds her spears.'

Then she lay down and went back to sleep again.

The five cooks slumbering around Solveig in the bows were so deeply asleep that they didn't twitch their little fingers, and neither did they stir when Solveig suddenly sat up again as day dawned. She stared at her broken fingernails, she stretched until her sore shoulders cracked. She groaned and she yawned, then she stood up and padded down the length of the boat.

It was just as Nico feared. The squall had bullied and scattered Harald's fleet, and there was no way of telling where the other boats were, or whether they were still afloat, even the two transporters.

Again and again Solveig scanned the skipping and skeltering waves as if her eyes must be tricking her.

'What I think . . .' Solveig began. 'What I hope . . .' She faltered into silence.

'Hope,' repeated the helmsman. 'Hanging on ropes of wind.'

Solveig looked at him fearfully.

Nico sniffed. 'Better to hope than not to hope. Hope's your good friend.'

'Your light friend,' said Solveig. 'And gloom is your dark friend.'

The helmsman nodded. 'Both will keep you company on your journey.'

As Solveig made her way back along the deck she heard someone singing, and it wasn't Vikings on a beach of bones or the wavering vowels of the wind.

Grimizo, thought Solveig. A voice fit for the gods; that's what Snorri says.

Solveig stopped to listen, but Grimizo was just ending his song: 'And yet . . . And yet things turned out better than I thought.'

Solveig advanced on Grimizo. 'What were you singing?' she asked.

'A song.'

Solveig waited but Grimizo said nothing more.

'A dawn-song?' asked Solveig, remembering Sineus and the song he had sung on the quay at Ladoga.

'A disgruntled song,' Grimizo replied.

'What does that mean?'

'What does it sound like?'

Solveig snorted like a sow.

'A grumpy song.'

'Oh!' said Solveig, and she couldn't help smiling. 'Will you sing it again?'

Grimizo didn't reply, but Solveig held her ground and after some while the German cleared his throat:

'Me? I got drenched. Soaked to the skin.
In that sudden squall our craft was mauled,
it was wrenched. My life was at risk
in this bucket – this bucking, oozing ousiai.
Call her a boat? I call her a joke.
To Hel with her! I've never seen
such a disaster. And yet . . . And yet
things turned out better than I thought.'

'Yes!' exclaimed Solveig, cupping her hands tightly as if they were guarding some truth. 'Yes, that's how it was. And how things are.'

The north wind hissed through a split in the square sail as long as a sword-blade.

'I like your words,' Solveig said. 'You play with them.'

The German met her eye for a moment, and gave her a nod, and then Solveig continued on her way between the banks of men slumped over their oars.

For the next three days, Harald Sigurdsson's crew sailed west without sighting a single one of their companions. To begin with, the stink of their own vomit and the stench from the horse-stalls knotted their throats, and their mouths were full of complaints that they'd left the Golden Horn in too much of a hurry, without making sacrifices or even saying charms. One guard pointed out that Empress Zoe's priests had wafted incense and sprinkled holy water over all of them in Hagia Sophia, but that was as nothing to most of the Varangians. As hollow-cheeked Priskin declared at some length, 'The god of the sea is Ægir, even if Nico and the Greeks have another name for him. Ægir's the god of the sea, and he always has been, and his wife with her drowning-net is Ran, and the god of winds and squalls and storms is Njord. If we don't pray to them, we're fools.

Men can die even when they're not fated if they're neglectful.'

Is this true? wondered Solveig. Is my life as uncertain . . . as chancy as that?

'You, Priskin,' said one guard, 'you make all your opinions sound like facts.'

'You should have been a temple priest.'

'Yes, words, words, always words.'

'Go on! Give half of them away to Grimizo!'

But as the wind went round to the south-east and ushered their boat towards Sicily, the mood aboard changed. The Varangians recovered their appetites, Solveig and two guards sat shoulder to shoulder stitching the rips in the square canvas sail, several Greek oarsmen searched out and stopped all the leaks, while a number of guards mucked out the horse-stalls and swabbed the deck. Often they shouted to each other, now and then they sang together, and Solveig saw how at midday, when the scorching sun rode high in the skull of the sky, they fell quiet, almost dazed by the brightness of the day. By the way the light seemed to fizz and the clouds seemed somehow to gather and rise – rise as if they were ascending to Asgard – and the sea was not one blue but every blue, not one green but every green, intense yet transparent.

'Little hops,' observed Solveig. 'Little skips and jumps.'

'All the way to Sicily,' her father replied. 'That's what Nico says. Already it's as if the squall were just a night-hag.'

'*Swa swa hit ne waes*,' agreed Solveig.

'What?'

'Edwin used to say that. *Swa swa hit ne waes*: as if it had never been.'

For a while the two of them stared at the waves, almost

mesmerised, and then Solveig said, 'I keep wondering about Edith and her baby. And her home in England.'

'What about us?' asked Halfdan. 'When will we see home again? It's more than halfway through Hay Month.'

Solveig filled her lungs with air, and closed her eyes, and very slowly let it all out again.

Oh! The sweetness and the ache. The sweep of the waves and the curving hill-brow above their farm, the sharpness of salt and the fragrance of hay, her two cows lowing and the croon-and-wash of the ocean, all her journeying and the womb of home: they were all part of each other.

'Everything is different here,' she told her father. 'Everything is strange. But it's less strange because we're here together.'

Halfdan put his arm round her shoulders. 'Solva!' he said fondly.

On the next day, Solveig again had to stitch tears in the ripped sail, but this time she was working on her own, and by midday she was flushed and her fingertips were red and puffy. She made her way to the bows and sat there on her own, sweating. She yawned. She measured the width of her scramasax in its sheath – just a little more than the distance from the tip of her middle finger to her second knuckle. Then she slipped off her belt and stitched three loops to the back of it so that she could wear her scramasax at all times.

Tamas spied her. He walked up and stood right over her.

'You're in my light,' Solveig complained.

So the young Viking sat down beside her, and for a while he watched her. 'You know what they say?' he observed.

'Who?'

'Men. About women.'

Solveig groaned.

'Wives and mothers, hearth-guardians, farm mistresses, feud-harbourers . . .'

Solveig groaned again. 'I've heard it all before. "Flying into rages . . . beautiful, dangerous . . . fickle . . . witches."'

Tamas pursed his mouth. 'But I've never heard them called warriors, well-armed, bloodthirsty, battle-hungry—'

'We're not!' exclaimed Solveig, and then she saw Tamas was making fun of her.

'You're giving women a bad name, Solveig,' Tamas said, and he poked her in the ribs with his left forefinger.

'Anyhow,' countered Solveig, 'what about the Valkyries?'

'They're not fighting women,' Tamas replied. 'They bring back slain warriors to Valhalla. Now, shall I help you to put on your belt?'

Solveig swatted him with the back of her hand. 'Go away!' she exclaimed.

'You do know how to wear it, do you?'

'My scramasax? Of course I do. Flat across the small of my back. The edge of the blade upward.'

The third day was no less peaceable, no less glassy than the first two, and Solveig at last completed her repairs to the sail. She flopped down on to the deck, just aft of the banks of oarsmen, and gnawed a rib of pork, most of it gristle, and swilled it down with sour milk. Then she delved into her bag of bones: one tine of a red deer's antler; an oval disc of walrus bone; lumps of whalebone and soapstone, both a bit bigger than her clenched fist, and a piece of amber twice as large as her thumbnail; bits and pieces of oak and maple that she had already begun to work into combs, pins and beads. Last

102

of all, Solveig pulled out the shoulder blade that she'd found at Stiklestad.

I don't know why I've brought it all this way, she thought. Or rather, I do. I'm going to carve runes for the battle-ghosts I heard singing in Trondheim fjord, runes for every Viking who has died in battle. The waste! Oh, the grief of it! Some so young. As young as I am . . . as young as Tamas!

Solveig flinched.

No! I wish I hadn't thought of that.

She groaned and rocked from side to side.

Sometimes, sometimes I can scarcely bear my thoughts and memories.

Solveig stared at the bleached shoulder blade. I don't know what the right runes are, she thought. Not yet.

Almost absently-mindedly, she delved into the bone-bag again, and grasped the wad of bog cotton at the bottom of it. Then she teased out her father's brooch nestling inside it and she squeezed it. She squeezed it until her blood warmed the gold.

Solveig picked up her little hammer and began to tap it on the deck. Without realising it, she was tapping the very rhythm, the double-beat, of her own heart.

I could carve a bone for Tamas, or cut a charm for Nico – one to send the sea to sleep.

Solveig stared down at her lap and the deck without really seeing them.

Or else Grimizo. Something to cheer him up. But I think he quite likes being gloomy.

The longer Solveig sat there, the more people she thought of. Oleg, the master carver in Ladoga, she could give him something on her way home; a bone comb for her little stepbrother Blubba who told her at midwinter that he wanted her to be happy again. Or Maria? What about Maria, surrounded but alone, her father dying, her mother locked away in a nunnery?

It's like this, she thought. Always. At first. I don't know what, don't know who for, don't know which piece of wood or stone or bone. Even if my skills were as great as those of Volund, the master smith, I still wouldn't know. I don't think I would. No, I have to wait . . .

Carving means warming your cold skills with all your thinking, your imagination, your feeling.

11

'Womanish! That's what you are!' exclaimed Skarp.
Snorri gave Skarp an affable smile and then slipped Solveig a wink.

'Soft!' said Skarp loudly.

'What a terrible insult, Skarp,' Snorri taunted him.

'I asked you what you thought about having a young woman aboard, not to sick up all your feelings. Since when were soft feelings a match for hard thoughts?'

'Poor Skarp!' observed Snorri. 'He doesn't trust his feelings. Doesn't he know there's woman in every man and man in every woman?'

'A young woman aboard,' Skarp repeated. 'I'm warning you – no good will come of it.' Then he jabbed his right forefinger in front of Solveig's nose. 'You're a bad omen.'

The afternoon air began to gather around them. It thickened into mist and blinded the glaring red eye of the sun. Its chill stopped the words in Snorri's and Skarp's throats.

'On my way to Miklagard,' said Solveig thoughtfully, 'the blacksmith told me about magicians who make death-spells.'

'That's right,' said Snorri. 'Sendings. In Iceland, they do.'

'Vapours and mists like this one,' Solveig went on. 'He said they can board boats and cross oceans.'

'There you are!' exclaimed Skarp. 'What did I tell you?'

The thick white sea mist closed around the *ousiai*. It clamped her in its grip, and the wind dropped, it fell away to nothing. The sip-and-suck of water around the bows sounded quick and keen, and so did the creak of the boom, but the shrieks of the seabirds following the boat and the sound of Nico's tolling stern bell were somehow muffled.

This mist has taken away my eyes, Solveig thought, and now it's taking my ears as well. The bell sounds so doleful. Even this sip-suck, slap-drip, it's like the sound of a hundred widows weeping.

Solveig shivered and wrapped her arms around herself. And then, without knowing quite why, she began to feel very restless. She made wings of her arms and pulled back her shoulders. She stood up again.

'What's wrong?' asked Snorri.

Solveig sighed. 'I don't know. I think I'll find my father.'

'Poor man!' said Skarp half-heartedly.

As Solveig glided along the deck, she called out her father's name several times, but now her own voice sounded muffled, almost lifeless. Twice she tripped over the legs of Greek oarsmen who swore at her, twice she apologised. She groped her way to the mast and leaned against it, cheerless.

Where is he? she thought. I haven't seen him all morning. How long until this sea mist lifts?

Solveig closed her eyes and started to murmur words, as if she were singing-and-saying a charm, and then she twisted them round each other:

'White shift
Blinding drift
Soft fist
Salt-kissed
  Please lift

Salt twist
White drift
Soft-kissed
Shroud shift
  Please lift'

The sending or the swirling sea mist or lung of Sicilian fog, whatever it was, heard Solveig. It began to lift.

Solveig kept screwing up her eyes, then opening them as wide as she could, blinking, and wiping her salty cheeks. Whatever she looked at swayed and danced – men made of flesh and bone, wooden crates, coils of hempen rope, even the thick torsos of the boom and mast – as if they were uncertain of their shapes.

Then she heard the bell. No longer tolling, no longer doleful, but clamouring, warning, as the helmsman thwacked it again and again with a mallet.

At once Vikings and Greeks were leaping to their feet all around Solveig, grabbing their weapons, their oars, getting in each other's way, yelling.

'There!' bawled the guard Gissur, pointing to starboard. 'There!'

Solveig stared. Everyone stared.

'Dhow!' shouted the helmsman. 'Saracen!'

The dhow sliced through the silken water alongside them. One hundred paces. No! Less than that. No more than an arrow's shot.

Then Solveig made out the row of men standing on her deck, watching them.

How did they know we were here? In all that mist? Did they throw its cloak over us? Was it them? Father, where are you?

'To your benches!' bellowed a voice right behind her. Harald Sigurdsson. 'Every man to his oars! Row, men! Row!'

Then Harald rounded on Solveig. 'Stay where you are, girl.'

'My father!' Solveig gasped.

'Stay by this mast! You've got your scramasax?'

The Greek oarsmen obeyed Harald. Following their strokesman, they all rowed as one, but it was soon apparent that the dhow was the faster boat.

As the last of the sea mist vanished and the sea glittered as if some god had showered it with scales of mica, Solveig could see that some of the men aboard the Saracen boat were waving curved swords.

'Sabres!' she whispered. Sabres, like the one King Yaroslav gave my father. Where are you? What are the Saracens doing? Why are they shadowing us?

'All right!' barked Harald, devouring the deck with huge strides, bearing down on Nico. 'All right! We'll ram them! Ram them and board them.'

Harald hurried back past her with battle-light shining in his eyes. He spoke to the strokesman, and the Greek immediately ordered the port oarsmen to raise their blades until the *ousiai* had swung round and was pointing just ahead of the dhow.

'Vikings!' yelled Harald. And he raised his massive battleaxe above his head.

All around Solveig, the Varangians were pulling on their padded jerkins and scrambling for their swords, their scramasaxes, their twisting-spears.

And then she saw them, emerging from the gloomy horse-stalls below deck into the dazzling light, first her father, then Tamas, and at once she called out to them. But what with all the rumpus on deck, neither of them saw or heard her.

'Row!' shouted the strokesman. 'Everyone! For dear life, row!'

Yes, thought Solveig. Life is dear. Every scrap and breath of it.

The *ousiai* began to pick up speed again. She surged through the sparkling water. And although the helmsman of the dhow saw what was happening, he had too little time to hand down orders to his crew or to change direction.

'Greasy!' yelled Nico. 'You sidling Saracen! We've got you!'

The helmsman of the dhow did his best to drag the double rudder towards him and veer away from the *ousiai*, but he couldn't escape. Nico drove the spiked ram right into the dhow just aft of midship and just below the waterline.

Oh! The jolt, the growl and then the splintering, the scraping and gnashing and grim grinding of it.

Solveig was thrown forward against the mast, and the great beam itself shook in its socket. Her teeth rattled. And then she heard the yelling and howling, the flapping and splashing.

Solveig could see the dark faces of the pirates, their pitch-black hair, the whites of their eyes. The iron ram had driven their dhow down and pinioned it, and they were trapped as the ravenous water rushed into the hold of their boat.

Hugging the mast, half-hiding behind it, Solveig watched one man climb right up on the gunwales of the dhow and then leap across, trying to board the *ousiai*.

Howling, he fell between the two boats.

'Careful!' said a voice behind her.

'Oh!' gasped Solveig. 'Father!'

'They've got spears!'

Solveig stiffened. Every muscle in her body.

'You're safe.' Halfdan stood behind his daughter and wrapped his strong arms around her. 'This mast's in front of you. I'm behind you. You're safe.'

Now Solveig was trembling – all of her. Her lips. Her fingers, her kneecaps, her toes.

'Pity!' growled another voice. Solveig tried to screw her head round to look up, but Harald Sigurdsson pushed the back of his hand against her cheek.

'Stay where you are!'

'Pity?' asked Halfdan.

'She's filling so fast that the water will drag her off the ram before we can board her.'

'Board her?!' gasped Solveig.

'And if we can't board her, it's goodbye to our booty.'

Solveig was dry-mouthed. She kept trying to swallow.

Then Nico began to thwack the stern bell again.

'In the name of Odin!' bellowed Harald.

He whirled round angrily. Then Halfdan loosened his hold on Solveig, and all three of them saw the helmsman was gesturing to starboard.

A second Saracen dhow was cutting through the water straight towards them.

'That's why!' cried Solveig. 'That's why the first boat was waiting.'

'Get your jerkin on, man,' Harald told Halfdan.

'Father!' wailed Solveig, and she grabbed his right arm.

'And your helmet. They're coming straight for us.'

Just for a moment, but it seemed as long as a lifetime, the three of them stood side by side gazing at the dhow, Solveig flanked by her father and Harald. Then Harald roared like a wild boar at bay, and the sound quickened the blood of every Viking aboard the boat.

Halfdan looked down at his daughter. 'Now then!' But before he could continue, their bow kicked up, and the whole boat rocked from stem to stern as the weight of the water dragged the dhow off the ram.

'What did I say?' Harald shouted, waving towards the sinking dhow. 'The water got there first. Right, Solveig. Follow me!'

Solveig could hear the cries of the pirates as the dhow sank under them. Some were still standing on deck; some had jumped overboard and were grasping crates, spars of wood, oars, anything that would float. And around her the Vikings were humming and buzzing, all on the same pitch, as if the *ousiai* were a huge hive and they a swarm of vengeful bees.

'Follow me!' Harald repeated, and he spun on his right heel and strode towards the stern.

Solveig looked beseechingly at her father.

'Do as he says,' Halfdan told her. 'He'd sooner lose his right arm than see anyone harm you.'

'That's not true.' Solveig shook her head.

Halfdan raised his hand and stroked Solveig's hair.

'What about you?'

'Shoulder to shoulder. Each for the other. Each for ourselves. Like it was at Stiklestad.'

Solveig hurled herself at her father. She dug her fingernails into the back of his leather jerkin. She grazed her left cheek against his bristling beard.

'Go on!' Halfdan told her. 'Follow Harald!'

'Solveig!' howled Harald. 'Now!'

For just a moment the two of them looked the other in the eye, and then Harald planted his heavy hands on Solveig's shoulders.

'Up here!' he told her.

'The backstay?'

'Go on.'

Solveig gazed up, up the thick rope to the top of the mast.

'Go on! Shinny up.'

'Down with the horses,' pleaded Solveig.

'Up, I said.'

'Wait,' Solveig told him.

'Where are you going? No!'

Solveig ran to her sleeping quarters just aft of the mast, swept up her canvas bag and hurried back to the stern again.

'My bones,' she panted.

'How dare you!'

'You don't understand.'

'No!' said Harald very sharply.

But Solveig defied him. She hung the bone-bag around her neck, reached up and pulled herself off the deck.

'Stand on my shoulders!' Harald told her. 'Go on, now.'

Solveig began to haul herself up the rough, taut rope.

'Go on! You're on your own.'

'I am!' gasped Solveig.

'Top of the backstay!' Harald called. 'The only safe place on this boat.' And then: 'If anyone comes up after you, use your scramasax. Poke his eyes out!'

The higher Solveig shimmied, the steeper her climb. Well before she was able to reach out and touch the mast, she was gasping. Her forearms and shoulder joints were aching and, tough as they were, her hands were burning.

More than forty feet below, the second Saracen dhow was sidling up to their boat, and Solveig could see that the men lining the rope rail were holding grappling hooks.

Then she saw how some of the pirates who had

jumped overboard were swimming round the back of the *ousiai* towards the second dhow.

Hanging from the backstay, Solveig watched the first dhow sink. Burdened by her cargo of water, she lay low, her gunwales scarcely clearing the waterline. Then, quite slowly, her bow rose, it rose upright. After that, the dhow went straight down, as if she were being pulled from below; gently she slipped below the wavelets. And above her, on the surface of the water, there was nothing but whorls of blue roses, black roses, scimitars of light, and a mass of popping bubbles.

Solveig gave a deep sigh. Several times more she dragged herself further up the backstay, and there she was! There she was, grasping the spar that ran along the top of their sail.

Solveig was able to swing one leg over the spar and sit on it as if she were riding a horse. She kept hold of the very top of the mast with both hands and, although the spar shifted from side to side and sometimes swung alarmingly, she felt reasonably secure.

Below Solveig, the pirates had gripped the *ousiai* with their iron hooks. They were vaulting on to the deck just aft of the banks of oarsmen. They were howling. Caterwauling. Whirling their sabres.

The Vikings waited for them, standing shoulder to shoulder. Almost fifty men.

Then the pirates leaped at them, and Solveig could see this was not a battle between a Viking troop and a pirate band but combats between pairs of men, pairs and sometimes trios, fighting to the death.

Solveig saw one Varangian swing his axe and cut off a pirate's hand. She saw the hand fall at his feet, saw his sabre skidding across the deck.

She saw one pirate lunge at a Varangian and drive his knife straight into his stomach.

Solveig saw her father far below her, she saw Tamas, and she clenched the mast as if she were trying to squeeze all the breath from its wooden throat.

Solveig saw scarlet blood. Blood pumping, blood oozing. She smelt it. She tasted it on her tongue, in her throat.

She didn't know whether the Vikings were winning or the pirates were winning. All she could see was whirling and swinging, hacking, chopping, slicing; all she could hear was clanging, smacking, howling and grunting and choking and gargling.

'Priskin!' screamed Solveig. 'Priskin!'

But Priskin couldn't hear her, and even as he jerked away from one lunging pirate, a second man buried his knife in the Viking's back.

Priskin howled. And reaching for his back with his left hand, he exposed his chest. His throat.

Solveig screwed up her eyes as the pirates finished him off. She sobbed and shook.

At first, Solveig felt as if each slash, each slice were wounding her as well. Cutting deep into her. But she was so horrified at what she was seeing that she became dazed and confused. Her mind was like tangled rigging.

Tamas!

What if they kill my father?

Nico . . . What if . . . ? No! No!

Vibrog? Edla?

Alnath! Alnath!

Tamas! You. Where are you?

As if Tamas had heard her thoughts, Solveig saw him looking up at her. His shining face, his acorn hair. He was waving and he was shouting, but she couldn't hear what.

Solveig leaned right forward. She took one hand off the mast and reached towards him.

114

That was when the slender leather band around her neck snapped. Before she could do anything about it, her bead, her violet-grey eye, the one Oleg had given her, plummeted to the deck. It bounced, and bounced again. She saw a Saracen swoop on it as if he were a predatory bird, but the bead eluded him, bounced a third time and disappeared over the gunwale.

My eye! My third eye!

Burning as the day was, Solveig shivered. She could hear the jerkiness of her breathing. The thumping of her heart. The pounding of her own blood.

What if?

My father . . .

Harald . . .

What then?

But it was otherwise. Although the pirates did kill three Vikings and grievously wound two more, they paid a terrible price themselves. Thirteen of them lay sprawling on the deck of the *ousiai*, dead or almost dead, squirming and twitching in their death throes.

Solveig didn't know who gave the signal, but all at once the Saracens disengaged. They reeled back to the gunwales; trying to shield each other they tugged at their grappling hooks, they grabbed their dhow's rope rails and threw themselves back on to her deck.

One young pirate wasn't so fortunate, though. Two guards, Bolverk and Egil, cornered him against the mast, and he dropped to his knees and begged them for mercy.

His eyes, thought Solveig. They're like Maria's. So dark and shining.

'Go down to Hel!' Egil roared.

'No!' screamed Solveig. 'Don't!'

But then Bolverk drove his scramasax into the pirate's throat, and his scarlet lifeblood leaped out of him. The boy fell over sideways.

Even then, the Vikings weren't finished with him. Staring down, aghast, Solveig could see the two men hacking at the boy's neck until they had severed his head from his body.

Egil lifted up the Saracen's head by the hair and glared at him.

'Pray for mercy!' he gasped. 'Beg for mercy now!'

Still holding the swinging head, Egil backed away from his companion.

'Ready?' he panted.

Then he cradled the boy's head and tossed it to Bolverk as if they were playing a game of catch.

Solveig screwed up her eyes. She began to retch. She wished she too were dead.

Ruthless as he was, and hungry for booty, Harald counted his dead and wounded companions and assessed it would be too risky to board the dhow. He called his men off.

Solveig heard him bawling, 'Enough! Enough! Let them carry the word!'

Carry the word! Carry the word! Solveig wasn't to know it, how could she, but those three words would keep her company – just as a refrain keeps company with the verses of a poem – for as long as she lived on this middle-earth.

Harald gazed up at her, still sitting athwart the spar above the sail.

'Come down!' he called. 'Solveig! Come down.'

But Solveig didn't want to come down. She didn't want to, not even when her father and Tamas joined Harald at the foot of the backstay. She sat in her high seat, feeling so numb, so empty, needing time inside herself before she came down into the world.

Her mind idled; over surfaces it drifted like a seabird on outstretched wings.

It's like this for Allfather, she thought, when he sits in his high seat. Odin witnesses everything that is – everything in the nine worlds. He remembers everything that has been and can foretell everything that will be.

All the pain. The horrors. All the cruelty . . .

Solveig swayed. She closed her aching eyes.

How can I belong? How can I?

They're animals. Vikings, pirates, pirates, Vikings.

This is not my world.

How can I go down?

12

The Vikings sailed west, boasting and jesting, but frustrated not to have boarded and plundered either of the Saracen dhows, and angry at the deaths of three of their companions, Priskin one of them.

'Mind you,' said Skarp, 'dying won't stop Priskin's mouth.'

'By now, he'll be sitting in Valhalla,' agreed Snorri, 'and boring Odin himself.'

'I never knew a man who talked so much,' Skarp added.

'And unless I'm mistaken,' Snorri observed, 'Halfdan here is bound to know some saying . . .'

Halfdan fixed Snorri with a knowing look. 'A wise man is wary,' he began. 'He listens with his ears, watches with his eyes, and keeps his mouth shut.'

'What did I tell you!' exclaimed Snorri. 'Poor Priskin! May those Saracens die a thousand deaths.'

'They have a saying much the same as ours,' Halfdan volunteered.

'Another time!' said Skarp, waving him away.

But Solveig's father had the last word. 'Nothing speaks more loudly than silence,' he announced. And with that, he spun slowly on the ball of his right foot and stumped off.

For her part, Solveig was sickened by the deadly

fighting she had witnessed at such close quarters, and troubled by the way in which the Vikings had been so unnecessarily cruel. She felt as if her blood were on fire inside her.

I've seen a man die before. I saw that Pecheneg arrow go straight through Red Ottar's mouth and stick out of his back. I was standing right next to him, I saw the scarlet bubble. But this was much more horrible. That head . . . How could they kill that boy when he was begging for mercy? And then dishonour him?

On the evening before they sighted Sicily, Nico told Solveig they were nearing land.

'How do you know?'

'How does a man know he is hungry? His own body tells him.'

'Yours doesn't,' Solveig said. 'You're too thin.'

The helmsman shrugged his bony shoulders. 'Look!' he exclaimed. 'That flock of birds. They only fly near shore. Look there! That cloud-cap. My eyes, tongue, my nose . . . everything tells me.'

'Mihran was like that,' Solveig said. 'Our helmsman – all the way from Ladoga to Miklagard. He could always tell.'

'God of winds lives in Sicily,' Nico told her. 'Aeolus.'

'No,' said Solveig, 'Njord – he's the wind-god, and he lives in Asgard.' She smiled ruefully. 'But as I keep finding out, people in different places have different names and stories for the same gods.'

'God of winds,' the helmsman repeated. 'God of fire. Mount Etna. You will see. You will hear.'

But all Solveig kept seeing was Egil and Bolverk playing catch, and hacking and slicing and chopping and blood, and all she kept hearing was yelling and howling and screaming. Nico understood how distressed Solveig still was. He took her chapped right hand

and placed it on the tiller and laid his own hand over it.

'Hope,' he reminded her. 'Don't forget your light friend.'

That night, Solveig lay under the stars with her head full of all kinds of bits and pieces with which the kind helmsman had tried to cheer her: how the Greeks call Sicily the three-pointed island and how it was once part of the Empire of Byzantium, how the great volcano Etna had once erupted and covered half the island with ash, how dark-skinned Saracens have ruled it for eight generations, and how most of the men have more than one wife, and all the women wear veils, and how a monster-dog with six heads used to grab six men for dinner from each passing ship, and how some islanders know how to stop ice from melting, even when it's blazing midsummer.

'Now sleep and wake,' Nico said, 'and when you wake, the island will be waiting.'

Nicolaus had steered traders to Sicily more than half a dozen times and knew exactly where he was heading, and where Harald Sigurdsson and the commander of the Imperial Fleet were to meet and combine forces.

First he steered straight towards the twin peaks of Mount Etna and then veered south.

'Round this cape,' he told Harald at daybreak, 'then west again. We make landfall at small bay . . .' The helmsman pushed out his lower lip. 'Cove near Girgenti. About noon tomorrow.'

'What about Maniakes?' Harald asked.

Nico shook his head. 'Already there? Maybe.'

Harald gritted his teeth. 'Thousands of Greeks,' he said. 'Thousands. And forty-seven Varangians.'

With both hands, Nico patted the air in front of him, calming Harald's impatience.

'And the girl?' Harald asked him. 'Solveig.'

The helmsman patted the air again. 'Time,' he said. 'She needs time.'

Under his breath, Harald growled. 'I should never have brought her.'

Once Solveig had helped the other women prepare food below deck – grilled meat and fruit, some of it rancid, some mushy, and none of it appetising – she picked her way to the bows and tucked herself into the space between the forestay and the stem-post. Her father and Tamas both saw her there, but each knew she wanted to be left alone. As for Harald Sigurdsson, he took the helmsman's advice about giving Solveig time, or else he was too preoccupied with other matters.

Solveig gazed at the island of Sicily spread out in front of her. It occupied the whole western horizon.

Later, she told the helmsman that it didn't look like an island at all, but Nico just shrugged and said that, even with favourable winds, it still took two days to sail the length of Sicily and more than four days to sail right round it.

It all looks so dead, thought Solveig. So dry. Burned.

Why would anyone live here when they could live where grass grows green and trees whisper and fields wear coats of many colours?

Why have so many people fought to win Sicily? Not just Saracens and settlers from Miklagard but Greeks and Africans and Romans and . . . I can't remember everything Nico told me.

As Solveig gazed across the jingling water, the large pancake of cloud over the island somehow congealed and darkened, and the wavelets between her and the shore looked quite steely.

Solveig sighed. Weather changes, she thought. And

my moods change. But I want one part of me, the core of me, not to change. So I can be afraid or hopeful or joyful, so I can be angry or ache like when I met Maria's father, and yet still be the same. I don't know how I can be like this, I don't even know how to say it exactly. But I know I must try.

In this way, sometimes staring out at the island, picking out squat white farmsteads and trees with one hundred begging hands, sometimes looking into herself, her own head and heart, Solveig slowly began to look forward again as well.

For much of the morning, Nico sailed their *ousiai* along the coast about half a mile offshore, passing several wide-mouthed bays. But then the land began to rise and become more rocky and almost at once the helmsman swung the boat round towards a much smaller bay – a cove almost – and called on the Greek oarsmen to man their oars.

As soon as they had driven the boat up the gravelly beach and the gangplank had been pushed out, Harald bounced down it and splashed ashore. He unsheathed his sword and shouted. The cliff guarding the far side of the cove heard him.

Harald rounded on the boat and his companions. 'Hear that?' he yelled. 'What I say, Sicily says.'

Then he turned again to the cliff. 'Sicily,' he yelled. 'Sicily, fall to me! Follow me!'

'Fall to me,' grumbled the cliff. 'Fall to me! Follow me!'

First the Vikings waddled and stamped around, finding their land legs. Then Harald ordered some men to scale the cliff-top and establish a lookout post there – and he showed others exactly where he wanted them to pitch their poled tents, on the stubby foreshore well above the tideline at the back of the beach. While he was doing this, Solveig sighted a ship heading straight for them.

Then another.

Almost at once a third.

'We're trapped!' she cried. And she leaped back up the gangplank and ran to the stern.

The helmsman scrutinised the three ships very carefully. His brow was furrowed and he pressed his lips together.

'Nico!' barked Harald from below. 'Who are they? Nico?'

'Dhows, are they?' Solveig asked him fearfully.

The helmsman didn't reply. He kept tugging his oily wisps of hair with his splayed fingers.

'How could they have followed us without our seeing them?'

Nico looked Solveig straight in the eye, and he smiled. 'No,' he said. 'No.' Then he leaned over the gunwales and called down to Harald. '*Ousiai!* They're *ousiai*. Your own companions.'

Hearing this, many of the men around Harald yelled and raised fists above their heads.

Harald himself stood still as a statue, gazing at the approaching ships, and Solveig couldn't be sure whether he was smiling or scowling.

Both at the same time, she thought.

Before nightfall, nine of Harald's fleet had sailed in, and the cove was crammed with Vikings and Greek oarsmen embracing their companions, talking, laughing, and establishing a first footing on the island. By the time another eleven *ousiai* had come in during the next morning, only three boats were missing. One old tub and the two transporters carrying all the Vikings' siege engines.

'The etesian!'

123

'Mother storm!'

'Whirled us round and round.'

'Yes, we saw them go down.'

'Three boats, yes. The two transporters.'

'Upended.'

'We couldn't get near them.'

'No one. No.'

Harald Sigurdsson filled his lungs with salty air and then slowly, very slowly, he expelled it all again. The press of men around him fell so silent that everyone could hear the wavelets chafing and chiding the bulwarks of the boats lined up along the shore.

'A cruel mistress, the sea,' observed Harald in an almost expressionless voice that somehow gave his words more force – words that at once reminded Solveig of Edith's song about a woman waiting for her husband, and how:

Unless he's sick or the sea stays him,
He sails home. The sea holds him in her hands . . .

'Yes,' said Harald, 'she makes wives widows, mothers childless, and children fatherless. That etesian . . .' Harald looked around him. 'Snorri! Where are you?'

'Behind you,' a voice replied.

Harald turned. 'Right! I want you to shape a poem about this disaster. Shape a poem. And you, Solveig, you cut Snorri's words, and we'll raise a stone here, beside the water.'

Solveig nodded. It's right to remember our dead, she thought. I know it is. But that pirate . . . Don't we dishonour ourselves when we dishonour our enemies?

'So these dead men will never die,' shouted Harald.

'Never die,' the cliff answered him.

'Never die!' shouted Harald again, and with that he

clamped his jaws and stalked across the beach until he was standing right under the cliff. He raised both arms and the great crowd of Vikings milled around him.

Harald's closest companions, Snorri and Skarp, flanked him, and Halfdan was next to Snorri, the four of them facing almost one thousand men.

Standing with the galley-women, Solveig saw her father was holding a furled banner.

Land-Ravager!

'Unfurl it!' Harald ordered Halfdan. 'Let it fly. We'll build new siege engines. We'll flatten all the Saracen strongholds.'

Then Solveig's father unfurled the banner. He held it high, and Solveig shone with pride. Harald Sigurdsson listened to the fierce shouts and whoops and cheers of the Varangians. He raised both hands and clapped them above his head.

'Vikings!' he proclaimed. 'You are Vikings, not southerners. You know how to fight better than any men on middle-earth. And you know who your best companions are. Grit. Guile. Ferocity. Yes, and you know what your rewards will be. Friendship. Fame. Booty.

'I know! We're fighting for a cause. I heard what Empress Zoe said as clearly as you did. We're fighting to clean this island of filth.' Harald raised his voice an octave. '"All the filthy Saracens who've swarmed in from north Africa. Drive them out. Better yet, put them to death." Fellow Varangians, we are fighting a cause. But . . .'

'What about Maniakes?' one Viking called out.

'Yes,' shouted another, 'Maniakes. Where is he?'

Harald Sigurdsson tossed his head. 'You heard the Empress. Her messengers have instructed him to meet us here. If he comes, he comes. If not, not. So much the worse for him.

'Vikings,' shouted Harald, 'we're fighting for good reason, but more than that . . .' He paused and looked around him, and almost every man there would have sworn he was looking him in the eye. 'Do you worship our gods? Or White Christ?' Harald's mouth curled. 'Ha! Or both? Be brave then, be loyal, and your reward will be great. Not only plunder! Not only safe passage! Fame here on middle-earth! And a second home in Asgard, or in high heaven. You are Vikings!'

Georgios Maniakes, commander-in-chief of the Byzantine forces and fleet, was a mountain of a man. Not only was he almost as tall as Harald Sigurdsson – himself a head taller than most other men – but he was built like a barrel. His shoulders were broad and his torso was like a tree trunk. He had huge hairy hands, square as spades, and beetling dark eyebrows.

From the moment he stepped ashore, Harald disliked the sight of him. And when Maniakes opened his mouth and Harald heard what he had to say, he disliked him even more.

After giving Harald a peremptory greeting in the name of Christ, the Emperor Michael and Empress Zoe, he demanded, 'What kind of place is this? There's no room here for all my men. Almost one thousand Turks and Greeks.'

Harald bristled. 'Not as many as we are, then,' he replied. 'We've been camping here while you kept us waiting. Seven days.'

'I keep no one waiting,' Maniakes retorted. 'People wait on me.'

'Anyhow, there's plenty of room for you and your . . . crew,' said Harald, gesturing towards the low land abutting the cove to the east. 'Over there.'

'Take down your tents,' Maniakes ordered him.

Harald Sigurdsson glared at the commander. His left eyebrow, the higher of the two, kept twitching and jumping.

'I take orders from no one except Empress Zoe and Emperor Michael,' Harald Sigurdsson replied.

Georgios Maniakes glowered, then he snarled like a wild dog.

The cove cliff heard him, it snarled back at him, and Harald Sigurdsson put his hands on his hips and laughed.

'I'm not camping over there,' Maniakes declared. 'Look how green it is. Damp. Boggy.'

'Suit yourself,' Harald told him.

Maniakes growled, and with his right hand he reached for his sword. 'Take your tents down. I'm your commander, and I'll choose where my men camp.'

Harald smiled. 'I thought we'd sailed here to fight the Saracens, not to scrap with each other.'

'For the third and last time,' Maniakes grunted, 'take down your tents.'

Harald Sigurdsson turned on his heel, stooped, and picked up a grey pebble a little smaller than his fist. He tossed it from hand to hand.

Then he stalked over to Snorri and Skarp. 'A brute!' he confided. 'He's an ugly troll.'

'A Turkish troll,' said Skarp.

'He may be a good leader,' Harald told them. 'A good strategist, that's what I've heard. But he's also a bully, and I'm going to teach him a lesson.'

'That's right,' agreed Snorri. 'Begin in the way you mean to go on.'

Harald kept tossing the pebble from hand to hand. He walked a little way around the foreshore on his own, weighing up what to do, and then he returned to Maniakes.

'You are commander-in-chief of the Byzantine forces and fleet,' he began.

Maniakes glared at him under his beetling eyebrows.

'All my men heard the Empress,' Harald told him. '"You will fight alongside Georgios," she told me. Alongside Georgios, not under Georgios.'

'Bah!' exclaimed Maniakes.

'We Varangians who serve the Emperor and Empress are free. We're independent. That's the right we've been granted, and—'

'No army can serve two masters,' Maniakes interrupted him.

'However,' continued Harald, 'you and I can't be having arguments all the time about whose ships are going to put in first, whose horses are going to be fed first, whose tents are going to be pitched where, and Thor knows what else. Now Empress Zoe . . . she commanded me to be even-handed with you.'

'You talk too much,' Maniakes said.

'I'll cast lots with you,' Harald volunteered. 'If my lot is chosen, we Varangians will have first choice. If your lot's chosen, you Byzantines will.'

Maniakes sniffed. He hadn't the least intention of sticking to any such arrangement, but seeing Harald Sigurdsson was so stubborn, he recognised that this could be the best way to settle their argument without shedding blood.

'Who'll draw lots?' he demanded. His dark eyes glittered.

'Oh!' said Harald, looking round him. 'An innocent eye. How about that young girl over there?'

Standing with the other galley-women, Solveig realised Harald was pointing straight at her.

'Innocent?' exclaimed Maniakes. 'Is that what you call your camp followers?'

Harald shook his head. 'No, no,' he said. 'She's just . . .' He waved his right hand in exasperation. 'Take my word for it.'

'I'll take your word for nothing,' Maniakes replied.

Harald inspected the stones at his feet and picked up a second large grey pebble much the same size and shape as his own. He passed it to the commander-in-chief.

'You mark yours and I'll mark mine,' Harald told him, 'and we'll each show our mark to our henchmen.'

'I'm not a child,' Maniakes retorted in a scornful voice. 'I don't need you to tell me how to cast lots.'

Then he and Harald Sigurdsson turned their backs on one another and drew their short knives.

Maniakes was still scratching a six-pointed star on his stone when Harald called out. 'Maniakes! Let me see your mark. What if we both marked our stones the same way?'

So Maniakes showed Harald the star on his stone, and Harald sniffed and backed away and scratched a mark on his own stone. He showed it to Snorri and Skarp and Halfdan.

'All right!' said Maniakes. He pointed at one of his men who was wearing a bandage around his head, and gestured to him to unwind it.

'Stop that!' Harald commanded him. He strode over to his horse and pulled off his saddle-cloth. 'Better sweat than blood,' the Viking observed, and he laid the cloth on the foreshore. Then he and Maniakes stooped and placed their marked stones on it, without allowing anyone else to see which stone belonged to whom.

'All right!' barked Harald. He turned to Solveig and called her forward.

'All you have to do,' Harald told her, 'is choose one stone. Choose it and say, "The man who marked this stone will have first choice." Isn't that right, Maniakes?'

'Get on with it,' Maniakes snapped.

'You heard him,' Harald told Solveig.

Solveig eyed the two identical grey pebbles . . . she wrinkled her nose . . . for a moment she hesitated, and then she picked one of them up. At once Harald snatched it from her, bent his arm and hurled it as far as he could into the dancing waves.

'Mine!' he yelled. 'You chose mine!'

Maniakes' dark eyes glittered like freezing stars. 'Why?' he demanded through his barred teeth. 'Why didn't you let anyone see it?'

'Ha!' exclaimed Harald. 'Look at the other one. You'll see it's yours. It's got your mark scratched on it.'

Harald scooped up the pebble.

'Leave it alone!' growled Maniakes.

Harald presented the pebble to one of Maniakes' henchmen, and the commander could plainly see the star on it.

Harald permitted himself a dawdle of a smile. 'Over there,' he said, waving at the boggy green field abutting the cove to the east where Maniakes had refused to pitch his tents.

'You snake!' Maniakes snarled. 'You won't get away with this.'

But Harald turned and walked away, taking Snorri and Skarp and Halfdan with him. Before long, Solveig heard the four of them laughing loudly. She was sure Harald had played some trick on the Byzantine commander, but she couldn't work out exactly what.

One thing I know, she thought. If Harald can't win by fair means, he'll win by foul. He'll use force or cunning. He tricked Maniakes, I'm sure he did.

Would he trick me like that? He's smiling on me now, but can I trust him?

13

'Clear off!' exclaimed Solveig.

With both hands she swiped them away, not all the tireless, jumpy sandflies attracted by her damp wrists, the insides of her elbows and salty folds of her neck, but the tiresome young Vikings who had a way of gathering around her, sometimes in small swarms.

Without making any particular effort to do so, she attracted them and made them somehow homesick, recalling their own sisters and mothers and the girls on neighbouring farmsteads, reminding them of the creature comforts of home.

Yes, sometimes they surrounded her, sometimes jostled her, and of course this didn't escape the attention of the other women accompanying the Varangian guards – Vibrog and Edla and the drudges who did the endless round of cooking and grooming the horses, Silkisiv and the women, tawny-eyed and dark-eyed as lionesses, with whom the guards pleasured themselves.

Vibrog and Edla were jealous of her and wagged their tongues at the way Harald Sigurdsson so favoured her, but the others simply ignored her. None shared secrets with her in the way Edith had done.

They're as tough as the men, Solveig thought. At least they pretend to be. Perhaps this is what happens to women who spend too much time in the company of mercenaries. They grow a shell.

Is there no room in our ranks for pity – or for grief?

Is a man less of a man if he allows himself such feelings?

Solveig braced her shoulders and stuck out her elbows. 'You're as bad as a cloud of mosquitoes,' she told the young guards.

'That's right,' said Egil. 'We drink blood.'

'Go away!' she exclaimed.

'Away?'

'Why?'

'When we're enjoying ourselves?'

'And annoying me.'

'Come on, Solveig. Life's for living.'

One guard, Gorm, put his arm round Solveig's shoulders. 'I can help you,' he said. But all he got was a sharp elbow in his ribs.

'Not a chance,' another guard told Gorm. 'She's sweet on Tamas.'

'I'm not,' Solveig protested.

'Yes, how long was she down in those horse-stalls with him?' asked Egil.

'Quite long enough!'

All the young guards, at least half a dozen of them, guffawed.

'Sweet!' they taunted her. 'Sweet!'

But even as she denied it, Solveig knew that she was.

At this moment, Harald Sigurdsson walked past.

'You layabouts!' he reproached the young guards, without breaking his pace. But then he thought better of it and swung round. 'Pestering an innocent young girl.'

'She was lonely,' said Egil in a mournful voice.

'And lovelorn,' added Gorm.

'Anyhow,' Harald told them, 'it will be a different

story tomorrow. I've got that obstinate Turk to see sense at last – after two precious days. We'll strike camp at dawn.'

The young Viking guards cheered and waved their fists, and Gorm put his arm around Solveig again.

Harald towered over them, squeezing his blonde beard. 'Yes, Solveig,' he said. 'I told you. You'll be needing your scramasax one way or another.'

Solveig lowered her eyes. 'I can look after myself,' she told him.

'And in the meantime,' Harald told her, 'go and look after your father.'

'Why?' asked Solveig. 'What's wrong?'

'Ask him,' said Harald. And he walked off.

'What is it?' Solveig asked her father once she had found him, sitting on one of the oarsmen's benches aboard their *ousiai*. 'What's wrong?'

Halfdan pushed out his lower lip.

'Your hamstring?'

'My gut.'

Solveig frowned. 'The pork? No, it can't be. I ate it too.'

'Nothing like that,' Halfdan said. 'My gut feels knotted. I can't explain exactly. All I can say is it doesn't feel right.'

You never complain, Solveig thought. Not about your hamstring. Not about anything.

'We're going to a hill fort,' Halfdan told her.

'To attack it?' asked Solveig, grimacing.

'To lay siege to it,' Halfdan replied. 'Slow strangulation, until the Saracens are gasping and begging for mercy.' He clasped his hands over his stomach. 'If this gets worse, I'll ride back here.'

'I'll come with you,' Solveig told him. She wrapped her gold-flecked arms around his neck and nuzzled him.

'Solva!' murmured her father.

Solveig swallowed and cleared her throat. 'Your Solva suspects you, though.'

Halfdan frowned.

'I know Harald tricked Maniakes,' she said. 'He deceived him. But you, you just laughed. Look at you, you're even grinning now.'

'A Turkish troll,' Halfdan grunted.

'Since when was it right to use deceit and cunning?'

Halfdan shrugged.

'You just laughed,' Solveig reproached him.

'If you're a fox, I'm your tail,' her father growled.

'What does that mean?' Solveig demanded.

'It means,' Halfdan said slowly, 'that it's better to meet cunning with cunning. Everyone says Maniakes is not to be trusted, so Harald decided to teach him a lesson.' He reached out to Solveig.

'No!' said Solveig angrily. 'If even his ally can't trust Harald, why should anyone else? Why should his friends? Snorri . . . Skarp . . . Why should you? Why should I?'

'Solveig,' said Halfdan quite gently, 'shhh! Each of us has our faults. Me . . . You! You don't want me to tell you all yours, do you?'

That evening, Solveig was in no mood for company. She felt as uneasy as the fjord sliding past her farm, its surface unbroken but tugging and turbulent in its depths.

I accused him, she thought. My own father. I've never challenged him to his face before.

My words were half-sheathed, and they didn't seem to upset him, but they've upset me! Is it wrong to say what I think and feel? I wonder whether Maria's father has ever angered her, and whether she has confronted him.

Thoughts such as these shape-changed into night-hags. Halfdan was accused of something, Solveig didn't know what, but she had to stand witness at her own father's trial. Halfway through, the law-sayer called out that they'd got things the wrong way round. He announced that Halfdan was entirely innocent and Solveig was the accused, and that her father must stand witness against her.

Solveig's heart-care only began to dissolve at dawn when the nightwatchmen blew their aurochs horns, and all the women and Varangians around her were soon stomping around, hawking and spitting, chewing lumps of pork, slurping ale, trooping off to the shit-pits, hauling down their tents and feeding and saddling their horses.

Tamas hurried up to Solveig, combing his tousled hair with his splayed fingers. 'We're striking camp,' he told her. 'We're heading for a hill fort. Do you want to ride Alnath?'

Solveig looked puzzled. 'Why?'

'Why not?' Tamas replied cheerfully.

'I mean . . . which horse will you ride?'

'Alnath.'

'Oh! You mean . . .'

'Me in front, you behind, so long as you hold on!'

The nape of Solveig's neck tingled. 'All right, then.'

Tamas smiled like a cherub, and Solveig waved at the throng of guards.

'I know,' Tamas said joyfully. 'They're envious.'

'Where to?' asked Solveig. 'Where are we going?'

The young guard shrugged. 'No idea,' he replied. 'Some hill fort.'

It was only a short ride – a couple of hours at the most – but Solveig never forgot it. The shouting and whinnying, harness clinking and jingling, leather creaking, hooves pounding and thudding as the Viking army left camp. The quickening heat of the day. Holding on to Tamas, her arms around his waist. Leaning into his broad back. Tamas spurring Alnath into a canter, a gallop, and Solveig crying out for the joy of it, and holding on to Tamas even tighter. The two of them laughing.

'The butting one!' Tamas yelled. 'Alnath! He'll butt the Saracens until . . . until they're shrieking.'

Solveig pulled away, then twice she rammed her forehead against Tamas's right shoulder. 'And I'll butt you!' she called out.

'I surrender!' Tamas cried. 'Oh! I surrender!'

Yes, the heat of the day. And the heat of Tamas's body. Her own body, burning. And the high hills of Sicily rising ahead of her, so dry, so scorched and thirsty.

Rafts of cloud, thin as spear-shafts but more ragged, feathery almost, stood over the island. Now and then, Solveig stared up at them.

They're out of breath, she thought. Like I am. But they're so calm they're scarcely moving.

My heart, it's racing.

At one moment the high hills looked rusty, at another dusty pink and even milky blue. But then the Varangians and Byzantines, almost two thousand of them, crested a ridge, and below them they saw a green-and-gold valley. At the heart of it stood a walled hill fort, round as a giant mushroom, built on a steep hillock.

At once Harald Sigurdsson shouted to his guards. His mounted men began to gallop and the men on foot ran down the long incline and across the plain towards the hill fort. They completely outstripped the Byzantines, who were obediently waiting on Maniakes' instructions and encumbered by their sundry siege engines.

Rapidly as the Varangians descended, they weren't quick enough to prevent four horsemen from clattering out through the gateway of the hill fort and making off as fast as they could.

'Carrying the word,' Solveig panted.

'What?'

'Carrying the word. That's what they're doing.'

'So are we!' Tamas shouted. 'So will you!'

'What do you mean?' Solveig asked. But what with Alnath's thudding hooves and her own ears drumming, and being front-to-back, she couldn't hear Tamas's answer.

Harald Sigurdsson and the Varangians crossed fields of wheat and watermelon, skirted a grove of pine trees and swept round the back of the hill fort. There, on rocky ground, Harald signalled to his men to catch their breath and take stock. The stout grey walls glowered above them.

'Why?' Solveig gasped. 'Why not in front of the gateway?'

'When the Saracens come out,' Tamas told her, 'they won't be jumping off these walls, will they?'

'Oh!'

'They'll come out through the gateway. So the first to feel their fury will be Maniakes.' Tamas threw back his head and laughed. 'Yes, and if we all storm the fort, Maniakes and his men will have to be the first to go in.'

Solveig unlinked her fingers and let go of Tamas.

Harald has tricked Maniakes for a second time, she thought. He's commander-in-chief, but Harald treats him like a fool. I thought they were meant to work together.

Tamas sensed Solveig's disquiet. He squirmed round in the saddle and looked at her over his right shoulder.

'Which would you prefer?' he asked. 'Dead Greeks or dead Vikings?'

'Neither,' said Solveig, in a sharp voice.

'Harald knows how to safeguard his men,' Tamas

137

told her. 'That's what counts. He wants fame, and you won't win a name by kneeling to Turkish trolls.'

'Or by trickery,' said Solveig, and she pushed herself backwards until she slid over Alnath's rump. 'I don't like the way you laughed.'

Just a moment before, Solveig had felt closer to Tamas than she had ever done to anyone except for her own father; now she was aware of a distance between them.

As soon as Snorri had unfurled Land Ravager and jammed it into a crevice, Harald Sigurdsson rode around, issuing instructions.

'Keep out of arrowshot. The Saracens will insult you and taunt you, they'll try to draw you in. Keep out of arrowshot or they'll pick you off.'

When he saw Solveig, Harald dismounted.

Solveig gave him a steely look.

'Your father?'

Solveig shook her head.

'Where is he?'

'I don't know,' Solveig said in a truculent voice.

'A fine daughter!' Harald said, and then he clicked his tongue. 'I've got no time for your women's games. You heard what I said about staying out of arrowshot?'

'Yes.'

'Right! We've got plenty of cooks – though where we'll get enough food is another matter. Your work now is to ready my men. Use your skills, Solveig. Sharpen their axes, their short knives, their scramasaxes. Understand?'

Solveig nodded.

'That, and grooming the horses,' Harald told her. 'Men at the ready! Horses at the ready!' He slapped Alnath on the rump. 'And not just this handsome Arab.'

Harald glared at Tamas under his eyebrows, remounted and rode off. And as he did so, he called out, 'This fort won't last long. You'll see.'

Harald Sigurdsson was wrong.

As one scorching day succeeded another, the Saracens watched and waited. But the Byzantines were unable to make much impression on the stout stone walls with their siege engines. The Vikings, meanwhile, tightened the noose so that no one was able to enter or leave the fort by day or night, either by slipping surreptitiously through the main gateway or by scaling the walls with a ladder, and waited for the Saracens to run short of provisions.

But there were wells inside the fort, and so there was no lack of water.

One day a Saracen appeared on the wall high above the Vikings. He propped up a dead man beside him and bawled something at the Vikings below.

Solveig was standing with her father and asked him what the Saracen was saying.

'He's speaking a kind of Greek,' Halfdan told her. He cupped his right hand to his ear.

The Saracen yelled again, and Halfdan translated.

'Here's a Christian! A fat Christian. You think we'll surrender? We'll eat all the Christians in this hill fort first.'

'Eat them?' exclaimed Solveig, appalled.

Then the Saracen hauled the dead man on to the top of the wall and shoved him over. His corpse hit the rocky ground in front of the Vikings with a dull thud.

Solveig covered her face; when she stared up at the Saracen again, he had disappeared.

'It's one thing to kill a man in combat,' she gulped. 'I know that if men fight, men must die. But it's wrong to . . . violate his body after he's dead.'

'Not if it helps to strike fear in your enemy,' her father replied.

Solveig screwed up her face, remembering what Egil and Bolverk did.

Each day, the Vikings and Saracens shouted insults and now and then loosed arrows at each other; and each day, Solveig moved from one tent to another, sharpening the weapons of the guards.

'You won't win without sharp weapons,' she told one cluster of men, 'but you can't win without high spirits.'

'Listen to you!'

'Yes, grandmamma!'

But although they teased her, the men knew that what Solveig said was true.

Harald Sigurdsson, too, was aware that his men's morale was in danger of dropping and, as the last weeks of Hay Month and the whole of Harvest Month burned away, he varied their responsibilities from day to day.

If a man kept watch on the walls, checking for signs of movement behind the arrow-slits, the next day he harvested wheat or watermelons or hunted for rabbits or snared the little birds that flew to and fro all day between their nests in the hill fort and the grove of pine trees on the plain; or else he helped the carpenters with the slow work of building siege engines to replace all those lost at sea, or rode off to one of the outlying lookout posts on the surrounding hills, or else relieved his companions who were keeping watch over their ships.

At night, the musicians played their humstrums and drums and horns, the guards sang story-songs, some aching, some bawdy, while the older men told tales that crossed the rainbow bridge to Asgard or galloped nine days northward and downward to the world of monsters and the dead, and the poets raised their voices and sang of love matches and those conquests that time cannot defeat.

For her part, Solveig remembered a riddle-poem that Edith had asked her.

'This wind bears little creatures
high over the hill-slopes. Black! They're black,
dressed in dark clothing. They travel in flocks,
singing loudly as they fly between the greenwoods
and the houses of men. Can you name them?'

'Mosquitoes,' said one guard, slapping his neck. 'From Hel.'

'Mosquitoes don't sing,' Solveig replied. 'They whine.'

'Gnats, then,' another man guessed.

'No,' said a third. 'Some kind of bird. Crows. Ravens. Death-birds.'

'No,' said Solveig. 'Crows and ravens squawk and yelp.'

'I know,' said Tamas. 'The birds we see here every day, they're the same as the ones around our farm. They nest in the eaves of houses, and fly to the greenwoods. House martins.'

Solveig clapped her hands, and for a moment the guards fell quiet, each remembering, perhaps, their own homes – so far away, so dear to them.

Solveig saw the light in Tamas's acorn eyes. She nodded, and smiled.

You're like I am, she thought. You care. Sometimes you pretend you don't when you're with the other guards. You bray and horseplay, but I've seen how gentle you are with Alnath.

And then, without thinking, she announced, 'I want to talk to you.'

'Well?' replied Tamas.

'Oh!' exclaimed Solveig, startled by the sound of her own voice. 'Later!'

I do, thought Solveig. I want to ask him what he really thinks about Harald's cunning and the whole army's greed. Their cruelty.

One morning, Solveig and Tamas disobeyed Harald's orders about staying beyond arrowshot.

'If I keep loosing my arrows from such a distance,' Tamas told her, 'I'm just wasting them. Most bounce back off the walls. Only one in ten flies over.'

So Solveig held up Tamas's shield, and the two of them cautiously advanced on the walls, Solveig in front and Tamas right behind her.

Solveig looked down at her feet, the only part of her left exposed. Then she remembered Sineus, and how a Pecheneg arrow had pierced and pinioned his left foot, and she wondered whether the Saracens poisoned their arrow-tips.

Nine times Tamas notched an arrow and stepped out from behind the shield. Nine times he drew his bowstring. He pulled it right back to his right ear and released it. The bowstring hummed and whirred and his arrow flew deep into the heart of the hill fort.

Now the Saracens began to shoot back at Tamas. Twice an arrow stuck into the ground only a few feet away from them.

To begin with, Solveig felt flushed – more feverish than scared, excited by sharing such danger with Tamas.

But all at once, in the way a cold sea mist seeps in and blots out the sun, the heat drained out of her and she felt afraid and chill.

'That's enough,' she pleaded.

'One more.'

'Nine's a good number.'

'Pff!'

'Nine worlds, Tamas. One arrow for each world.'

'I know a charm,' Tamas intoned, 'to speed an arrow

to its target. A shrieking Saracen!'

Then Tamas notched the tenth arrow and stepped out from behind the shield. He drew the bowstring, back, right back . . . His bowstring hissed and it snapped. It whipped Tamas's face and left a red line down his right cheek.

'No!' Tamas shouted. 'Back! Careful!'

So while more Saracen arrows whirred around them, Solveig and Tamas quickly retreated until they were safely out of arrowshot again.

Tamas gazed at his bow. Then he opened his eyes wide and pouted at Solveig.

He's like a child, thought Solveig. Like Blubba caught dipping his forefinger into the honeycomb.

'The trouble is,' Tamas told her, 'I haven't got any spare strings. I left them aboard the boat.'

'You can borrow one.'

Tamas shook his head. 'Precious as fiddle strings,' he lamented. 'Precious as heartstrings.'

No sooner had the thought crossed Solveig's mind then she acted on it. With her right hand, she reached round to the small of her back.

'What are you doing?'

Solveig didn't reply.

'Solveig!'

Solveig drew her scramasax from its scabbard and brandished it. She grabbed a hank of her long fair hair, pulled it sideways and, before Tamas could stop her, sliced it off.

Solveig gazed at Tamas, pink and triumphant. 'I'm making you a new bowstring,' she told him. Her voice was low and quivering.

The messages passing between Harald Sigurdsson and Maniakes grew more terse and tetchy. Neither leader

143

was ready to risk his troops in an onslaught on the hill fort's huge iron gates or by scaling the walls with long ladders.

'Be patient,' Maniakes counselled Harald, 'if you know what that word means.'

But one day, while watching a flock of twittering martins fly back from the pine grove to their nests in the hill fort, Harald's eyes lit up.

The Viking leader instructed his bird-snarers not to wring the necks of the birds they caught but to bring them to him alive.

The guards brought Harald nineteen birds, some flapping inside a floppy catching-net, some keeping their heads well down.

Harald ordered his catchers to make a mixture of warm wax and fire-powder and a few pine needles, and to smear a glob on the tail feathers of each bird.

'One spark can set fire to a city,' he told them. 'That's what Saracens say. And it's what I say.' He raised both arms. 'Odin, be with us!' he called out. 'Christ, be with us. Our cause is a just one.'

Then Harald ordered his men to light the wax and the powder and the pine wicks, and to release the nineteen birds. The poor house martins hurtled back to the high hill fort, their nests in the eaves, their fledglings.

Thatched roofs crackled; timber frames caught fire. Very soon a thick plume of black smoke began to rise over the hill fort, and there was nothing whatsoever that the besieged men, women and children could do about it.

They opened the gates and streamed out of the hill fort, surrendering and imploring Maniakes for mercy.

The commander-in-chief instructed his men not to draw their swords or swing their axes or harm their captives in any way.

'My work,' Maniakes told Harald later that day, 'is

to win back Sicily for Emperor Michael and Empress Zoe.'

'You should have strung their leaders up,' Harald replied. 'At least that. As an example.'

Maniakes gave him a withering look. 'Vikings!' he said. 'You're vile. You're always violent. Sometimes mercy is a better weapon than butchery.'

'If I'd followed your advice,' Harald retorted, 'we'd still have been here this time next year. You with all your men and siege engines and your sickening patience. In one short hour I achieved what you in six long weeks could not.'

14

Although Harald Sigurdsson had found a way to capture the hill fort, it was the Byzantines who profited most from it. They were billeted in front of the gateway, and they were first through it. They swept from house to house like a second wave of fire, seizing gold, silver, weapons and other valuables, and leaving the Vikings only poor pickings.

Tamas's share consisted of two little salt spoons, shaped like scallops.

He pocketed one, and in full view of Vibrog and Edla presented the other to Solveig. She wrinkled up her face and tried to give it back to him.

'Put it in your bone-bag,' Tamas told her. 'Forget about it.'

Very soon after this, Harald and Maniakes decided to go separate ways – Maniakes to a hill fort further west along the coast, Harald to a walled town in the scorching heart of Sicily.

Neither of them was in the least sorry about it.

'Good riddance!' Harald declared. 'The man's a bully and a cheat.'

So says Harald, thought Solveig. But I wonder what Maniakes has to say about him. I don't suppose he'll be singing praise-poems.

Harald's men were relieved to step into a greenwood

after a long morning's ride-and-march. While they waited for their companions who were pushing their newly made siege engines to catch up with them, they stretched out, and many of them dozed.

Not Harald though. As was his habit, he did the rounds, here and there pausing to encourage his guards. When he came upon Solveig, sitting on her own with her back against a stunted oak, he pursed his lips.

'Hmm!' he purred. 'One-breasted women, I've heard of them, but not one-plaited women. You'll have to do better than this.'

'Why?' asked Solveig.

'If you want to be a Valkyrie—'

'I don't,' snapped Solveig.

Harald raised an eyebrow.

'Carrion crows! That's all they are.'

'I see,' said Harald. 'You don't think slain warriors should be raised to Asgard.'

Solveig closed her eyes and sighed.

'Solveig,' began Harald, 'I can see you're far from happy. I was fifteen once . . . once upon a time. The year I fought at Stiklestad and overwintered with you. You must learn to accept.'

It's true, Solveig thought. I do keep wrestling with myself. With everyone else. I know Harald's men have to fight – that's why we're here. But that doesn't mean they have to be cruel. And I know we're here to win back Sicily, town by town. But our weapons are swords and scramasaxes, not cunning and deceit. We're humans, not animals.

Harald waved at the men dozing all around them. 'This is an army. This is how armies are. You begged to come, and I allowed it. Now you must do as we do.'

'But . . .' Solveig began. 'How can I accept without questioning? How can I accept what troubles me?'

'Your father can,' Harald replied.

Solveig lowered her eyes.

'Now! What about that scamp? Is he pleased with his bowstring?'

Solveig sighed. 'No. He says it's not as good as a real one.'

'There's gratitude for you,' barked Harald. 'You cut off half your hair and Tamas complains! He's wrong, anyhow. Hair stretches just as willow bends, but it doesn't break.' He reached down and gave Solveig's plait a friendly tug. 'A man's strength,' he said, 'and a woman's beauty. That's what hair is. And it goes on growing after a person dies.'

Solveig frowned.

'So do fingernails and toenails,' Harald told her. 'Christians clip them off and worship them.'

The two of them caught each other's eye and laughed.

'Come on, now,' Harald told her. 'I like to hear that laugh. And your hair will grow back.'

'Harald,' said Solveig in a serious voice.

'What now?'

'Maria.'

Harald frowned. 'Maria.'

'Do you know . . .'

'What?'

'. . . know how . . .'

'How she carries her heart around on a platter, and keeps offering it to me,' Harald replied brusquely.

'Will you marry her?'

Harald stared at Solveig. He glared at her. 'Here I am,' he said in a low voice, 'here I am in the middle of a scorching day in the middle of a campaign in the middle of Sicily, and you're asking me whether I mean to marry Maria.'

'Will you, though?' Solveig persisted.

Harald sucked his cheeks and spat on the ground.

A bluster of hot wind rattled the leaves of the oaks.

'In a man's life,' observed Harald, 'there are many turnings. What is it your father always says? "Words and intentions come cheap, actions can be costly."'

Solveig sat still as a nut. She waited.

'You young women! You always want to talk about feelings. Use your head and let your heart follow, that's what I think.'

Solveig screwed up her face.

'Not now, Solveig,' Harald told her, and Solveig could hear that just for a moment he sounded understanding, even tender.

Harald Sigurdsson sniffed. 'Nothing happens until it happens,' he said.

'You boors!'

'Boiled lobsters!'

'Men or women, which are you?'

'Men-men are spawning babies on your sweethearts.'

'Yes, and on your sweet sisters.'

'Shitpool-hogs.'

'No! A clutch of hens.'

'Look at you! Peeping round your shields.'

No sooner had the Varangians reached the walled town, set in a valley in the high hills, and planted Land Ravager in front of it, than the Saracen inhabitants began to rain down insults on them.

'You limping lumps of filth!'

'Pagans!'

'Trolls!'

'Come on!'

'Come in!'

'Yes, and welcome! We'll teach you how to fight.'

'Look! Our gates are open.'

'Ignore them,' Harald instructed his men. 'Pitch your tents beyond arrowshot – and out of earshot. Whatever you do, keep away from those gates.'

So that's what the Varangians did, and two weeks passed before they and the Saracens engaged again.

But before dawn on the fifteenth day, while the stars were still sparkling seeds of light, three nightwatchmen – Grimizo was one of them – heard noises coming from the top of the town walls. Quite a hollow sound. The bumping of wood against stone, was it? Then a man's brusque voice. And a strange scratching and scraping.

Grimizo and his companions drew their scramasaxes and raised their shields, daubed as dark as night. Stealthy as cats, they advanced towards the walls, and were crouching at the bottom when three people came slithering down a rope towards them.

A boy. Ten years old perhaps. Then a little girl. And then a man, quite old, with no teeth and a face like wrinkled leather. All three of them were carrying buckets.

The Varangians pounced on them, and although the girl squeaked and the boy wrestled and tried to bite, they were completely overwhelmed.

'Buckets,' said Grimizo. 'That's the noise we heard.'

'Throats?' asked one of his companions.

Grimizo shook his head. 'No! Hostages are worth more than corpses.'

'One of those plots over there,' growled the third man. 'That's where they were going. Where they grow their beans and eggplants.'

'We've eaten them already,' Grimizo said.

The nightwatchmen found Harald Sigurdsson awake, early as it was.

Harald inspected the three hostages and sniffed.

'Bottom of the barrel!' he observed. 'A toothless old man and his two grandchildren. Hang them!'

That speedwell dawn, Solveig woke to the sound of three gallows being built by the Vikings, and she was horrified to see that her father was one of the carpenters.

'You can't,' she insisted. 'No matter what Harald says.'

Halfdan didn't reply.

'You can't.'

'Devils!' muttered Halfdan. 'Dark ones! Do away with them!'

'Talk to him, can't you? Harald listens to you.'

Again Halfdan didn't reply.

'He asks your advice.'

Solveig begged, she implored, she accused, she kicked at the gallows-frame, she clutched Halfdan's right arm until, impatiently, he shrugged her off.

'You're not my father!' she cried. 'Two children. An old man.'

Halfdan's eyes darkened. He avoided his daughter's gaze.

'In this army, you're a different person. This is worse, much worse than Harald's trickery and cunning. These two children, they're even younger than Kalf and Blubba. Look how that girl keeps hiding behind her grandfather.'

Halfdan didn't reply. Not one word. He pressed his hands against his stomach as if he were trying to hold in his guts, gave a deep sigh and got on with his ghastly work.

The confrontation between Solveig and her father didn't escape the other women, of course. Drudges and camp followers alike, they noisily scorned her for being soft as eiderdown, and for failing to show the respect due to her own father.

'She says one thing but does another,' Edla complained in her wheedling voice.

'Exactly!' agreed Vibrog. 'Not so long ago, she was happy enough to accept Saracen booty – that silver salt spoon Tamas gave her.'

'Solveig's always right, and everyone else is wrong.'

'She's her own worst enemy.'

The lioness Silkisiv stretched her golden limbs. 'Solveig's still a child,' she said, 'not a woman.'

'Hang them!' That's what Harald said, and that's what Halfdan and his companions did. They hammered the gallows into shape. They erected them. They looped and lashed the three nooses and secured them. Then they dragged the two children and the old man apart from each other.

'I'll hang them,' said Bolverk. 'You can help me, Egil.'

'Not so fast,' said Halfdan. 'The hangman always gets paid for his work. We'll draw lots.'

So Halfdan and Bolverk and Egil drew lots with the other guards who had helped to build and erect the gallows – Gorm and Turgeis and Karly and Ulf.

'Gorm!' said Halfdan. 'Gorm's the hangman. Karly, you're his assistant.'

'Robbed!' growled Bolverk.

'The girl first,' said Gorm. 'Let's get her out of the way.'

So Karly lifted the little girl bodily on to the wooden platform of the gallows, and she just lay limp in his arms, as if she were dead before she was dead. When Gorm strung her up, she gazed at him with her big dark eyes and just whimpered a little.

After this, Gorm and Karly strung up the little boy, and unlike his sister he kicked and yelled.

Then the two guards hurried the old man up on to the platform. He said something, he kept saying it, but they didn't know what it was, and they didn't care.

'Right?' asked Karly.

'Now!' said Gorm.

The two Vikings pulled away the wooden platform.

They hanged the old man and his two grandchildren by the necks until their tongues lolled out of their mouths.

'Leave them there,' Harald told Halfdan. 'As warnings. Witnesses. Leave them until they turn purple.'

Whatever Solveig did during the remainder of that day went wrong. Trying to sharpen the battleaxe of one of the guards, she sharpened her right forefinger instead. Her bright blood filled the cup of her left hand, and she trembled; late in the afternoon she began to incise a flat green stone with three stick figures – two little ones and a larger one – but the stone split in two; and when at dusk she ate for the first time that day, a sharp needle of bone stuck in her throat and made her gag.

That night the mood in the Viking encampment was sombre.

The jokes in the men's mouths were bitter; their ale tasted sour.

Only Harald, it seemed, remained in good heart, whistling as he rode right around the city walls, now and then issuing instructions, now and then proclaiming:

'Leaders ride alone . . .'

'No man favours his leader, no one forgives him . . .'

'Men obey their leader. Their leader answers to the gods . . .'

15

The next day, Harald took steps to raise the spirits of his men and at the same time show his contempt for the Saracens.

'We have this town by the throat,' he told Snorri and Skarp. 'Time is our worst enemy, just as it was before, with Maniakes. Time starves a walled town, but it also exhausts the men besieging it.'

'Yes,' said Snorri. 'Time's a horseman. One day he gallops past, another he ambles and almost stops.'

'Time's a sword, more like,' Skarp corrected him. 'Unless you parry it, time's sword can wound you.'

'Exactly,' agreed Harald. 'Tell all my men that today is a day for games. Running, wrestling, weightlifting, leaping.'

Snorri and Skarp nodded and smiled.

'Tell them to leave their helmets and shields and all their weapons in their tents. Have them gather at noon on the flat ground over there beyond the lemon trees, and tell them to ignore the Saracens.'

Although the Saracens could see that the Vikings were not carrying a single sword or scramasax between them, they were still suspicious. They walked to and fro along the ramparts, they watched, they waited, but the Vikings competed and shouted and brayed all afternoon, and took not the least notice of them.

154

The next morning, Harald Sigurdsson instructed the Varangian guards to return to the plain at noon for a second day of sport of all kinds. Not only running and wrestling and weightlifting and leaping but flag-waving, beam-balancing, stone-putting, catching and kicking bladder balls . . .

'But not stallion-fighting,' Harald Sigurdsson instructed his men. 'No kicking. No biting. We can't afford to lose a single one of our horses. They're too precious.'

The spirits of the Vikings rose and, seeing that they were still completely unarmed, the Saracens didn't bother to weigh themselves down with their scimitars and shields and spears. They paraded along the town ramparts in the sunlight, and so did pairs and small groups of veiled women, some of them holding their babies.

Then the Saracens boldly raised the town gate for the first time since the siege had begun, and several groups of black-bearded men hurried out to the little plots of eggplants and watermelons and other produce untouched by the Vikings because they were so dangerously close to the walls.

'Ignore them!' Harald told his men. 'Take no notice of them whatsoever.'

Unarmed Vikings, thought Solveig. Unarmed Saracens. It's as if both sides have worn themselves out. Maybe even men can grow tired of war.

At the back of her mind was something Edith had said-and-sung about a place where there was no fighting, not between humans, not between animals or birds . . . But what were the words? Solveig yawned. She felt so tired.

Anyhow, she thought, I'm sure this is no more than a time between times. Harald's a trickster. He's brutal. He hangs little children. What is he up to now?

On the third morning, Harald Sigurdsson invited his men to return to the plain again.

'Leave your shields in your tents,' he instructed them, 'but wear your helmets under your hats. Strap on your swords and scramasaxes under your cloaks.'

Seeing none of this but only that the Vikings had once again left their shields in their tents, the Saracens raised the great iron gate for a second time, and a few of them hastened to plots well away from the safety of the walls to see whether they could salvage anything from them.

Once more, the Vikings ignored them. But soon after the sun had reached the crown of the sky, and was glaring down at Vikings and Saracens alike with her cruel, blinding eye, Harald Sigurdsson summoned Snorri and Skarp and Halfdan.

'Now,' he said. He pursed his chapped lips and sucked his cheeks. 'Wrap your cloaks around your left arms. Round and round.'

'Our cloaks?' exclaimed Skarp.

'Instead of shields,' Harald told him. His voice was iron hard. 'Tell all our men to do the same.'

'But, Harald . . .' Snorri began.

'Here and now!' snapped Harald. 'We'll butcher them! Slit their bellies! Men, women, children. Each and every one. No mercy! None!'

As soon as Tamas heard the instructions, he came bounding over to Solveig, who was standing alone outside the women's encampment.

'We're going in!' he announced. His eyes were shining.

Solveig screwed up her eyes.

'Yes!' Tamas exclaimed. 'Are you coming too? My cloak, Solveig. Shall I cut it in two?'

Solveig shook her head so fiercely that her one plait whipped from side to side. 'You're worse . . . worse than my father.'

At this moment, Halfdan limped up to them. 'This'll lift your spirits, girl,' he announced. 'We're going in.'

Tamas threw both his arms round Solveig and squeezed her tightly.

'You drink blood,' she said miserably.

'Now,' said Halfdan, 'don't you go a step nearer the walls than this. Solva, my Solva! There'll be booty for us all.'

Then both men turned away, her limping father, her tousled admirer. Solveig's eyes filled with tears and she trembled.

Already, the first group of Vikings was running towards the town gate, and they reached it before the Saracens could lower it. Hundreds more followed them, and Harald, Snorri and Skarp brought up the rear.

But the Varangian guard who was bearing Land Ravager was struck by an arrow – first it pierced the standard, then the man's ribcage. It felled him.

'See that?' barked Harald. He turned to Skarp. 'Your turn, Skarp! You carry it.'

Skarp rounded on his leader. 'Me?' he retorted. 'When you're leading from the rear?'

Harald Sigurdsson bared his teeth.

'I'm not bearing your banner for you,' shouted Skarp. 'You're a mouse of a man!'

Harald opened his mouth and, like a midnight hound, he bayed.

'Harald, you coward!' yelled Skarp. 'Trolls can carry your banner for all I care!'

Then Harald broke into a run. He ran towards the gates of the town, waving his sword and roaring.

Still rooted to the place where her father and Tamas had left her, Solveig shook. As the Vikings charged into the town, bawling and howling, she was blinded by her own tears. Her fear, her pity, her sorrow.

And then, all at once, as if everything blurred had become clear again, quite clear, Solveig hurried back to the tent she shared with Vibrog and Edla. Without looking at either of them, and without saying a word, she picked up her bag of bones and carving tools and swung it over her right shoulder.

'Going home, are you?'

'Good riddance!'

'You sniveller!'

Deaf to their spiteful words, Solveig turned away.

She tried to steady her jerky breath.

She raised her eyes to the waiting, wild hills.

16

She had to get away. She had to distance herself from everyone. Everything. She didn't know where she was going, and to begin with, she didn't care.

Her head was hammering, and her heart . . . it felt as if someone had carved into her chest and was dragging it out.

Several times Solveig cried out, but only the circling birds of battle heard her. The ravens. The buzzards.

Solveig hugged herself. Not since that day, she thought. I haven't felt like this since the day my father left me. Now, he's left me again. He's different; he's not the same.

Where can I go?

At home, I'd go up into the hills. Away. That's what I'll do.

I'll find food, I'll find something. Some stream, some dewpond. Some peace.

Solveig followed a string-thin path away from the walled town, and not until she stood high on the scorched hillside did she begin to think of the dangers. Not just hunger and thirst, but hungry beasts, wolves, wild boar maybe, those and beasts of men as well. Bandits, body-snatchers, murderers.

But I'm fifteen, she thought. Fifteen summers. I know I can't speak Saracen, but I've learned to look after myself. I've crossed the mountains from Trondheim to Sigtuna, and sailed to Ladoga and Kiev, and survived the cataracts . . .

'Every day's a cataract!' That's what Red Ottar said. 'Difficulties, dangers, choices . . .'

Solveig climbed right out of the valley until she could see back over the besieged town to the hills beyond it, and the hills beyond them, all of them as bare and blotchy and unwelcoming as the hillside she was standing on.

Yes, I can look after myself, she thought. I can.

Solveig didn't know where she was going, only that she was getting away, and she didn't know she would meet not a single person nor see one sign of human habitation during the remainder of that day. She didn't know she would find nothing to eat, nothing to drink, and would have to sleep under the stars.

Several times Solveig's path crossed other paths, if that's what they were.

But there's no one up here to make them, she thought. Sheep-runs, then. Rabbits, even. But I haven't seen any sheep, or any rabbits either.

Ghost-paths . . . Thought-paths . . . I don't know.

Several times, too, Solveig's path forked and she had to decide to go left or right.

I'd better keep climbing, she thought. This way I'll come to the next ridge, the next valley, and I'll find a farm or a settlement.

No, she found nothing of the kind. Solveig walked until it was dark and she could no longer see where to plant her aching feet. She sighed and lay down and curled into herself at the foot of a rocky outcrop.

What are those words? she wondered. The words of the High One about how a traveller must always carry sufficient food and drink, and sufficient clothing.

Solveig shivered. Just as the days in Sicily were blistering, the nights were blustery and chilly, and even her cloak was insufficient to keep her warm.

As for her companions, they were flickering moths, looping-the-loop bats, busy beetles, squirting lizards, and one swooping, screeching bird of prey impatient to claim Solveig.

If Grimizo were here, thought Solveig, he'd make up one of his grim songs about how bad things are, the ones that always end 'And yet . . . and yet . . . things turned out better than I thought.' And if Snorri were here, he'd tell me some story to make me laugh. And if Tamas were here, he'd whisper something like he does to Alnath, to keep me warm . . . And if my father were here . . .

Solveig sat up.

'Father!' she exclaimed. And she reached out for him.

But there was no one there, nothing but the shape of the night-wind. Solveig gulped and lay down again and tucked her knees under her chin.

I was so angry, she thought. So upset. And you, you wouldn't reply. Not one word. I begged you, and you shrugged me off. But now, I wish you were here. One flesh, one blood . . . We've no need of words, we do understand each other.

Solveig gulped again. Her throat felt rough.

Father, where are you? And you, Tamas?

Are you searching for me? Have you even thought about me?

Long before sunrise, Solveig opened one eye and saw the outcrop above her was glistening. Cobwebs, she thought. Gossamer. No, tiny silver rock-scales. She reached out, and touched the rock with one finger. It was cool and wet.

At once, Solveig levered herself up, and groaned because she ached so much. She put her tongue to the rock face and began to lick it. The night mist. The dew. Whatever it was.

Yes, the grim rock face was weeping and Solveig began to weep. Her feet ached, her ankles ached, her calves and kneecaps ached, her whole body ached. She had cramp in her empty stomach. Above all her heart ached, and she closed her eyes.

Father, I've troubled you. I've dishonoured you by leaving. I can never belong in an army of men, but I know that doesn't mean it was right to leave. What if I've angered Harald? Will he be angry with you?

I'll go back, thought Solveig. I'll go down. Father, Father! Please understand. Don't tell me I was wrong to come.

Quite how it happened she never knew, though in the mountains it's easily done. Following what she thought was the way back to the walled town, Solveig took the wrong path and didn't realise she had done so until it was too late. She lost herself in the brutal hills.

High over her head, the sun hammered her golden gong.

Solveig's sweat kept stinging her eyes; then she stumbled into a pillar of rock, she grazed her right wrist and bruised her forearm. Almost at once a blue lump as large as a blackbird's egg welled up under her skin.

The sun . . . the sun . . .

She's never like this at home, thought Solveig. Not at summer solstice. Not even in Hay Month or the start of Harvest Month.

I followed the strong sun east and south, but I never knew her eye could be as fierce as this.

Not as wild and murderous as this.

Voices. That's what Solveig could hear.

Some were bright and quick and clear, like spots

of sunlight dancing on a marl floor; some were cool-tongued, flowing around her. Some were more like humming.

Solveig couldn't understand a word they were saying but that didn't matter. It didn't matter at all.

Scents, that's what she could smell. A confusion of dried thyme and marjoram and sage and vervain and lemons and clover and cut nettles and many kinds of wildflowers. She didn't know the names for all of them, not in Norwegian, not in any language, but that didn't matter. Her head was buried in a nosebag, a whole headbag, of mountain scents.

When at last Solveig opened her eyes she could see a circle of goats and sheep peering down at her. She could hear hens squawking, cattle lowing, one dog barking. This is the kingdom of animals, she thought. I didn't even know there was such a place.

When she twisted her head, Solveig could see she was lying in a wooden manger.

She murmured. Her eyelids felt so heavy. She fell asleep again.

When Solveig opened her eyes for a second time, she saw she was surrounded not by goats or sheep but children with shining eyes, their skin almost as dark as dates, and women wearing black veils.

Then one boy and girl leaned right over Solveig and they laughed. They laughed for joy.

The hanged ones, she thought. They're the little ones we hanged. I'm in Asgard!

Solveig's eyes ached, her head was hammering. But she gave a sort of long, sighing smile, and fell asleep again.

The veiled women smeared soft wax on Solveig's cracked lips; they wrapped cool damp rags around her swollen arm; they kept refilling a little wooden water

163

cup and cradled her head while she drank; they helped her to sit up against a pad of straw, and laid in her lap a platter of curds infused with honey and lavender. And seeing how Solveig had turned away from the dark and chosen the path of life, they gladly helped her along it with little mouthfuls of prayer and snatches of song.

On the third day after the mountain people – that's how she always remembered them – had found Solveig beside the rock pillar where she had been felled by the sun, she stood up for the first time. She shared bread and cheese and drank milk, she sucked the juice out of blueberries and chewed bitter, pale green almonds.

Solveig listened to the music of their language, and smiled when the mountain people smiled. She knew she would have to return before long to the baking plain, the walled town, return to all the stares and barbed words and sharp questions, but she wasn't ready to think about all that. Not yet.

There were eleven children in the high village, not counting three babies still in their cribs, and no goddess ever had such close and faithful attendants as did Solveig. They led her up and down and around, whisking and frolicking like wavelets. And when Solveig sat down, they ranged themselves around her knees and pressed against her legs. Now and then one of them took her hand, and said something to her, something Solveig knew was very serious because all the other children solemnly nodded their heads. Or else one child asked her a question, and when Solveig smiled and shook her head and said she didn't understand, they all laughed as if she'd told them a wonderful joke. The smallest children very lightly pinched her fair skin, and stroked her golden hair, and touched her right under her eyes with their soft fingertips.

The children wanted to know what Solveig kept in her canvas bag. They were eager to see everything in it, but although she showed them the discs and slivers of oak wood and walrus bone, Solveig stopped them from rummaging because her father's gold brooch was still buried at the bottom of the bag, and so was the silver spoon Tamas had given her.

On the third day after Solveig had come back from the dead, everyone assembled in the dusty space at the heart of the village: women walked in from their herding and milking, men from the new stable and stockade they were building, old women emerged from their squat stone bothies, and all Solveig's young worshippers rejoined their parents.

Some of the men had two veiled women standing beside them, and one man had three. But none of the women had more than one man next to her.

Solveig frowned. What does that mean? she wondered. Do some men have more than one wife?

If not, where are the missing men? Where have they gone? Are they down in the plains, fighting?

Then one old man cried out, calling to heaven seven times. A few of the people in the enclosure – the cloister, she didn't even know what to call it – a few of them turned to face the east. They got down on to their knees, they pressed their foreheads to the ground. But Solveig saw that most of the villagers were reaching out towards a second old man who had mounted a block of stone and was holding a wooden cross above his head. Then these people, too, quietly got down on to their knees, their elbows, and prostrated themselves in front of the cross. They stretched their arms right out. Each of them made a cross of their own bodies.

Solveig held her breath. She stared around her, astonished.

Christians, she thought. Muslims. Muslims, Christians. Together. Praying together.

She bowed her head. Then she too got down on to her knees.

The enclosure began to hum – the hum of hundreds and thousands of words all becoming one word – and the old man who had called seven times to heaven picked his way towards Solveig through the press of villagers. He took her right hand.

'*Dhimmi?*' he said, and Solveig knew he was asking her something important. '*Dhimmi?*'

Solveig frowned.

'*Dhimmi?*' insisted the old man.

But Solveig could only shake her head and shrug.

The old man gently laid his left hand on the top of Solveig's head. Solveig could feel the warmth of it infusing her, filtering down through her body.

Then the old man gently smiled and lowered his hooded eyelids. He turned away.

Still the cloister hummed. Not urgent but intent; devoted; dedicated.

Something was tickling the back of Solveig's right ear. She reached up. She felt for it and touched it with her fingertips. Then she placed her hand on top of her head and drew it forward: a gauze so fine it could have been made of bees' wings and long-legged insects, the fluffy tail feathers of fledglings. Oh, mulberry and indigo and watermelon – its dark green skin – and hazelnut and chestnut, silver, lavender: the quiet, subdued colours of the mountains and the mountain people.

Solveig gazed at it. Her eyelids flickered.

Up here, she thought, war is only a murmur.

I don't know where I am. I don't know who these people are. And I know I can't stay here. But these people

166

have saved me. Solveig fingered the delicate gauze and wondered at it.

I wish I could save them. Save them from everything.

I'll carry them with me. I'll carry the word.

That afternoon, Solveig's little acolytes led her out of the village to their secret places: fissures in the rocks where blueberries grew, a hilltop cairn to which she added a stone, the stump of a fir tree she danced around with all the girls, and the mouth of a cave that opened into a chamber under the mountain.

Solveig wanted to go right down, the cool of the mountain reached out for her, but two of the children – the same ones she had imagined were the little boy and girl hanged by the Vikings – shook their heads and pulled her back.

'I understand,' Solveig said out loud. 'I think I do.'

But what about everything I don't understand? she thought. When will I ever, ever understand?

That evening, a storyteller sat on the stone in the middle of the village, and while he said-and-sang, Solveig incised a disc of bone.

She cut the sweeping contour of a high hill. She cut the cairn on the hilltop and, beside it, two stick-figures.

That was all.

No, not all. Very carefully she incised little strokes on either side of the two stick-figures standing next to the cairn on the high hilltop. Eleven of them.

Then Solveig looked around her and pressed the disc into the storyteller's left palm. With her little finger she pointed to the stick-figures.

'Eir,' she said in her light voice. 'Eir the goddess,' she repeated, 'and Solveig –' she pointed to herself – 'and eleven children standing on the Hill of Healing. Now I'm part of your story, and you are part of mine.'

The storyteller raised his eyes. Gravely he gazed at Solveig. Then he nodded and smiled.

Solveig knew the time had come. She gave the sign and very early next morning the mountain men guided her down from their village. They kept her company along the string-thin paths to the far plain.

17

'Where is this?' Solveig pleaded. 'I keep telling you this isn't right.'

The mountain men shrugged.

'This isn't the town where they are – my father and everyone.'

Inside the gate, the three men were uncertain which way to go, but a growing group of townspeople accompanied them through a warren of little twisting streets until they came to a stone-walled house in the heart of the town.

One of the mountain men turned to Solveig. 'Abu Touati,' he said.

Solveig frowned and shook her head.

'Abu Touati. Abu Touati.'

Then her guides stepped aside and gestured to Solveig to step through the low gap in the wall. In the middle of the courtyard stood a large mulberry tree, and all around it there were blazing flowers: orange and scarlet and vermilion and ochre. Even the blooms of the long-legged blue flowers looked as if they were alight. They were growing in big tubs and little earthen beds, reaching along stone ledges and climbing up the walls.

While Solveig looked around her in delight, a wiry little man walked out on to the porch, then stepped down to greet her. He bowed and took Solveig's fair hands between his own.

'Abu Touati,' he said.

'Abu Touati,' Solveig repeated courteously.

The Saracen looked slightly puzzled, then amused, but he didn't laugh. Lights danced in his eyes.

They're mountain pools, Solveig thought. The ones that are peaty and deep and clear. I could drown in them.

'Have you come from Norway?' asked the man in perfect Norwegian.

Solveig gasped.

'Or Sweden? Denmark?'

'Norway,' Solveig said eagerly.

'I thought so. Yes, and your name?'

'Solveig.'

'Solveig? Are you sure?'

Solveig looked at him uncertainly. 'What do you mean?'

'Solveig . . . Not Abu Touati?' The Saracen's eyes were dancing again.

'Oh!' she exclaimed loudly, and she laughed at herself. 'Oh, no! I'm Solveig.'

'That's a relief,' the Saracen said. 'One of me is quite enough. Now then, first things first. The day is hot. Would my guest care to quench her thirst?'

'More than anything,' Solveig replied.

Abu Touati spoke to the mountain men. 'I was saying,' he explained to Solveig, 'that you will be safe with me and that their work is done. They are free to go.'

'Who taught you my language?' Solveig asked. 'You speak it as well as I do.'

The Saracen simply raised his right hand in a sign that she should be patient, and so Solveig turned to the mountain men. She reached out and embraced each of them and they left only with great reluctance.

'This will be the first time,' Abu Touati told her, 'that they've been embraced by any female except their own mothers and wives and daughters. A Viking girl, indeed!'

Solveig remembered how some men had been accompanied by two women to the prayer assembly in the mountain village, and one by three.

'Do Saracens have more than one wife?' she enquired.

Abu Touati nodded. 'Some do.'

'Why?'

But at this moment, a servant stepped down from the porch and proffered a tall glass cup to Solveig.

'What is it?' she enquired. 'Yellow as cowslips. Foaming.' And then, when the servant placed it between her hands. 'Oh! It's so cold! How can it be?'

Abu Touati smiled and stroked his well-trimmed grey beard. 'You Viking, you should know.'

'It can't be,' said Solveig. Then she dipped her right thumb and forefinger into the glass and pulled out a small lump. 'It is! Ice in midsummer!'

She pressed the ice against her forehead, and against her throat and the back of her neck.

'From the mountains,' Abu Touati told her.

'They're burning. There's no ice up there.'

The Saracen smiled. 'We cut it and bring it down in winter.'

'But . . .'

'When the Romans came to Africa, they taught us how to conserve ice in summer. We Muslims know many skills forgotten by Christians.'

I wish my father were here, thought Solveig. This ice would cool his gut.

'Now!' said Abu Touati. He gestured to Solveig to sit on the bench in the shade of the mulberry tree and then straddled it himself. 'You've come to Sicily with Georgios Maniakes?'

Solveig shook her head. 'He's the commander of the Byzantines. Our leader is Harald. Harald Sigurdsson.'

Abu Touati grimaced.

'I've come with my father. I followed him.'

'To do – how do you say it? – to do dirty work for Empress Zoe.'

'She told everyone her cause is a just one.'

'Leaders always say their cause is just,' Abu Touati replied, 'and most of them believe themselves. What I say is, each of us can be a leader so long as we're not led by one! Each of us must think for ourselves.'

Solveig raised her glass cup to her lips and swilled another mouthful of the delicious lemony drink around her mouth.

'What is your faith?' the Saracen asked her. 'Are you Christian?'

'I don't know what I am any more,' said Solveig.

Abu Touati shook his head. 'Impossible,' he exclaimed.

'I do pray to Odin and Freyja and Eir,' Solveig told him, 'she's the goddess of healing, but . . . but I'm Christian too.'

'We Muslims in Sicily,' said Abu Touati, 'we allow all the Christians and Jews to worship in their own way. We say they are *dhimmis*.'

'*Dhimmis*,' repeated Solveig. 'I heard that word in the mountain village.'

'Not Muslim,' the Saracen told her, 'but not pagan. But the Christians in Byzantium, they vow to drive each and every Muslim out of Sicily – or even better, kill them. This is not just. And it is not wise.'

Solveig slowly shook her head. She didn't know what to think. She remembered that in their little dugout, Edwin had said the Vikings were always vengeful and Christians were compassionate; now Abu Touati was saying the Muslims were compassionate and the Christians brutal.

Abu Touati looked at her kindly. 'No easy answers,' he said.

'In the mountain village,' Solveig told him, 'everyone prayed together. Christians, Muslims, everyone.'

The Saracen pursed his lips and smiled. 'They are not bedevilled,' he said. 'Down here, we talk too much and argue too much and know too much, at least we think we do. Here in the plains, traders and emissaries and travellers, they all come and go, armies assemble and fight and win and lose, but up there, war, war . . .'

'Is only a murmur,' said Solveig with a wistful smile.

'Exactly,' said Abu Touati. 'War is only a murmur. Half forgotten or still to come.'

The Saracen sighed and, without knowing quite why, Solveig reached out to him and laid her fingers on his right wrist, light as a butterfly. For a little while she left them there.

'Blessed are strangers!' the Saracen said. 'That's what the Prophet said, and what we all say. Blessed in themselves, because they're strangers, and blessed because they give us back ourselves.'

'We have many sayings about strangers and how we should welcome them,' Solveig told Abu Touati.

'I would willingly sit here all day,' Abu Touati said, 'listening to leaves whisper and your green words. What could be more agreeable?'

'You were going to tell me,' Solveig said. 'How did you learn Norwegian?'

'Be patient,' the Saracen told her.

'I never am.'

'I was saying I would willingly sit here all day, but nothing in our lives happens wholly by chance. You have been sent to me in my hour of need.'

'What do you mean?' Solveig asked him.

'This,' said the Saracen, and he stood up, still straddling the bench. 'In this town live Saracens and Greeks and Jews and black-skinned people from the deserts of Africa, and the people who settled on this island before we conquered it. Settlers from all around the Great Sea. Traders come here from beyond the gates of the Great Sea and from east of the Black Sea . . .'

'The Black Sea!' Solveig exclaimed. 'I crossed it on my way to Miklagard.'

'And here,' continued Abu Touati, 'we learn from each other and about each other. That's how we live in peace.'

Solveig frowned.

'On this afternoon each week, six or seven of my friends come to my courtyard. We talk, we argue.'

Then Abu Touati gave Solveig a little bow and led her by the hand up the steps to the chair on his porch.

As soon as his companions had quaffed lemon sherbet and settled themselves around the small courtyard, Abu Touati beckoned Solveig back down to join them.

'This is my guest,' he explained. 'My . . . Viking guest, come from afar. Solveig.'

Solveig looked at the seven men. Not one smile. Not even a nod. Just seven pairs of dark, watchful eyes.

'Sit here on this bench,' Abu Touati invited Solveig. 'Next to me.'

One squat man growled something.

'What did he say?' Solveig asked.

A daddy-long-legs of a man with bolting eyes and protruding cheekbones nodded and jabbed towards Solveig with his right forefinger.

'Let them spit it out,' Abu Touati calmly advised Solveig.

'What are they saying?'

'Battle-mongers! Blood merchants! War wolves!'

'I'm not,' protested Solveig, and she felt scared.

'Last week,' Abu Touati told the men . . . but then he turned to Solveig. 'I'll translate what I'm saying,' he told her, 'phrase by phrase. Don't be afraid.'

Solveig avoided the men's angry eyes. She stared at the ground.

'Last week . . .' Abu Touati began again, 'my friend Mansur told us about his pilgrimage to Jerusalem. Today, I'll tell you about how I sailed across the Black Sea and stayed for three months with Viking traders.'

Oh! thought Solveig. That's when you learned to speak our language.

'The finest people to look at on Allah's earth,' Abu Touati told his companions. 'They're tall as date palms and their skin is reddish in colour. Their hair is red-gold.'

As Abu Touati described the Vikings' clothing, their boats, and what they had brought with them to sell in Kiev, his companions listened intently.

'Skins of all kinds – sable and squirrel and ermine, black and white foxes . . .'

'And marten and beaver,' added Solveig without looking up. 'And sealskins.'

'Yes,' said the Saracen, 'and wax and birch bark – people use it for writing as we do papyrus. Globs of amber, and honey the colour of amber, and hazelnuts and cattle and horsehides, yes, and slaves.'

Abu Touati grasped Solveig's arm. 'Look at this girl! She's no warmonger. Of course she's not.'

Solveig felt troubled and near to tears.

'The Vikings have very different customs to us,' Abu Touati went on. 'Different manners, a different language, different beliefs. Their women are more free than our women.'

One of his companions, the squat one, angrily shook his head and growled again.

'Much more free. They can leave their husbands if they choose to. If they don't want to keep their babies, they can drown them like kittens.'

Now several of the Saracens protested, and one spat on the ground.

'No Viking women wear the hijab or the abaya. No, they darken their eyelids and eyelashes with dyes to make themselves look more beautiful, and flirt with men who are not their husbands.'

'Viking women,' Abu Touati declared, 'do not worship Allah or even Jesus Christ and his mother Mary. You know me, all of you, my companions, my friends. I'm no pagan. I'm Muslim. I do not believe in false gods, and Viking customs anger and trouble me.

'Now the Vikings and Byzantines have travelled here to Sicily and they're trying to win it back with swords and scramasaxes. But do you suppose that when we came to this island, we won it with embraces and kisses?'

He screwed up his face like a walnut and sighed. 'And so it will go on, on and on. Until we all come to understandings.' He gave Solveig and his companions a lingering smile. 'Travel,' he said. 'Why do we do it?'

'One part of hell!' exclaimed one of his companions, a man wearing a white scarf over his head.

'Exactly! Travel tires us out – the boat, the beast we're riding, our companions and the flea-beds we have to share with them, the rotten food: they're all uncomfortable, or unpleasant, or anyhow unfamiliar. And there's always some hazard around the next corner.

'Yes, one part of hell,' Abu Touati repeated. 'And yet travel's a kind of medicine, isn't it? People who stay at home for season after season become like stagnant water. They smell sour. They taste sour. Not so the traveller. The traveller finds out. New countries, new people, new beliefs. He finds out about himself. And when at last he –' the Saracen smiled and translated for Solveig – 'he or she comes home, she values her family and friends all the more dearly.

'And so, my friends, unless I travel, unless I find out . . . unless I try to understand . . . and unless we all come to understandings . . .'

'Rest now,' Abu Touati advised Solveig. 'Then you will be ready.'

Solveig stared at the Saracen. She felt completely worn out.

'My servants have prepared a room for you.'

That night, Solveig slept deeply, and for most of the next day she sat in the shade of the mulberry tree, sometimes picking a squashy berry and then sucking her stained fingers, sometimes nibbling at figs and dates and apricots, or sipping foaming, icy lemon.

'The path to healing is understanding,' Abu Touati told her, smiling, 'but after reaching our destination, the next step on our path is to turn back.'

'I wish I had a gift for you,' Solveig said.

The Saracen gently shook his grey head. 'You've already given it to me,' he said. 'Now, I've asked three guides to ride with you, but I can't pretend they're not fearful. You'll find your companions have moved on since you last saw them. Another town. Another siege.' The Saracen sighed. 'You'll have to walk the last mile or two on your own.'

Solveig nodded.

Abu Touati gazed at his guest, unblinking. 'But what can compare with the pleasure of coming home?' he asked in his firm, calm voice. 'When at last a traveller returns home . . . Ah, Solveig! Your own husband. Your own children. Your family and farm. Your friends. May the Prophet protect you. May Allah go with you.'

18

'So where have you been?'

The two cooks appraised Solveig.

'Your poor old father.'

'You've finished him off.'

'What?' cried Solveig. 'What do you mean?'

'Sick,' wailed Edla. 'Sick with sorrow.'

'As for Tamas . . .' groaned Vibrog, rolling her eyes.

'Lovesick!' sneered Edla. 'He rode out of camp, searching for you. Harald had him beaten.'

Solveig blinked. She kept sucking her cheeks and swallowing. 'I'll explain,' she said. 'I can.'

'He'll have you beaten too,' Vibrog told her. 'When he gets better, he will.'

'You're women!' cried Solveig.

She expected of them at least some concern, some understanding, even if no gentleness. But she didn't go on. She bit on her tongue.

'And you, Solveig, you're a child,' Edla told her. 'Learn before it's too late.'

'What do you mean, when Harald gets better?' Solveig asked.

Vibrog sniffed. 'He caught a fever. A few days after.'

'After what?'

'We ransacked that town. The one you ran away

179

from.' She smirked. 'We killed the whole lot. Every man, woman and child.'

'And looted it,' Edla gloated. 'Rich pickings, Solveig.'

'And then set fire to it,' added Vibrog with grim satisfaction. 'Every building. But on our way here, three days later, Harald felt unwell.'

'He gave us orders to pitch his tent over there,' Edla said, pointing to a single tent standing well back from the circle of Viking tents surrounding the city. 'So he can sleep.'

'But my father and Tamas – are they all right?'

'Harald sent your father back to the boats. To recover.'

'He wasn't wounded?' Solveig asked anxiously.

'Only by you, Solveig,' Edla told her. 'Only by you. But he swears a snake's worming round inside his gut.'

Solveig stared at both women, dismayed. 'What shall I do? I mean . . .'

'When people suit only themselves,' Vibrog added, 'they shit on others. That's what your father told me.'

That's not what he said about me, thought Solveig. It can't be. But she was half afraid it was.

In the gloom of his tent, Tamas looked up at her. His eyes were shining.

Solveig, she looked down.

'You've come back,' he said. His voice was soft and almost expressionless.

'Ohh! Tamas!'

Solveig got down on to her knees and laid her right wrist on his brow as lightly as the mountain man had laid the gauzy veil on the top of her head.

Tamas was feverish.

'Because of me,' she whispered.

'No,' said Tamas. 'You didn't ride out. I rode out. I disobeyed orders.'

Solveig felt stricken.

'I'll heal,' Tamas murmured. 'I'll be whole again. They say I will.'

Solveig stroked his forehead. Gently she stroked it.

'Well enough to fight again,' murmured Tamas.

Solveig felt such utter tenderness. In her heart and head, each limb of her body. She longed to encircle him, encompass him, heal him.

His eyelids closed, his long eyelashes flickered. Solveig looked at him and knew she loved him.

Harald, meanwhile, lay in his tent on his straw mattress, and his companions were ants and beetles and jewel-eyed lizards, half memories, half waking dreams.

One afternoon, he saw himself aged three, looking up at King Olaf. The king was glaring at him and trying to drill through Harald's head with the augers of his eyes, but Harald stared right back at him. Then the king grasped a handful of Harald's hair and twisted it and pulled it. And little Harald? He reached up, grabbed the king's moustache and pulled it.

King Olaf laughed. 'No one's going to get the better of you,' he said, and then he turned to Harald's mother. 'A king-in-waiting. You're bringing up a king. A warrior whose name will never die.'

'Stand beside my Harald,' his mother said. 'Watch over my son.'

'I will,' said the king. 'For as long as I live and after I'm dead.'

When Harald opened his eyes and returned from his dream, he realised he had grabbed his own moustache and was still holding it in his right fist.

The Saracens were puzzled. For seven days the Varangians had encircled their town but they hadn't hurled a single stone from one of their three siege engines. They hadn't loosed so much as an arrow.

So the townsmen sent two Christian priests over to their encampment to try to find out what was going on. Each man was carrying a large wooden cross, and they had instructions to make the Vikings an offer.

'You've no need to lay siege to us,' the priests told Harald's shoulder-companions, Snorri and Skarp. 'The leaders of our town will give you great riches if you lift your siege and leave us in peace. And this is one of the richest towns in Sicily.'

'We'll put your offer to Harald,' Snorri told them, 'as soon as he's well enough.'

'Well enough?' enquired the priests.

'That's what I said,' Snorri said, and he bared his teeth.

'Their leader is ill,' the two priests reported to the townsmen later that day. 'Harald Sigurdsson himself. Very ill, maybe. His men fear his strength is failing. Two of them told us he will soon die.'

But the moon waxed . . . and because of the concoctions he gulped down after refusing to be bled with leeches, or because of the sheer strength of his own will, Harald began to recover. He sat up, he ate watermelon and drank milk.

When he was informed that Solveig had been able to find her way back to them, and was in their new encampment at that, Harald just growled.

And when his men told him about the Saracens' offer, Harald glowered and said nothing.

But late that night, alone in his tent, he had an idea.

Very early next morning, he summoned Snorri and Skarp, and the two men got down on their knees on either side of Harald's mattress.

'As you know,' he told them, 'a siege can last for

182

months, and that's the last thing we want, with winter on its way. From what I've heard, this hothouse of an island quickly turns very cold. We must reduce this town as quickly as we can.'

Snorri and Skarp agreed.

'I want to sail back to Miklagard before the end of Slaughter Month. We'll overwinter there and come back next spring.'

'What about Maniakes?' Snorri asked.

'What about him?!' retorted Harald. 'Now! I hear some men were fool enough to tell those priests my strength was failing and I might even die. So . . .' said Harald, and he pursed his lips, '. . . I've decided to die.'

Snorri and Skarp frowned.

Harald gave them a crafty look. 'I want you two to walk up to the town gates. Unarmed. Completely unarmed. You understand?'

Snorri and Skarp clamped their jaws.

'If Halfdan were here, I'd ask him to go with you. My three best men.' Harald paused and stared at Skarp. 'I know,' he said, 'you insulted me. You refused to carry Land-Ravager. You incensed me.' Harald shook his head. 'But I also know I need henchmen who say what they think. I need you, Skarp.'

Skarp grunted.

'Yes,' continued Harald, 'I'd have asked Halfdan to go over with you. But seeing as he's not here, his daughter can take his place.'

'Solveig!' exclaimed Skarp with a contemptuous laugh.

'Why not? An innocent young woman. There's no better way to persuade the townsmen to trust you.' Harald narrowed his eyes. 'In fact,' he said slowly, 'she needn't even know I'm still alive, need she? Tell her I died during the night. It's better she believes that I am dead.'

183

Snorri and Skarp slapped their knees.

'But when we reach the gates . . .' Snorri began.

Harald didn't reply. And then, talking more to himself than his henchmen, he growled, 'I'll spare her a beating. This time.'

'At the gates?' Snorri asked again.

'Tell the Saracens I've died,' Harald instructed him. 'Tell them I'm dead.'

Snorri and Skarp leaned forward. The three men's heads were almost touching.

'Wait until you're sure you're speaking to their leader, their chief . . . whatever the Saracens call him. If you can, talk to him on his own, or with just a few followers. No crowd makes a good decision.'

'And when we've told him?' asked Skarp.

'Say my last wish was to be buried on holy ground – one of the churches inside the town. Ask his permission to bring my coffin through the gates and bury me in a Christian graveyard.'

Snorri and Skarp both rocked back on their haunches, laughing.

'And say this too,' added Harald. 'A few days ago they were offering us vast riches to lift the siege and leave them in peace. But now we're offering them even greater riches – gold, jewellery – if they agree to this.'

'They may ask what we Vikings mean to do,' Snorri said, 'after we've buried you.'

Harald Sigurdsson nodded. 'Tell them you'll lift the siege. Say you mean to leave Sicily and return to Miklagard.'

'As we do,' declared Skarp.

At noon, Snorri and Skarp walked soberly up to the town gates. Tear-stained, Solveig walked between them.

'Three well-aimed arrows, and it will be all over,' Snorri observed.

But the Saracens wanted to hear what the two men had to say and, whatever their thoughts and feelings, they received the news of Harald Sigurdsson's death without undue emotion.

'Death's a black camel,' their leader said. 'Sooner or later he kneels in front of each of us.'

'Any man who dies for a cause, a just cause, a vile cause, will be remembered by it,' one of his henchmen added.

No, thought Solveig miserably. No. That's not true, that's not how I'll remember you.

Oh, Harald! I can see you lifting me off my feet and whirling me round and round. I can hear you telling me my father's worth two men. I'll remember how you allowed me to come to Sicily, and your almost-patience with me, even when I know you were impatient. And the look of you, Harald, the look of you . . . All of Norway will mourn. And who here will lead us?

When the Saracen leader and his henchmen heard about Harald's last wish, their dark eyes shone. And while Solveig went on sniffing and sometimes gulping, they began to bargain with Snorri and Skarp, and to write down on papyrus the exact weight of gold and silver and precious stones the Vikings were prepared to offer.

'Harald was Christian,' Snorri told them.

'Well, no less Christian than pagan,' Skarp added, but the Saracens didn't understand quite what he was saying, and it was probably a good thing they did not.

'Christian, yes,' Snorri said very firmly. 'Wherever he is now, he will be blessing you.'

Then Snorri and Skarp and the Saracens discussed arrangements for the burial. The Saracens agreed to raise the gates at noon so that the town's Christian priests could come out to meet the funeral cortège.

'We have five churches in this town,' the Saracen leader told them, 'and you can be sure their priests will argue over where Harald is to be buried. They argue about everything.'

'Ohh!' wailed Solveig. 'I've failed my father. Harald, I failed you.'

All the men ignored her.

Why should it matter in which churchyard he's buried? she thought. Death is death. What matters is the stone we raise and the words carved on it. No one has even mentioned that.

I wish . . . I wish I could carve it. Words to honour Harald . . . I hope I can.

All that interests Snorri and Skarp and these Saracens is money. Profit. Harald Sigurdsson lies dead, and these men stand haggling over his grave.

After assuring the Saracens once again that they would lift the siege as soon as Harald had been buried, Snorri and Skarp returned with Solveig to the Viking encampment, and it was only then that the two men informed her that Harald Sigurdsson wasn't quite so dead after all.

Solveig shuddered. Her head and heart whirled. First she felt relief, even joy that Harald was still alive. Then she became angry, very angry, at the calculating and cruel way in which she had been deceived and, without any regard for her feelings, Snorri and Skarp had used her grief to trick the Saracens. And after this, she felt a surge of sheer terror at what was to come.

*

Next morning, a horseman rode from tent to tent around the Viking encampment repeating this message:

'Harald Sigurdsson's strength has not failed. He will not die. Nevertheless, we will hold his funeral today at midday. Half of you will join the cortège, with your axes and swords concealed inside your cloaks, and half will stay here in your tents, armed and ready, until you hear the trumpeter. Every woman in the encampment is to join the procession.'

At midday, the town gates were slowly swung open. Then the leader of the Saracens and at least fifty townsmen came out to meet the funeral cortège. The five priests and their acolytes accompanied them, carrying shrines and holy relics, and the five priests were all still arguing, all intent on burying Harald in their churchyard so as to secure additional rewards from the Vikings.

The Vikings dressed themselves in their finest clothing – what survived of it after the murderous encounter with the pirates and three months in baking Sicily. Brick-red tunics with long narrow sleeves. Sealskin boots. Scarlet and purple cloaks fastened by a brooch at the right shoulder.

Most guards combed and tidied their red hair, their moustaches and beards.

Not Tamas, though. 'What's the point?' he asked Solveig when she hurried over to his tent and sat him on a stool so that she could dress the oozing wounds on his back. 'It only curls again.' He reached up and ruffled Solveig's hair. 'Yours is growing back now.'

'You can't join the cortège,' Solveig told him. 'Your back hasn't healed yet.'

'No choice,' Tamas said curtly. 'We've drawn lots in this tent already.'

'But . . .'

'No choice,' Tamas repeated.

'I'm coming too,' Solveig told him. 'All the women have to.'

Tamas shook his head very slowly. 'That's wrong. Quite wrong. Not honourable.'

'Shhh!' Solveig cautioned him. 'He'll have you beaten again.'

'This is men's work,' Tamas said forcefully, 'not women's work.'

'Shhh!'

Tamas stroked Solveig's soft cheek. 'Solveig,' he said tenderly. 'Solveig.'

Solveig felt flushed. She could feel her breath quickening. Slowly she dipped her head towards Tamas' pink, upturned face.

Their eyes met. Just for a moment.

Then their lips met. So warm. So yielding.

Tamas pulled Solveig down towards him and Solveig wrapped her arms around his neck. She closed her eyes.

She felt so utterly tender, so vulnerable. She could feel her whole body quickening.

Tamas sighed, and under his breath he murmured, 'You are wearing it. You are, aren't you?'

'My scramasax?' Solveig replied at once. 'Yes. And I'll wear the veil they gave me on the Hill of Healing. I'll be all right.'

The funeral cortège stretched all the way from the Viking encampment to the soaring walls of the Saracen town.

It took six men to carry Harald Sigurdsson's stout oak coffin, and it was surmounted by a canopy of precious purple silk. His standard Land-Ravager was laid along the top of it.

But all of a sudden, as they were passing beneath the town gates, the six pall-bearers wheeled round and lowered the coffin to the ground – a wedge between the gates.

A Viking guard blew short, sharp bursts on his trumpet.

Then Harald hoisted the lid of his coffin and scrambled out, roaring.

All around him, his guards were yelling and baring their shining swords, their axes and scramasaxes, while more Vikings at once came running from their tents to join them.

The Vikings made no distinction between men, women, children, Christians, Jews, Muslims, priests, laymen. They whooped and swung their weapons, they hacked their way into the town.

The Saracens may have been unprepared, but not all of them were unarmed. And they were no more fastidious than the Vikings.

They attacked the Varangian guards; they swung their scimitars and lopped off the limbs of the screaming women.

Then Solveig saw a burly woman running down the narrow street towards her, grasping a knife.

Not me, she thought.

Solveig reached around to the back of her belt and, biting fiercely on her lower lip, slid out her scramasax.

The dark-skinned woman headed straight for her, wide-eyed and wailing. She aimed the point of her knife at Solveig's heart. Solveig watched, alert as a cat, she waited, she sprang aside and jabbed her scramasax into the woman's stomach.

At once Solveig jerked her arm back. The Saracen woman reeled away, gasping; she tried to clutch at the stone wall, and collapsed into the dust.

Solveig stared at her scarlet blade, horrified.

Then a man came charging down the narrow street towards Solveig. He levelled his spear at her.

'Down!' bawled a voice from behind her. 'Solveig!' Then one of the Varangian guards knocked her forward on to her knees, her elbows.

The Saracen leaped right over Solveig, howling. He drove his spear straight through the body of the Viking behind her.

The young man fell on to his back. His eyes were bolting and his face fringed with acorn curls. He shuddered. He kept shuddering.

Then, with his right hand, he reached towards Solveig.

He shuddered again.

He lay still.

Solveig howled. She threw herself over Tamas's pierced, broken, bloodstained body. She clutched him. She wrapped him in her arms.

Down, down, Solveig drowned in her own darkness.

She knew nothing at all of how, that day, Harald Sigurdsson and the Vikings put every single Saracen to the sword – each man, each woman, each child – and how they ransacked all the churches, all the guardrooms and houses, and rounded up more plunder and rich pickings than they could carry. She knew nothing of how Harald decided to keep almost all of it for himself and for his men, and pass over no more than a pittance to Empress Zoe.

Solveig was numb. She no longer cared whether she were dead or alive.

Tamas.

Tamas.

She couldn't even remember how, late that afternoon, she had been half dragged, half carried back through the town gates. She didn't know how Harald's men had dug a long, shallow grave in one of the churchyards and laid Tamas and all their dead in it. Forty-three young men.

The Vikings buried them, they sang a dirge over them and blew their aurochs horns, they called on the Valkyries to fly down and lift those dead warriors to Asgard.

The next dark morning, still wearing her gauzy veil, Solveig rode Alnath back to the boats, sick in her head and heart.

19

It was there, inside her. As Solveig rode with the Varangian guard and their retinue along the sun-scorched valley between bare hills, and across the great baking plain towards the sea, it was always there: sometimes a lumpy stone lodged in her heart, sometimes a cold emptiness, an absence. It was there at first waking, and all day, and there when she tried to escape into sleep – her tearing grief for Tamas.

Only when Alnath plodded across the foreshore and Solveig saw her father standing on the gangplank, waving, did she realise how deeply she had missed him and how long it was since she had last seen him.

Not since she had begged him not to hang the two children and their grandfather, and accused him of drinking blood. Not since, in the dark, she had called out for him on the rocky mountainside, and he was not there. Not since the mountain people had rescued her and she had seen Christians and Muslims, Muslims and Christians, praying together. Not since she had met Abu Touati. Not since . . .

'Your hair's growing back,' Halfdan called out. But then, seeing his daughter's face, puffy and stricken, and at once understanding what must have happened to Tamas, he awkwardly pulled her to him.

'Solva, my Solva. Solva, my Solva.' That's all he said

and kept saying, and all Solveig needed, just as a baby needs only a simple lullaby. 'Solva, my Solva.'

Even as she shook and sobbed, feeling the warmth and strength of her father's love, Solveig recognised how stiff in his body Halfdan was. Because of his size, she thought. His hamstring. Because of the worm in his gut. But he's my father. My own father. My obstinate, awkward, loyal father.

As soon as the helmsman, Nico, had weighed anchor and swung round their *ousiai* to the east, Solveig had to work in the stables and with the cooks in the galley, but always Tamas was there too, in her head, in her heart, always there.

When she and her father did find time to talk, and Solveig asked him about the worm in his gut, and which medicines he was taking for it, she kept seeing Tamas spreadeagled, eyes bolting, with the Saracen spear in his gut.

And when she began to tell her father about the mountain people, Halfdan interrupted her and said he knew how Tamas had disobeyed orders in an effort to find her, and got beaten because of it, and that's when he had known for sure how much Tamas cared for her.

Yes, Tamas was there and the scramasax was there, scarlet, dripping.

After Solveig had been pulled away from Tamas's body and half dragged, half carried through the town gates, she had walked back to her tent as though she were in a trance, and it was only when she sat down that she realised she was still holding her bloody scramasax. She had wiped the blade with tufts of grass and then with a strip of canvas, and secured it to the back of her belt. But she knew it would never be clean, and kept drawing it to check it wasn't scarlet and dripping again.

Solveig's scramasax – it was there when at sunset she looked at the orange-and-pink blades of the sea and their dark undersides. It was there when she told her father about Abu Touati and how his mulberries had stained her fingers; it was there when she remembered pressing the lump of ice against her throat and the back of her neck.

After a second day's work, Solveig told her father about Abu Touati. But he wasn't all that interested, though he did relish the Saracen's description of the Vikings he had met on the River Dnieper.

'The finest people on earth!' he repeated cheerfully. 'That's what he said?'

'"The finest people to look at",' Solveig corrected him. 'On Allah's earth. And he told me the next step on my path is to turn back,' Solveig told her father.

'Turn back where?'

'Home.'

'What does he know about it?'

Everything, thought Solveig. Everything. He's a wise man.

'Mmm,' growled Halfdan, and he slowly shook his head. 'He's right, of course. An army like this, it's no place for my daughter. I know that.'

Solveig began to sniff. '"Your own husband." That's what Abu Touati told me. "Your own children."' Her eyes flooded with tears . . . and she began to sob.

'"May the P-P-Prophet protect you. May Allah go with you."'

Halfdan grunted.

I haven't told him anything, Solveig thought. I told him almost nothing.

But one way and another, Halfdan understood. He understood from the little his daughter had told him and from her silences. The sudden leaping terror that convulsed her body, her faraway looks of loss and hopeless longing. He understood from what Snorri and Skarp told him about how they had deceived Solveig, and how Tamas had saved Solveig's life at the cost of his own . . .

Wearily, Halfdan waved the two of them away. He gritted his teeth.

This middle-earth, he thought, it's on the rack. It's cankering. It's rotting from the inside out. Like my poor body.

I'll get back to Miklagard, no doubt. But after that? What?

And you, my Solva? What will you do then?

Solveig knew how her father shouldered his own sorrows, and suspected he was hiding the worst from her. When she asked him how he was feeling, more often than not he dismissed her enquiry with a grunt and a wave, or with some terse reply that his illness was a gift from the gods or that men must learn to accept their fate, whatever it was.

Accept, thought Solveig. Accept. That's what Harald kept telling me I must do. Learn to accept.

I know it's no use banging my head against a door like a battering ram. But if I accept without asking questions, I'll become mild and milky and toothless. Why else should I think and feel, and listen and argue, and learn, and compare?

On the third morning after leaving Sicily, Solveig woke not with a lightness of heart but with some new sense of purpose. Thinking what Tamas would say to her and want her to do, she stretched her arms and legs, and briskly walked up and down between the bows and the stern.

Yes, she said to herself. He would. He'd say I must look forward as well as back.

195

Solveig felt as if she were waking from a suffocating dream that kept winding its dark tentacles around her, and she began to look around.

'How long?' she asked Nico.

The helmsman shook his head and shrugged.

'But how long?'

'Five days with this wind behind us.'

Solveig opened her eyes and stared ahead. She thought of seeing Maria again, and wondered whether her old father was still alive . . . Alive, she thought, when Tamas is dead. That's the wrong way round. Then she started thinking about the Saracen woman she had killed, and wondered whether she was a mother, and whether her old father was still alive . . . And then, amidships, she saw something jammed between the bottom stringer and the deck timber. Something shining.

She knew what it was at once. She swooped on it.

Her violet-grey eye, her third eye that Oleg had given her in his little workshop in Ladoga.

I saw it, thought Solveig; it bounced three times and escaped that clutching Saracen and jumped over the gunwales. But my eyes tricked me.

For a long while, she cradled the little stone in the warm palm of her right hand and examined it – the way it shone with its quiet inner light.

It was waiting for me. Patient. Unblinking. Why has it found me now?

'Maker's eyes,' came the reply. 'You have maker's eyes.'

Solveig drew in her breath. It's true. I haven't cut and carved for so long, because there's always so much work to do. It was the same in Sicily. Snorri and I didn't even have time to word and cut the stone for all our companions who were drowned in the great storm. But now I'll carve again as soon as I can.

'They won't attack us again, will they?'

Nico scratched his red neck. 'Why not?'

Solveig stared at the helmsman, dismayed.

'Our best weapon is forewarning.'

'Lookouts, you mean?'

Nico nodded. 'You showed a clean pair of heels when you shimmied up this mast-stay. Go on!'

Solveig shook her head, and for just a moment she saw herself straddling the spar, and a young man with tousled acorn hair gazing up at her, waving and shouting.

'No,' she said. 'If I go up there, I'll see it all again. Every stroke. Poor Priskin.'

'Priskin!' repeated Nico, wrinkling his nose. 'What kind of name is that? People's names should . . . shine. Up you go!'

But Solveig shook her head again. 'I've got work below,' she told the helmsman. 'More than enough. Down in the horse-stalls.'

Solveig was kept busy that afternoon, and by evening she was smeared all over with dung and felt exhausted. First she had to groom Alnath, but although she gave of her best, he kept stamping and swishing his tail and giving her mournful looks.

'Don't be gloomy,' Solveig urged him. 'Please don't. We must help each other.'

How Solveig wished she knew the secret words to whisper in Alnath's ears, and how she longed to tell him how brave Tamas had been. She laid her forehead against the Arab's brow, as she had seen Tamas do, and put her arms around his neck.

After this Solveig went straight through the open entry into the kitchen in the front part of the hold, only to run into a volley of abuse from Edla and Vibrog.

'Suit yourself!'

'She always does.'

'We've skinned the rabbits already.'

'And chopped them up.'

'You're too late, Solveig.'

'No!' protested Solveig. 'No! I had to . . .'

But she was drowned out by more taunts that she was Harald's little darling and deserved a good beating, and threats that they'd chop her up too and add her to the bubbling cauldron.

That evening, several of the guards set aside their portion of stew, complaining that it tasted wrong.

Vibrog planted herself in front of them. 'Wrong?' she exclaimed.

'Mine's full of horsehair.'

'More sinew than flesh.'

'Thirteen rabbits and a lolloping hare,' Turgeis interrupted. 'I netted them the day before we left Sicily.'

'That's normal,' said Karly. 'Still, it's the meat that's wrong.'

'Rotten!' exclaimed another guard.

Vibrog glared at them and put her hands on her hefty hips. 'You . . . monsters!' she yelled. 'You wretches! There's nothing wrong with my stew.'

There was, though. Those men who had set it aside and eaten only bread and mashed turnip slept, or did their best to sleep, while around them their companions belched and groaned and farted, and got up in the dark, clutching their stomachs and cursing.

Solveig woke early in the women's quarters, but not as early as Edla, and still lying on their pallets they faced one another.

'Didn't you eat any?' Edla asked her.

Solveig shook her head.

'Why not?'

198

'Why do you think?'

Edla gave her a slow, spiteful smile. 'Nothing tastes good to you. Everything tastes of death.'

While many of the guards were still slumped over their oars or lying higgledy-piggledy on the deck, drained by their sorry night's work, Solveig picked her way along the deck to the place just aft of the oarsmen's benches where she'd sat and carved before the pirates had attacked them.

Once more she untied her filthy canvas bag and delved into it. First she drew out the fine gauze the mountain people had given her, and in the sea breeze it trembled and kept changing colour – calm colours, peaceful colours, mauve and olive, almond, woad and amber. Then, just for a moment, keeping a firm hold on the corners to stop it from blowing away, she laid it on the top of her head and at once she felt the same comforting warmth as in the mountain village.

Solveig gazed at the square of material. She squeezed it and pressed it to her heart.

Then she slipped the gauze back into her bag and began to pull out all her bones: the rough hunks of antler and walrus bone and soapstone and the combs and pins and beads she had already half carved.

The blade of white bone – the shoulder blade Solveig had found on the battlefield at Stiklestad – was wedged at the bottom of the sack with only the gold brooch beneath it. Solveig dragged it out into the whisking wind and bright light.

'One of us?' she could still hear her father saying. 'One of them?'

And her reply: 'Any of them . . . All of them.'

I know I want to carve runes on it for everyone who has died in battle. Tamas! Tamas . . . That girl we hanged . . . the woman I killed . . . Everyone.

Until now the time wasn't right. I wasn't ready. But now I am.

Solveig sat with her long legs stretched out in front of her, and the shoulder blade laid over her thighs, and her fair hair hung like a curtain between the bone and the sun. Then she began to carve.

Very poor company, the guards told each other, the few who had refused to eat the stew. No company at all. Not one word. Not one smile. It's best to leave her on her own.

At noon, Halfdan came and sat on the bench beside his daughter. For some while he watched her carving. Then he gave a deep sigh.

Solveig looked up. 'All right?' she asked.

'Remembering,' he told her.

'It's time I got down to the stables again,' she said, opening the mouth of the bone-bag and starting to stow her bones in it. 'Remembering what?'

'Stiklestad. You don't always know it, not at the time, but in each of our lives there are happenings that change everything.'

'The battle, you mean?' asked Solveig.

'What happened after. Harald staying in the farm. Our friendship. Life on middle-earth is . . . so chancy. We try to steer a straight course but can't tell what'll happen from one day to the next.'

'I think that's why Christians are Christian,' Solveig observed. 'They know that whether their lives are rough or smooth, long or short, they'll rise to a safe home in heaven. That's what Edwin told me.'

Halfdan fell silent again.

'Some things do last, though,' Solveig went on. 'They do, don't they? Not lives, not laws, not kingdoms. But . . .' Solveig delved down to the bottom of her bag again, fished out the brooch Harald had given her father, and offered it to him.

'Not now,' said Halfdan, hurriedly looking around him. 'Put it away, Solva.'

'A gold brooch,' insisted Solveig. 'A gold brooch lasts. Carved silver, carved wood, carved stone, carved bone, they last. And what about words? Songs and sayings and stories last. If they're well-made, they do.'

'Ha!' exclaimed Halfdan. 'You've reminded me.'

'What?'

'Harald says it's time for Grimizo to sing and Snorri to tell stories. Nico too, maybe. And you, Solveig . . .'

Solveig blew out her cheeks. 'Only after I've finished in the horse-stalls.'

'This evening.'

By no means everyone aboard felt well enough to listen to stories and songs, let alone to tell and sing. After eating the rabbit-and-hare stew the previous evening, some of the guards were still loping around as if they feared the worst, while half a dozen lay flat on their backs; and although Edla's insides were as tough as her leathery skin, Vibrog had succumbed and was lying on the deck, wheezing and spouting like a stranded porpoise.

No matter. When Harald had made up his mind, there was no dissuading him and no way of resisting his powers of persuasion.

Solveig felt weary after carving all morning and mucking out the stables and grooming horses all afternoon. But for all that, Harald soon had her telling a story.

'It's one I've known,' she began, 'for longer than I can remember.'

And then, below the golden stars appearing one by one in the darkening sky, and above the silver stars glittering in the darkening water, Solveig told everyone in her light, pretty voice about the young woman whose spirit rode nine days northward and downward from middle-earth to the underworld.

'Down through swirling mist,' she said, 'down through freezing mist. She was so ill that she knew she would soon die, so she thought she would go down to the underworld of her own free will.

'But Hel,' said Solveig, 'the ruler of the underworld, told the young woman it wasn't time for her to die. He told her to ride back up to middle-earth again.

'Hel was heart-warmed. She was stirred by the young woman's bravery.

'"You can take whatever gift you like with you," Hel told her.

'Loyalty, the young woman thought. No. Love! Or laughter? Or children? Song?

'Do you know what she chose?' Solveig asked.

The stars sang their silent songs; wavelets throbbed against the planks of the *ousiai*.

'There's one gift, the young woman thought, that's made up of all those gifts, and many more besides.

'"Storytelling," the young woman told Hel. "I'll take the gift of storytelling."'

In the dark, the Vikings smiled and nodded.

'When the young woman came back to her home and her body,' Solveig told them, 'she found the ravens had already pecked out her eyes. But for the rest of her life, she travelled from village to village, a blind woman, storytelling. Telling stories of loyalty and love and laughter and children and song . . . Telling this story I'm telling you now.'

After Solveig had finished, Grimizo sang one of his grim little songs that made listeners thankful they were still alive and breathing, and Skarp scared everyone with a story about a ghost in Iceland, and half a dozen guards sang a bawdy song about a pretty girl and all the loaves in her oven.

'Ale!' shouted Harald. 'More ale for everyone!'

But not everyone felt like drinking, and by the time Snorri began his story, many of the guards were unable to stay awake. As best Solveig could remember, it was a story about a man made of ice and fire – a mountain of a man who came from the north.

'His sword was a blade of ice, his scramasax an icicle. He sailed south and nothing could melt him. Not the warm snare-words of an old empress, not the hot blood of a young princess, not . . .'

Even though Solveig thought she recognised the hero of this tale, she couldn't stay awake. But sometime later that night she woke with a start and realised that Harald himself was standing right over her and her father.

'All right, are you?' he growled.

'I fell asleep.'

'So I saw.'

Solveig shook her head and yawned.

'You missed a good story.'

'I know.'

'A story without an end.'

'No stories end,' Solveig said. 'Once they begin, they last for ever. They never end.'

'Unfinished, I mean,' Harald replied curtly. 'An unfinished story.'

Solveig yawned again.

'Your father – he's all right?'

'He never says,' whispered Solveig. 'Not as good as he makes out.'

'I count on him. I need him.'

Solveig slowly nodded. 'He knows that,' she replied.

'It strengthens him.' She yawned for a third time. 'I was dreaming. About Maria.'

Harald said nothing and, in the dark, Solveig was unable to make out his expression.

'I'm longing to see her. Are you?'

20

It was almost as if the two servants were awaiting her. Silently they glided her to her own chamber in the palace. They tipped basins of warm water into the circular marble trough in the far corner, and they brought her sweet-smelling unguents, undergarments, sweeping dresses.

Solveig trailed her chafed fingertips over the silken oatmeal bedcover. She picked up one of the little roses strewn all over it, and sniffed it. She pressed her forehead against the shining marble wall. She scoffed one of the marzipan sweetmeats set on a table at the end of her bed, and then a couple more, but not before noticing each was decorated with a crystal flower. She listened to the caged canary in the far corner of her chamber singing, singing . . .

How could I have forgotten? she thought, wrinkling up her peeling nose. How could I possibly have forgotten all these delights? But I did. They aren't delightful, anyhow. Not for Maria. She's a prisoner. Not for me, either. I don't belong here any more than with an army of braying, brutal men.

For some while Solveig padded and stalked around the chamber, and then she realised another reason she felt so uneasy was because she hadn't been on her own like this – not for weeks and weeks, not since she had walked up into the hills in Sicily. But at length she unpeeled her filthy clothing. She stepped into the trough, scrubbed herself from top to toe and washed her hair, as well as splashing a fair amount of water over the marble floor.

Then Solveig stepped out, naked as a needle, and unsheathed her scramasax. She stared at it and turned it over and over between her hands. Then she laid it into the shallow water.

Christians say Jesus died for them, she thought, and if they truly repent He forgives all their sins. Is that true? Is it as easy as that? Can you really wash guilt away?

Just as Solveig was securing the last hook on the front of her dress – the one across her throat – Maria's servants knocked on the door and entered the chamber.

They walked in just like this before, she thought. There must be a spyhole in the wall. I'm sure there is. In this palace, everyone's watching each other, and watching out for themselves.

The servants led Solveig to Maria's chamber, and the moment she saw her, Maria gave a little cry, stood up and embraced her. And then, still keeping her hands on Solveig's shoulders, she took one step back and inspected her.

'The same,' Solveig told her. 'Not the same.'

'Your hair.'

'I know. I was going to tell you.'

Maria looked puzzled. 'One side, not the other side.'

'Oh, Maria. So much. There's so much to ask and tell.'

Both girls were quite breathless, almost nervous, as if each feared the person standing in front of her might not quite measure up to the one she remembered and had so often thought of. Maria's eyes were shining, but Solveig could see the muscles in her neck were twitching, and could feel how she was slightly trembling herself.

'Man?' Maria asked bluntly.

Solveig lowered her eyes. She slowly nodded.

Without asking any more than that, Maria somehow understood. She embraced Solveig again, and didn't let go, and Solveig felt as if she'd stepped into a richly perfumed garden.

'I'll explain everything,' she whispered. 'I will. Your father – is he . . . ?'

Maria shrugged. 'Still in that stone house,' she replied. 'Damp.'

'Alive!' said Solveig, her eyes shining.

Maria held out both hands, and then lowered them degree by degree.

'Monster!' said Solveig indignantly.

'Shhh!'

'A dying man.'

'Just as she plans,' said Maria under her breath. 'I should be looking after him.'

'I should look after my father too,' Solveig said, 'but I don't even know what's wrong with him, and he doesn't want to talk about it.'

'Same,' said Maria.

'Anyhow,' Solveig went on, 'I hope I can visit your father again.'

Maria smiled. 'He hopes,' she replied.

Solveig gazed at Maria. 'Harald . . .'

Maria's lips slightly parted; her dark eyes were dancing.

'Harald wants to see you,' Solveig told her. 'We talked about you last night, and when we were in Sicily. I told him how I was longing to see you, and I know he is too.'

Maria slowly ran her fingertips through her luscious dark hair.

'Oh, Maria! Wait until he sees you.'

'Solveig,' whispered Maria, and then she took Solveig

into her arms so there was no chance whatsoever of anyone else being able to hear her, 'I've seen him.'

'What?' cried Solveig.

Maria nodded.

'Harald?'

Maria drew back and put her right hand over her heart. 'He came straight here.'

Solveig felt quite breathless. Then hot tears welled up behind her eyes.

'He says he'll come back this evening.'

'Oh, Maria!'

The two girls embraced again.

'But what about the Empress?' Solveig asked. 'Harald's first duty is to report to her.'

'"She can wait." That's what Harald said. "Duty, duty, nothing but duty for day after day and month after month. Duty and hardship. Hardship. Maria, the hardship of our separation!"'

'Harald said that?' exclaimed Solveig.

She remembered how brusquely Harald had told her that Maria carried her heart around on a platter and kept offering it to him; she recalled how he had refused to answer whether he meant to marry her.

Maria pushed out her puffy lower lip. 'What are you thinking?'

Solveig slowly shook her head. 'Sometimes,' she said, 'Harald's my almost-brother. Sometimes he's . . . a sun-god.'

'Sun-god,' Maria repeated happily.

'He believed he would be a leader when he was only three,' Solveig told her. 'When they were little boys, one of his elder brothers wanted more cattle than anyone else, and the other more corn, but Harald wanted warships. Warships and warriors.'

Maria smiled.

'He looks like a leader. When he says something, he expects people to listen to him. And they do. They believe in him.'

'Me,' said Maria.

'I know,' Solveig replied. 'You told me once that "Harald is most man," and that's true. And then you said, "His heart batters in his chest." That's true as well.'

'Very brave,' added Maria.

'Very brave,' agreed Solveig, 'very quick to decide. He knows who his henchmen are and keeps faith with them. He's been loyal to my father. Without Harald, the Varangians would never have won those three towns in Sicily. But, Maria . . .'

Maria could hear the caution in Solveig's voice.

'He's greedy. Very greedy. And he –' Solveig hesitated – 'he's brutal. He's cruel.'

Solveig spoke with such force that Maria opened her cinnamon eyes and looked quite startled.

'I know there's good and bad in each of us, and maybe more of each in great men and women. But please be careful.'

'Careful?'

'Harald's . . . dangerous.'

'No,' said Maria flatly.

'Yes. He's cunning. He's a deceiver.'

Maria shook her head. 'I know Harald.'

'He is. I saw how he tricked Georgios Maniakes, his own ally. And then three times he tricked the Saracens.'

Maria shrugged. 'Normal,' she said.

'He deceived me,' Solveig insisted. 'He used me and my feelings. If it's his fate, Harald will be a great king, I know that. But when it suits him, he uses people . . . and then disposes of them.'

Maria sighed, and turned away from Solveig.

'Oh, Maria!' persisted Solveig. 'I scarcely know what

to say – I want to be true to Harald and I want to be true to you. Please be very careful.'

'The Divine Empress!' scoffed Skarp, and the other guards accompanying Harald brayed.

'What was it she said in Hagia Sophia?' Snorri asked Harald. 'Just remind me.'

'"Harald,"' said Skarp, aping the Empress's voice, clipped but quite soft-spoken, '"Harald, I'll give you my treasures . . . and grant you favours . . ."'

The guards laughed.

'Her treasures,' jeered Skarp. 'Her favours, Harald. What kind of favours would they be?'

'I saw how her thin lips stretched and her grey face crinkled,' Snorri told Harald. 'And how you lowered your eyes.'

'We all did,' said Grimizo. 'In disgust.'

Harald Sigurdsson said nothing. He ignored the lot of them and on stiff legs stalked towards the golden chamber.

'Don't forget your hood,' Snorri told him. 'Otherwise . . . chop-chop. The Divine Empress will cut off your head.'

Dressed in royal purple from their heads to their heels, Empress Zoe and Emperor Michael were already ensconced on their high-backed seats on the stone dais, ready to receive Harald and his shoulder-companions. As soon as the Varangians entered the hall – led in by the same boy as before, in his baggy yellow trousers – the seats of the Emperor and Empress began to ascend on their stout marble columns.

Harald Sigurdsson and his henchmen bowed and got down on to their knees. They pressed their foreheads against the cold marble floor.

'Rise!' the Empress instructed them.

The Vikings got to their feet, and bowed again.

Harald glanced around him at all the courtiers and pageboys and servants, the priests, petitioners and the like in the great hall, and he picked out Solveig and Maria, fair and dark, standing side by side.

Maria sighed. Her lips parted.

Then the Empress showed Harald Sigurdsson the palms of her misshapen hands by way of inviting him to speak.

'We are grateful to you for your audience,' Harald Sigurdsson began in a very formal manner. 'We are thankful to set foot again in Miklagard.'

'More thankful than I am,' the Empress called out. 'I instructed you to clean the whole island of filth. All the filthy Saracens who've swarmed in from north Africa. I ordered you to drive them out, or, better, put them to death. I scarcely expected to see you again within three months.'

'Lady . . .' began Harald, and then he corrected himself. 'Empress! On our way to Sicily, we lost three galleys. Three tubs!'

'Lost?'

'To storms,' said Harald calmly. 'And two of them were carrying our best siege engines.'

'Only a bad workman blames his tools,' Emperor Michael observed, 'and only a bad mercenary blames his weapons.'

'You can scarcely blame weapons you do not have,' Harald replied sharply.

Solveig stared at Emperor Michael. He looks even younger than he did before, she thought. Less than half as old as the Empress. His moustache and beard, they were just sprouting, and they've scarcely grown since I last saw him.

'But we locked horns with two dhows,' Harald continued. 'West of Chios.'

'Booty?' asked the Empress.

Harald shook his head. 'We rammed one, but she sank before we could board her. Then we fought the pirates on the other dhow. Hand to hand. We lost three men. No, we had to sail on, and when we reached Sicily, my carpenters had to make new siege engines. Empress, we laid siege to three Saracen towns. For you and your empire, we've already won three great towns.'

Empress Zoe nodded. 'And you've brought back a hoard of gold, silver, treasures?'

'Lady—' Harald began.

'Empress!'

'Empress,' repeated Harald in a measured voice, 'not as much as I'd wish, and not as much as you'd wish.'

Solveig saw Empress Zoe draw herself up in her seat as if she were a snake about to strike. She glowered at Harald from under her hooded eyelids. 'That's not what I've been told,' she said in her soft-spoken voice.

Harald didn't reply.

'My commander-in-chief,' the Empress continued, 'Georgios Maniakes, he has informed me there were huge riches in the first town – the one you besieged together.'

'His men were encamped outside the gates. Right outside them. They were first in.' Harald balled his right hand into a fist and punched his left palm. 'They ran riot, they rifled the place and left us very poor pickings.'

'Is that so?' Empress Zoe replied. 'Maniakes informs me that you divided the booty equally. One-quarter for him and his men, one-quarter for you and your greedy Varangians, one half for my treasury.'

'That's a lie!' Harald Sigurdsson retorted. His voice bounced off the arched roof of the golden hall.

'A lie?' said Empress Zoe in a measured voice. 'You're calling Georgios Maniakes a liar.'

'A hog!' shouted Harald. 'A Turkish troll! Nothing but a baggage-man!'

'And you, Harald,' the Empress continued calmly, 'Maniakes says you tricked him. He says you deceived him.'

Solveig half turned to Maria, but Maria stared straight ahead. Then she blinked and swallowed noisily.

Harald raised both arms and looked to left and right at his shoulder-companions. 'He insulted me in front of my men. I told him, "I take orders from no one except Empress Zoe and Emperor Michael."'

'Deceived him,' the Empress repeated, 'so your ships would always put in first, and your horses would be fed first, so you'd have first choice as to where to pitch your tents . . . Harald Sigurdsson, I warned you to be even-handed in your dealings with each other. I told you misfortune always follows on the heels of too much greed.'

'He got his deserts,' Harald said gruffly.

Empress Zoe raised her claw of a right hand and pointed at Harald with her hooked forefinger. 'Georgios Maniakes,' she stated in an unhurried, deliberate voice, 'accuses you of deceit and theft.'

'Where is he?' growled Harald like a wild boar.

'And I accuse you, Harald Sigurdsson, of defrauding the Empire of Byzantium.'

For a moment, everyone in the golden hall held their breath. The canaries in their cages stopped singing. Time itself held its breath, and listened.

Solveig took Maria's right arm.

'I sentence you to imprisonment.'

'In which case . . .' Harald replied, and for a moment he paused. 'In which case, Empress, I will no longer

213

serve you or fight for you. Here and now . . .' His voice was rising. 'Here and now I stand down as leader of your Varangian guard.'

'Take him away!' screeched Empress Zoe.

At once half a dozen of the Byzantine guards surrounded Harald Sigurdsson and his henchmen, but not one of them dared touch Harald.

Harald glared at them disdainfully. 'Which one of you,' he challenged them, 'will lay a single finger on me?'

Then the Viking gazed up at the Empress and the Emperor. He bared his teeth, and his piercing blue eyes drilled through them like augers.

'Take him away!' the Empress screeched again.

Harald bestowed a grim smile on her. He didn't bow, let alone prostrate himself; he didn't back away. He glanced towards Solveig and Maria and then swung on his right heel. Followed by Snorri and Skarp, Halfdan and Grimizo, he strode out of the golden hall.

Commotion!

Everyone was agog. Aghast.

Dark eyes burning, Empress Zoe raised her mottled right hand, and the racket around her hushed into a shocked silence.

The Empress searched out Solveig and Maria. She reached out towards them.

'You!' she said in a hoarse voice. 'Harald's light angel, his dark angel. I know you better than you know yourselves.'

The two girls stood so close together they could feel each other's warmth.

'You can't rescue him,' Empress Zoe told them, and now her voice was caustic and bitter. 'Don't think you can help him in any way. Maria! Solveig! Don't go near Harald. You're not to take a single step towards him.'

The Empress flexed and tried to straighten her crooked hand. She drew it across her throat.

21

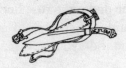

Maria squeezed her wrists. She got up from her silken sedan, and then sat down again. She sighed noisily.

'The Black Tower,' she wailed. 'Black as the hole to hell. Have you seen it?'

'If anyone can escape, Harald will,' said Solveig.

'Prisoners get thrown in but carried out. Everyone knows that.'

'There must be some way.'

'There's only one door,' Maria told her. 'A thick oak door with many locks. Inside, there's a platform and a ladder into the dungeon. As soon as a prisoner has climbed down, the warder pulls up the ladder.'

Solveig quaked. 'And above the platform?' she asked.

'Nothing. Not a single window. Not even a roof.'

'No roof?' exclaimed Solveig.

'So the walls of the tower bake in the sun,' Maria continued, 'but after a rainstorm they're cold and slimy and, the dungeon's ankle deep, shin deep in water.'

'My father and Snorri and Skarp,' asserted Solveig in a very firm voice, 'they'll . . . I don't know what, but they will!'

Maria shook her head. 'Only a master of magic could,' she replied. 'That door's always locked and guarded.'

'In Sicily,' Solveig told Maria, 'we were sitting round

the fire talking about prisoners and escapes, and one guard told us how dozens of women had cut off their hair . . .'

Maria waved a pudgy hand. 'And knotted it into a long rope,' she said. 'That's just a story. It's not true. And what good did it do you or Tamas when you cut off your plait?'

The tower is guarded, thought Solveig . . . and we can't dig a tunnel. So how can we help Harald to escape? He can't pretend he's dead – that wouldn't work without a coffin . . . In our fjord, there's an old woman who knows spells to send people to sleep . . . Maybe Harald could send a message to the Empress . . . What would he say, though? 'Maniakes is right and I'm wrong. I've cheated and defrauded the Empire of Byzantium. Yes, and I long for you to grant me your favours!'

Solveig screwed up her face.

'What are you thinking?' Maria asked her.

'Bad thoughts and worse ones,' Solveig replied.

'I'll talk to my father,' Maria said. 'When I see him tomorrow, I'll ask him whether he knows the warder of the Black Tower.'

'And I'll find out what my father and Snorri and Skarp are thinking. They won't rest for as long as Harald's in that dungeon.'

It was quite a long while, though, before Solveig was able to cross the palace to the Varangian guardroom, because as soon as she returned to her chamber, worried and weary, four servants carefully carried in the most beautiful glistening silk dress.

It was woad and ice and bluebell. It kept changing colour and Solveig recognised it at once. That silk we saw in the silken paradise, she thought. This dress has been woven by those Jewish weavers.

Tears filled Solveig's eyes. Quickly she put on the

dress, and her servants buttoned all the buttons and fastened all the fastenings. The silk rustled, it gleamed, and Solveig retraced her footsteps to Maria's chamber.

'I had it made for you,' Maria told her.

Solveig grabbed her and hugged her fiercely. 'Oh, Maria!' she whispered. 'It's made of light. Northern light.'

'It becomes you.'

'The light that never darkens,' Solveig said, 'not even at midnight. It's the most lovely dress I've ever seen.'

Only very reluctantly did Solveig change back into the day-clothing Maria had lent her and, when she had done so, she set off for the Varangian guardroom.

There were more than a dozen men there, some perched on low stools, some sitting on the floor with their backs to the wall, and they all stopped talking as she walked in.

'Oh,' said Skarp. 'It's you.'

'Only me,' Solveig replied.

'My one and only,' groaned Grimizo, reaching out for Solveig. 'I feel so lonely.'

Solveig shook her head. 'We are all lonely . . .'

But Snorri interrupted her. 'We've just seen a friend of yours,' he began.

Solveig looked puzzled.

'He sailed in this morning.'

'The one with teeth like a jack-rabbit,' added Skarp. 'Englishman.'

'Edwin!' yelped Solveig.

Snorri nodded. 'The word-spinner. That man can thread a word through the eye of a needle.'

'Where is he?' asked Solveig.

'Up his own word-spout!' Skarp exclaimed.

'He's gone to arrange an audience with the Holy Mother,' Snorri informed her.

'You've . . . you've told him about . . .'

'Of course,' said Snorri, and then he lowered his voice. 'Actually, your Edwin says he knows someone. And that someone knows someone who . . .'

'He does?' said Solveig eagerly.

'Well,' said Skarp, 'we're beggars. We haven't got one bright idea between us.'

'Edwin's our best chance,' Snorri continued.

'Our only chance,' Skarp said flatly. 'The only one, so far as I can see.'

'Words,' observed Solveig, 'words sometimes win what weapons cannot.'

Skarp smacked his forehead. 'Like father like daughter!' he yawned.

And at that moment, as if Solveig's saying or Skarp's response had summoned him, Halfdan appeared in the frame of the door. He stepped into the guardroom.

'Very good!' he declared with a broad smile.

'Very good?' Snorri repeated. 'What's very good?'

'What's wrong with Halfdan?' asked Skarp. 'Glum and gurgling for weeks, what with his gut ache, but now that we're all joyless, every single one of us . . .'

'And leaderless,' added Snorri.

'And lonely,' said Grimizo in a hollow voice.

'It came out,' Halfdan announced in a loud voice. He thrust out his right fist.

All the guards turned to look at him.

'Out?'

'Uh?'

'What did?' asked Gorm.

'The worm!' proclaimed Halfdan. 'The worm, Gormless! I felt it coming, and then it came. One moment it was crushing me. Strangling me.' Halfdan clutched his stomach and screwed up his face. 'The next, it was oozing out. Right out! Taller than I am.'

'Never!' exclaimed Skarp.

219

'As long as the Midgard Serpent. Writhing and shrithing. I chopped it into pieces.'

Heavy-hearted as they were, some of the guards hooted, some clapped their hands, and Solveig took her father's right arm and squeezed it fiercely and didn't let go.

Halfdan beamed at everyone. 'I feel,' he said, 'as if I've lost a companion. A deadly companion. And I've won back my life.'

'Father!' cried Solveig, and she swung around in front of him and grabbed him by the waist.

'Now for Harald!' boomed Halfdan. 'What's the plan?'

But Edwin didn't come back to the Varangian guardroom that day or that evening or even the next morning, and the guards grew as gloomy and humourless as Solveig had ever seen them. They were men of action, hobbled by uncertainty and by having to wait. They were followers, half lost for want of a leader.

When they bragged, their boasts echoed in their own ears; when they made gibes, they became fractious; when they mended their tunics, they punctured their own thumbs; when they talked about Sicily, they remembered the dead friends they had left behind. The more ale they drank, the more melancholy they became, while Halfdan's unquenchable good cheer only made them more sour-mouthed.

Solveig grew impatient with Karly and Ulf and Gissur and Gorm – she became annoyed with the whole lot of them.

And when Egil told her to go away and play somewhere else, that's exactly what she did.

'You dismal gang!' she cried. 'Is there no one here who can rescue Harald?'

She stalked out and slammed the heavy door behind her.

Skarp turned to Halfdan. His mouth curled. 'Shcum!' he growled.

Halfdan glared at him. Then he belched.

'Shcum!' repeated Skarp. He stood up and pointed at Halfdan. 'Tomash . . .' he began, and he frowned, trying to work out the dead guard's name. 'Tamash – he gave his life for your daughter, and she shtands here, accusing us.'

By now, Skarp was bellowing. Snorri stood up as well, and put a hand on his shoulder.

'Enough!' he said firmly. 'Much more of this, and it'll come to blows and blood.'

Solveig strode across the palace courtyard and, just outside the high walls, she saw a big man bundling towards her.

'Edwin!' she cried. 'Edwin!'

Solveig lengthened her stride and fairly hurled herself into the Englishman's arms, all her impatience and frustration dissolved in a moment.

When at last she stepped back, she saw Edwin's mouth puckering, and the very sight of it reminded her of what he'd said almost four months before.

'Well, Solveig, maybe there are camels in Sicily.'

'Edwin!' she said breathlessly. 'Edwin, I thought I'd never have a chance to ask you. Was it you who persuaded Harald to take me to Sicily?'

Edwin gave a self-deprecating smile. 'Oh, I wouldn't say that.'

'Wouldn't you?'

'Not really. Sometimes we say things, we suggest things already in another person's mind.'

'Oh, Edwin!' exclaimed Solveig. 'I'm so very glad to see you.'

'And I'm glad to see you,' the Englishman replied. 'Especially here, outside the palace.'

Solveig waited for him to explain.

'Well away from all your countrymen! Down in the mouth, all of them, glaring and glowering.'

'I know,' said Solveig, pressing her lips together. 'I've had my fill of them too.'

'They're afraid,' Edwin told her. 'Harald's their man-god, and with a snap of her horrible hooked fingers . . .' Edwin paused and smiled. 'Well, with a twist of her tongue, the Empress has done away with him. Dropped him into the dungeon.'

'Can you help?' Solveig asked him. 'Snorri says you know someone. And—'

'First things first,' Edwin said, and he inspected Solveig from head to toe. 'What do I see? A rather beautiful young Norwegian girl. Fifteen summers old.'

'And rising,' Solveig told him with a half-smile.

'Yes, fifteen and rising,' Edwin agreed. 'A girl with a plait on one side of her head, bristles on the other. A new fashion?'

Solveig lowered her eyes.

'A girl who has witnessed and listened and . . . loved . . . loved, yes, and suffered. Suffered much.'

How kind Edwin's voice was. Solveig smiled and warm tears slipped down her cheeks as they slowly walked away from the palace and across the concourse towards the Constantine column.

Through her tears, she told Edwin how hateful she found Harald's cunning and the unfeeling way he used other people for his own purposes; she told him about the cruel hanging of the two young children and their grandfather. She told him how she had come to realise she could never belong in an army of men, and how she had broken rank and climbed into the high hills; she told him about the mountain people and the wise Saracen traveller Abu Touati.

Edwin paused. He put a hand on Solveig's right shoulder.

'And –' he hesitated – 'you loved a young man. And he loved you.'

Solveig's face crumpled. Edwin accepted her into his arms, and for a while they stood there in the middle of the concourse, Edwin so patient, Solveig so stricken.

After some while, the two of them began to walk again, quite slowly. To begin with, they felt no need to say anything, but then Solveig asked Edwin about Edith and her baby.

'A daughter,' Edwin said. 'As she foretold. She went into labour in Kiev. A fine red-haired daughter.' Edwin paused. 'No Pechenegs!' he declared. 'God be praised! And none on the way back here either.'

'Is Edith with you?'

'No, no. She'll be more safe in Garthar until I can ship her home.'

'Will you go with her?'

Edwin smiled. 'You and all your questions.'

'You . . .' rejoined Solveig. 'You and all your word-fencing.'

Edwin blinked and waved an arm. 'Her name is Kata.'

Solveig frowned. 'Edith said she might call her that. Is it English?'

Edwin shook his head. 'I thought it was Viking.'

'No,' said Solveig. 'Not that I've ever heard.'

'After all,' reasoned Edwin, 'her father was a Viking.'

The two of them met each other's eyes, and smiled.

'And Sineus?' asked Solveig. 'His foot?'

'Poor man,' Edwin replied. 'He lost it. His whole leg. So he's still stranded where you last saw him, on Saint

223

Gregorios. I'll be sailing east and north again as soon as I can, so I can help him back to Kiev.'

'You've come with a message for Empress Zoe,' suggested Solveig.

'Have I?'

'And one for Harald.'

When Edwin didn't reply, Solveig recalled how Edith had laughed and told her that trying to get him to say something when he didn't want to was like squeezing a stone for water.

'You told me before,' Solveig reminded him, 'it would be a strange messenger who travelled so far and for so long with only one song in his mouth.'

'Is that what I said?' enquired Edwin with a polite smile.

'Harald, then,' said Solveig firmly.

'I can scarcely give Harald a message, can I,' Edwin replied sharply, 'if I can't even speak to him?'

'Can you help?' asked Solveig for a second time. 'Can you?'

'It seems I have no choice,' Edwin replied in a dry voice, as if assisting the Varangians were something he had no particular wish to do, 'if I'm to speak to Harald myself.'

'You know someone,' Solveig prompted him.

But Edwin was in no hurry to answer, and for a while they walked on through the streets of Miklagard without saying anything further.

'Yes,' said Edwin thoughtfully. 'Yes.' And then, in a much more definite voice: 'You're about to meet her.'

Edwin halted. He chafed his tongue against the back of his buckteeth. 'A woman,' he announced. 'A noblewoman.'

'Who?' asked Solveig.

'A child of the crossing-place,' Edwin said rather

grandly. 'Her mother was a great lady here in Miklagard, and she was given in marriage to a great Varangian.' He took Solveig's left arm. 'Five years ago,' he went on, 'this lady became ill. Very ill, and near to death. No doctor knew what was wrong with her, though many pretended to, and no amount of money given to the priests in their chantries was able to save her. She turned yellow, she turned grey. On her deathbed, this lady prayed to mighty Olaf, the king, the saint who brought the word of Christ to Norway . . .'

'I know,' said Solveig. 'He died when the wolf swallowed the sun.'

Edwin nodded.

'My father and Harald fought beside him,' Solveig told him. 'At Stiklestad.'

Edwin nodded again. 'This lady, she called out to Olaf to pray to Jesus to save her life – she called out without knowing that the king lay already dead on the battlefield. There and then, this lady began to recover! Her servants had given up all hope, and they began to hope.'

Solveig twisted her golden plait, she tugged a little at it.

Edwin smiled, and the two of them fell into step once again. 'This lady,' he assured Solveig, 'owes Saint Olaf her life, and she has vowed to repay him for healing her.'

'But . . .'

Palms uppermost, Edwin balanced his hands as if they were a pair of scales.

'Norwegian . . .' he said, 'Byzantine. Byzantine . . . Norwegian. Believe me, Solveig, there's no one here worth knowing whom she doesn't know.'

Edwin guided her into a gloomy, narrow lane, very much like the one where Leo, Maria's father, lay slowly dying.

'Down this one, I think,' Edwin said. 'Then left at the bottom. Yes, this noblewoman, she's vowed to repay Saint Olaf. I've spoken to her already, and tonight she'll try to rescue Harald.'

Solveig drew in her breath. She grabbed Edwin's right arm.

'Rescue Harald,' he repeated. 'No matter what the cost.'

22

Whether first dark is more dense than the later watches of the night, Solveig was unsure, but that is how it seemed to her. Just as we dive at first into deep sleep, she thought, before we sleep in the shallows among our coloured dreams.

Wrapped in thick shawls to conceal their faces and figures and to ward off the cold, the noblewoman and Solveig picked their way down one narrow lane after another. The bulky Englishman walked just in front of them, carrying a small lantern and wearing the becoming bonnet he had stuffed into his pocket after his audience with the Empress and Emperor. Now and then he rubbed his ears to keep them warm.

'What shall I call you?' asked Solveig.

The lady didn't reply.

'I don't know your name, and I don't know where we're going,' Solveig said.

'Knowing what we don't need to know can become a burden,' the lady told her. 'It can be dangerous.'

So Solveig didn't know the lady's name, and she wasn't to know, either, that they weren't alone. Four clusters of the lady's servants were already converging on the Black Tower from different quarters of the city, three of them carrying ladders, and the fourth a great length of thick, knotted rope.

'Ugh!' exclaimed Edwin. He slipped, recovered his footing, and turned round to face the two women.

'What?' asked Solveig.

'Mind your step. Someone's dinner.'

Now and then the three of them passed a person hurrying in the opposite direction – someone just as careful not to be recognised as they were themselves.

'Goat-feet,' murmured Edwin. 'Horned men. Harlots. Grave-robbers. This is no place to be, not for you, lady of ladies . . .'

'Lady Nameless!' exclaimed Solveig.

'Lady Nameless!' repeated Edwin with a little smile. 'Not for you and not for this Norwegian girl, strong as the sun.'

'Not for you either,' Lady Nameless told him. 'You strange . . . inscrutable Englishman.'

Solveig didn't know what that word meant, but there was no time to ask because at that moment she heard ghastly shrieking ahead of them, scything through the darkness.

Solveig gasped and the three of them halted. They said not a word.

The shrieking stopped. The silence felt even more intense than before. Killing, thought Solveig. Blood. More blood. She screwed up her eyes.

Lady Nameless slipped a hand out of her woollen shawl and grasped for Solveig's right arm. 'And some things,' she whispered, 'some we do better not to know. But look now, Solveig. Right ahead.'

Solveig looked.

It was growing out of the night, even darker than the darkness imprisoning it.

'The Black Tower,' murmured Lady Nameless.

Black, thought Solveig. She stared up at the bulk – the

grim fist and force of it. Pitch. Jet. Crows and ravens. It's like the lower half of Hel's body: corpse-black.

Solveig stared so intently that the tower seemed to rear up and begin to topple over her. She felt quite dizzy.

Who gave the signal Solveig wasn't sure, but when it happened, it happened very, very quickly.

The servants carrying the ladders and rope converged on the tower. They met outside the massive oak door. And there, by the light of Edwin's lantern, Solveig could plainly see the bodies of two wardens lumped against it. Their throats had been cut.

Quickly the men bound ladder to ladder, and then they hoisted them, creaking and wobbling, and propped them against the outside of the tower.

Two of Lady Nameless's servants started to climb, hauling a knotted rope behind them.

But high up, the man at the top lost his hold on the rope, and it took some time and cursing for him to haul it back up again. Then a rung snapped, and he trod on the left hand of the second servant.

The man yelped, and the tied ladder shook and swayed.

When he finally reached the top of the Black Tower, the first servant began to feed the rope over the coping and down, down into the dungeon.

Then two servants started to thump the door with their oak staffs in case it was possible that Harald had slept through the terrible shrieking. All around them, it seemed to Solveig, the night awoke and complained.

Dogs yapped and howled; gulls and pigeons squawked; in their graves the dead stirred and moaned.

Three more men started to climb the long ladder now. Holding the rope, they stood head to toe, head to toe below those at the top, taking the strain.

'What are they doing?' asked Solveig in a hoarse voice.

Lady Nameless didn't reply, but within two minutes, two minutes or three, Harald Sigurdsson had swarmed up the knotted rope inside the Black Tower. He grabbed hold of the coping, swung himself over and planted his feet on the ladder's top rung.

Solveig and Edwin and the lady stepped forward to the bottom of the ladder. They met Harald as he came back to earth.

By the light of Edwin's lantern, Harald Sigurdsson glared at the Englishman. Then at Solveig. Then at the lady without a name.

'Hou-arrch!' he growled, and he spat at their feet.

Aloof and glowering and bedraggled, he looked like some very badly ruffled giant bird – a stork, perhaps, or one of those flamingos Solveig had seen sitting on their rag-bag nests at the entrance to the waterway leading to Miklagard.

Several times Harald stamped. He shook himself.

'I was dreaming,' he said in a curt voice, as if for all the world he were rebuking them for having interrupted his dream by rescuing him. 'Then I heard voices and that rope chafing . . . Daydreaming, dungeon-dreaming!

'I was little, very little, and my mother was saying to King Olaf, "Stand beside my Harald. Watch over my son." And King Olaf replied, "I will. For as long as I live and after I'm dead." The same words I heard him say in my dream in Sicily.'

'Oh!' cried Solveig.

'And then,' Harald told them, 'I was down in that foul dungeon again, but King Olaf was there too. He was standing beside me, and telling me, "I will save you. Harald, I will rescue you."'

At once the lady without a name subsided on to her knees in the filthy street.

'A miracle!' she exclaimed. 'A second miracle! *Deo gratias! Sancto Olavo, gratias!*'

'Harald . . .' Edwin began.

The Viking leader raised Lady Nameless to her feet.

'A message.'

'Later.'

'Now,' said Edwin, very firmly.

Harald grunted.

'King Yaroslav.'

Edwin put his lantern between Solveig's hands, and he and Harald turned away into the dark.

'You heard what Harald said?' the noblewoman asked Solveig. 'His dream.'

'Yes,' whispered Solveig. 'And Edwin told me you vowed to repay King Olaf . . .'

'Saint Olaf,' the lady corrected her.

'. . . repay Saint Olaf, because he heard you.'

'And healed me,' the lady said. 'He guided the Englishman Edwin to me, and he heard my prayer.'

'And Harald,' marvelled Solveig, 'down in this dungeon, he knew Saint Olaf was watching over him. He was dreaming he would be rescued.'

'He had faith,' Lady Nameless said. 'As on my deathbed I had faith. Faith makes the impossible possible.'

Then the lady softly summoned all her servants. She praised them and promised them rewards; she reminded them of the utmost need to keep their night's work secret. Then she dismissed them.

Solveig, meanwhile, stood quietly in the dark, thinking about what she had just witnessed – the dream, the vision, the marvel, the miracle, call it what you will.

At length, Harald Sigurdsson and Edwin reappeared out of the darkness.

'Lady . . .' the Viking began. 'Lady Nameless.' He gazed at her and, even in the flickering lantern light, Solveig could see the light in his eyes, blue as blue stars. 'Because of you,' he declared. And he slowly spread his arms.

'Because of Saint Olaf,' the noblewoman replied.

'I'll have prayers said for him and prayers said for you,' Harald promised her. 'Here in Miklagard. In Garthar. In Norway.'

The lady gracefully inclined her head.

'You'll never be safe,' Harald said, 'if it becomes known who rescued me. But I tell you, lady, that even without a name –' Harald paused, pushed out his lower lip and nodded several times – 'even without a name, you'll be far better known than many men and women well known in the northern lands.'

Then Harald turned to Solveig. She was still holding the horn lantern and he laid his big hands over hers.

'Not sun-strong,' he said, 'not quite. But bright, and constant, and crucial. Where would we be without your light?'

Solveig supposed he was talking about her and not the lantern, and she wasn't quite sure whether he was praising or mocking her.

'This is what must happen,' Harald told her. His voice was very quiet, and very determined. 'I'll go straight from here to the Golden Horn. Down to the Varangian quay. I'll board my boat. It's already laden – yes, it's crammed with all my silver, all my gold, all my weapons and silks, everything from Sicily. We'll set sail at first light.'

'But . . .' began Solveig.

'No,' he said. 'I can't go back to the palace.'

So many questions were whirling around Solveig's head. Who will lead all the guards? What will become of me and my father? And Maria? What about her? Will the Empress take vengeance? Where will Harald go?

'You, Solveig,' said Harald in a voice that brooked no argument whatsoever, 'you'll go back to the guardroom.

232

On your own. Be very careful not to draw attention to yourself. Don't scoot, don't run, but be as quick as you can.'

Solveig looked up at Harald, wide-eyed.

'Tell Snorri and Skarp and your father that Harald Sigurdsson is free.'

Harald released Solveig's hands and clenched his fists. 'Have them hurry my men down to the quay and board our two boats there. Two hundred men. No more, no fewer. And then, my little sister, tell your father to shoulder Land-Ravager, my battle standard. You understand? All this?'

'Yes,' whispered Solveig.

'Listen!' Harald told her. He hesitated. 'In each of our lives, little sister, there come moments such as these. Everything depends on you; success or failure depends on you.'

Solveig held her breath.

'Snorri and Skarp must find their way to Maria's chamber,' Harald told her in a low voice.

'Oh!' exclaimed Solveig. From the top of her tingling head to her toes, her blood thrilled inside her.

'Maria's chamber,' Harald repeated.

'I'll show them.'

'Very good,' said Harald, as if this were Solveig's idea and he hadn't already thought of it.

'Nothing is to stop them. If anyone challenges them . . .' Harald clenched his fist. 'They're to bring Maria down to my boat.'

'You mean—'

'Tell them to bind and gag her, just in case . . . You, Solveig, you come with her and reassure her.'

Solveig was quite breathless now. 'Oh, yes!' she gasped. 'Yes, I will.' Her eyes filled with tears of joy.

Harald! Harald Sigurdsson! He was such a man! So

strong. So bold. So brave. Such a leader. There, at that moment, in the darkness of Miklagard, Solveig would have done anything for him.

Listening to all this, Edwin kept shifting uncomfortably, first putting his weight on one foot, then on the other. Several times he cleared his throat, and seemed about to interrupt Harald, before thinking better of it.

'And you, my friend,' Harald said to him, 'you'll escort my saviour, my nameless saviour, back to her house.'

'I will,' Edwin reassured him. 'And then I'll come to the Varangian quay. By the light of the Morning Star.'

23

'Now!' growled Harald.

Nico thrust his head forward and peered down the length of the boat. He checked the twenty-five pairs of Viking oarsmen were all at their benches. Then he stared out across the Horn, still night-grey, still gloomy. He glanced up at the mast and down at the quay.

'Get on with it!' croaked Harald.

'Ship the planks!' Nico called out. 'Slip the knots!' And then he waved to the helmsman of the second Varangian boat, tethered to the bollards behind him.

As soon as the oarsmen had levered the boat away from the stone wall of the quay, Nico ordered them to bend their backs.

'Twenty strokes,' shouted Harald. 'In . . . out. Two . . . out. Three . . . out!'

Nico screwed up his brown, weatherbeaten face. 'Twenty?'

'Then let the other boat come alongside,' Harald told him. 'Seven . . . out. Eight . . . out.'

Solveig was standing with her back to the mast, both arms wrapped around Maria, and Maria, still gagged, was wearing nothing but her silken nightdress, that and a creamy woollen shawl. She was trembling and kept making muffled squeaks, like a little animal in terrible pain.

I'm untying the gag, thought Solveig. Here and now. I don't care what Harald says.

'It's all right,' she promised Maria. 'You're going to be all right. Harald told me to reassure you.'

Solveig reached up behind Maria's head and began to tease the knot, but before she was able to loosen it, her father plunged past her shouting, 'Harald! Harald!'

'What?'

'The chain!'

Several voices at once echoed him. 'The chain! Yes! The chain across the Horn!'

'Nineteen . . . out. Twenty . . . out!' Harald raised his right hand, and the pairs of oarsmen rested their oars, the boat gliding across the glassy water. 'The chain,' he barked. 'Do you really suppose I've forgotten it?'

Halfdan raised his shoulders.

'I can scarcely ask the Empress's harbour master to remove it, can I? My friend, we're sea horses. We're sea stallions. Side by side, we'll charge at the chain.'

'Charge?!' exclaimed Halfdan.

'Like as not, we'll snap it. If not, we'll ride over it.'

Harald impatiently waved Halfdan away, and then he saw Solveig was untying Maria's gag and curtly told her to leave it alone. Keeping an eye on the second boat as she drew alongside, packed with so many men who had served with him and under him, Harald checked all his own oarsmen were at the ready. He missed nothing, nothing at all. He was like a blond giant with eyes at the front and the sides and the back of his head.

'Now then . . .' he said under his breath. 'Now then.' He raised both arms and beckoned everyone except his oarsmen to join him in the stern of the boat. The Varangian guards, the cooks, everyone.

'You, too,' Harald shouted to Solveig. 'Maria. Everyone.'

Shoulder to shoulder, cheek by jowl, more than fifty lives crammed into the space between the mast and the helmsman. Seeing what was happening, all the guards and women on the other boat, everyone except the oarsmen, did exactly the same.

Then Harald ordered his oarsmen to row, row straight at the chain stretched across the Golden Horn.

The two boats reached the chain at exactly the same moment. It grated and ground and scrunched against their keels, and at once Solveig remembered the ghastly grating and gouging when her little skiff collided with a sheet of ice in the fjord. She hugged Maria and screwed up her eyes.

Many of the Vikings began to yell and wail, but Harald's voice soared above them. 'To the bows! The bows! All of you!'

'Follow me!' yelled Halfdan.

At once Solveig's father hurried down the length of the boat, picking his way past the oarsmen, and shouting, swearing, stumbling, tripping, everyone followed him.

For a moment Harald's boat seemed almost to seesaw on the chain, no longer in the water but out of it, swaying between imprisonment and freedom. Then, quite slowly, she tilted forward and slid gracefully into the wide, welcoming channel beyond.

But even as some of Harald Sigurdsson's men began to cheer and embrace, others saw what was happening to the second boat.

The chain did its grim work: it cut deep into the keel, it opened the seams between the planks, and when everyone aboard waded to the bows, the timbers groaned, they growled and screeched. Then the keel itself snapped. The boat's back broke.

The chilly, dark water was full of flailing Vikings, Egil and Bolverk and Gissur among them, and Harald and

Nico were unable to save them because the tide pouring into the Horn was driving their drowning companions away from them, and they were on the other side of the iron chain.

By having his oarsmen stay their boat, Nico was able to rescue half a dozen men who had grabbed hold of the chain, but that was the sum of it; and even then, one guard lost his grip while he was hauling himself up the slimy rope Nico had dropped over the stern. He was swept away, gargling.

For some time Harald stood on his own, and no one thought it wise to speak to him, not even Snorri or Skarp or Halfdan. He surveyed the broken boat; he listened to the last cries of his companions and, after them, the suck-and-sob of the saltwater.

At length Harald turned to Nico. 'I hold Empress Zoe responsible for this,' he said, his voice dark and deliberate and angry. 'Empress Zoe and the boy-man. They will pay for it.'

In the bows, Solveig at last managed to remove Maria's tight gag and was shocked to see it had left a welt on either side of her mouth.

'You'll be all right,' she kept saying, but Maria couldn't stop shaking and sobbing.

'You're safe,' Solveig told her. 'We all are. You'll be all right.'

Solveig hugged Maria again. 'I'll go and talk to Harald now. I'll ask him to come to you. He'll tell you himself.'

Solveig kept an eye on Harald while he talked first to Nico, then to Snorri and Skarp. She heard him becoming more animated; she overheard him saying that at least all the booty they had brought back from Sicily – the silver, the gold, all the ivory and coins and church plate – was safe in the hold of their boat; and when

Harald threw back his head and roared with laughter at something Skarp had said, she judged she could approach him.

What a maelstrom of a man he is, she thought. Turn by turn he's wild, grim, resolved, caring, a cunning trickster, a loyal friend. I'll never understand him.

'Little sister!' Harald exclaimed.

Solveig gazed at him. She shook her head.

'The gods wanted them,' Harald said in a hoarse voice.

'The waste!' cried Solveig. 'The waste of it.'

'Tamas!' exclaimed Harald. 'Priskin. Egil. Bolverk. Gissur. All my young men.'

At once Solveig's eyes grew hot and bright with tears.

'The gods loved them,' Harald told her. 'They needed them.'

'I loved him,' choked Solveig. 'I . . .' But then she minded why she had come to speak to him. She swallowed and rubbed her eyes with the sleeve of her cloak. Then she almost cupped her hands between her breasts, as if she were offering him something precious.

'Well?'

'Maria,' whispered Solveig.

'Thanks to you!' Harald replied at once. 'Without you, she wouldn't be aboard this boat. If you hadn't carried my message from the Black Tower to Snorri and Skarp, none of this . . .' Harald spread his hands. 'Our success, Solveig, depended on you.'

'Are we sailing to Kiev?' Solveig asked him.

'We are, and as quickly as we can. Before ice locks the great river.'

'And that's where you'll marry her?'

Harald Sigurdsson frowned.

'Is it?'

'Marry her,' Harald repeated.

239

'Maria.'

Harald puffed out his cheeks, his hot breath blasted Solveig in the face. 'Marry Maria!' he exclaimed. 'Where did you get that idea?'

Solveig stared at Harald, aghast.

'I'm not marrying Maria,' Harald told her, almost laughing. 'I'm marrying Ellisif.'

'Ellisif! But I thought . . . I thought . . .'

'No, no! Ellisif. King Yaroslav's daughter.'

'I know who she is,' Solveig said fiercely. 'I've met her.'

'That was the message Edwin brought me,' Harald went on. 'If I'd agree to return to Kiev at once, with two hundred men, and help King Yaroslav to fight the Pechenegs, the king would give me the hand of his youngest daughter, Ellisif.'

'She's only twelve,' cried Solveig.

Harald shrugged. 'I'll wait,' he said. 'We'll marry when she's fourteen.'

Solveig buried her face in her hands. 'But Maria,' she half sobbed. 'Maria.'

Harald said nothing.

'What about Maria?'

Nothing.

'Why? I mean . . . Why did you ask me . . . ?' Solveig felt utterly helpless; she couldn't even find the right words.

'You're asking me why Maria's aboard this boat?'

Solveig nodded.

'She's my hostage,' Harald said in a cold voice. 'I'm taking her to Kiev to show Empress Zoe just how powerless she is.'

Solveig glared at Harald Sigurdsson. She bared her teeth; her eyes blazed.

'How can you?' she demanded. Her voice was

quivering. 'You went to see Maria alone in her chamber as soon as you disembarked. You led her to believe. With your words and body you did. You misled her to suit yourself.'

'Little sister—' Harald began.

'I'm not!' snapped Solveig. 'I'm not your sister. You, Harald, you tricked me when you asked me to lead Snorri and Skarp to her chamber and told me to reassure Maria. And you've not only deceived her, you've cut her off. How can you?' Solveig could hear her voice rising, but she also knew that she was saying exactly the right words, the words she wanted Harald to hear.

'I was stricken! I was so sorrowful when my father left – left after promising that if ever he went away, he would take me with him. All winter I was wounded. Then I sailed away from home, I crossed the mountains, I turned my back on Mother Norway. But you, you've cut off Maria from her dying father, her imprisoned mother. How can you? You're a monster! A man without a heart!'

Then Solveig shrieked and threw herself at Harald Sigurdsson. She reached up and clawed at his face and tried to gouge his eyes out.

Harald stayed her flailing hands, but not before she had striped his forehead and left cheek and drawn scarlet blood.

Harald roared. He put his hands round Solveig's throat and she thought he was going to strangle her.

But no, the Viking grabbed her by the shoulders and roared. He simply threw Solveig away; he hurled her so that she slammed into the gunwales and then collapsed on to the deck, unconscious.

With that, Harald turned his back on Solveig, he strode past poor Maria without even glancing at her, and stalked up to the bows.

*

'Solva,' murmured a voice.

The sound of it reminded her of something. Many things. Bees happy and humming in the lavender bushes. What else? No, she couldn't remember.

'My Solva.'

She felt warm and comfortable. Cradled almost.

'Solva.'

When Solveig opened her eyes, the daylight was too bright. Her eyelids flickered; she began to drift again.

When she opened her eyes for a second time, she realised she must be lying on the deck with her head in her father's lap. The world swirled around her, and she kept screwing up her eyes. But when at last she stood up, feeling very shaky, she knew at once where the boat was: the mouth of the Bosphorus, with its shadowy rib of land to the south, its hills climbing away to the north.

Solveig kept taking deep breaths and trying to clear the mist from her head as Nico steered through the swarm of little fishing boats with their brightly coloured sails, mint-green, heron-blue, flamingo-pink.

'Why are we heading for the shore?' she asked her father.

Halfdan didn't answer her.

'What's happened?'

Nico drove the boat up on to the shallow sandy beach, and at once Harald ordered a couple of men to shove out the gangplank. Then he swung himself over the gunwale and bounced down on to the foreshore.

'Bring her down!' Harald called out. 'Solveig too!'

Four guards lifted Maria bodily over the gunwales. Cautiously she shuffled down the gangplank. They followed her.

'Solveig too, I said,' Harald shouted.

Not until Solveig and Maria were standing side by

side on the chilly strand did their eyes meet, and each saw in the other her own stark fear.

Harald Sigurdsson scowled at the pair of them.

Stony-eyed, Solveig returned his gaze; Maria lowered her cinnamon eyes.

'Look at me,' Harald told her.

Maria slowly raised her eyes.

Then Harald backed the girls up against the bows of the boat so that everyone aboard could hear what he was saying.

'Maria!' he declared. His voice was clear and loud. 'I'm setting you free.'

Maria licked her lips. Her eyes were bolting. Then her legs buckled under her. She lurched and fell forward on to her hands, and Solveig helped her back on to her knees.

'Free!' repeated Harald. 'And you can thank Solveig for your freedom.'

Harald stepped right up to the two girls and spoke more quietly, so that only they could hear what he was saying.

'Solveig has told me of her grief, her winter-sorrow when she was separated from her father, and how she crossed half of middle-earth to find him. Maria, I will not separate you from yours.'

The tears glistening in Maria's eyes began to flow, and for a moment Solveig thought she was about to clutch Harald's fingers and beg. But if so, she thought better of it. She stood up. Noiselessly, she wept.

'I want no grief aboard my ship,' declared Harald. 'I want high hopes, a peaceful voyage back to Kiev, a new beginning.'

Harald glanced up at the gallery of guards ranged along the gunwale.

'Free!' he called out for a third time. 'And you can tell

your . . . poisonous aunt that she has no power over me. None whatsoever.'

Hearing this, many of the guards began to jeer.

'None!' repeated Harald. 'She couldn't save her own niece. And she couldn't have stopped me even if I'd wanted to marry you.'

Every nerve in Solveig's body trembled for Maria; every bone ached.

He's so used to cruelty, she thought, I don't think he even knows how cruel he is. He can't open his mouth without cruel words coming out.

Harald Sigurdsson turned to the four guards standing on the foreshore.

'I'm detailing you men to escort Princess Maria back to Miklagard,' he told them. 'Guard her life with your lives. She's to come to no harm: not one eyelash, not one hair.'

The four guards looked at their boots.

'Horses?' asked one man.

Harald pursed his lips. 'Sea horses,' he replied, 'if you know how to catch and ride one. Or else you can walk it. Thirty miles. You'll be there in two days.'

'Not with her,' said another guard.

'Not one eyelash,' Harald warned them. 'Not one hair. If I hear otherwise, you'll pay with your lives.'

With that, Harald stared at Maria. All he had been to her, pilgrim-guard and companion, friend, teacher, yes, and lover, perhaps lover, he no longer was – or else no longer allowed himself to be. Stern and proud and unyielding, he stared down at her, and then strode up the gangplank on to the boat.

Wild-eyed, Maria turned to Solveig, and Solveig drew her close.

'Help me!' Maria whispered like a little child. 'Come with me.'

Solveig screwed up her eyes and for a while she held Maria in her arms. 'I can't. You know I can't. If only I could.'

'S . . . s . . . s . . .' Maria stuttered-and-sobbed, but she couldn't articulate the words.

Still keeping her hands on Maria's shoulders, Solveig took a step back.

'Maria, oh Maria! Your life will be . . . will be more . . . your life will be less troubled without this man. Please believe me. One day you'll believe me. Harald would never honour you, he'd never love you as you need and deserve.'

Around them on the chilly beach, the sand shimmered like wild silk. Silver-gold sheets swept along the strand.

Njord, god of winds, opened his mouth and bellowed. The veil of sand sidled, it swayed and lifted, it gagged the two girls. Grit grazed their sweet faces.

24

Harald Sigurdsson steered clear of Solveig. He didn't send her to cook in the galley alongside the other women. He avoided catching her eye. He appeared to take no notice of her.

Halfdan understood how Solveig's sense of betrayal and her fury had completely numbed her, and he watched over her. When he asked her how well she had slept or whether she'd had sufficient to eat, he didn't press her when she gave only a brief, bleak reply. And sometimes he simply sat beside her in companionable silence.

On the second afternoon, though, Solveig asked her father about his gut.

'Twice the man I was with that tapeworm inside me!' Halfdan exclaimed. 'I'm alive, girl! And you, you're alive, when so many of our friends . . . The Norns have smiled on me, and they're smiling on you.'

Awkward and fond, Halfdan shifted nearer to his daughter so that they were sitting shoulder to shoulder. She's healing, he thought. Thinking of me. She's starting to feel again.

'Alive,' repeated Halfdan in a thoughtful voice, 'and she's beautiful too.' He sounded as if he were talking to himself. 'The gods have given her beauty, and it's time she . . . groomed herself as young women like to do.'

Solveig nudged her father's shoulder. Then she clasped the right side of her head – the side where her fair hair was short and still bushy. 'How can I?' she demanded.

But Solveig, too, sensed she was healing. She was glad of it, but now and then she felt utterly desolate because she knew time was also taking away the sharp edge of her feelings for Maria . . . and for Tamas.

Time gives, she thought. But time takes away.

One morning, Solveig began to tell her father more about her meeting with Abu Touati.

'He said it's true that anyone who travels finds out much more about herself,' she remembered, 'but that nothing can compare with the pleasure of returning home.'

Halfdan took a deep breath. 'And that's what you think?'

Solveig slowly nodded.

'That's where we're going, Solva. I'm taking you back to the fjord, back to our farm.'

'Is that what you want?'

Halfdan shrugged. 'First things first,' he replied. 'You don't belong here with this army of men.'

'No,' agreed Solveig.

'And I've been thinking,' Halfdan continued, 'on the way home, we'll be able to see that carver you've told me about.'

'Oleg!' exclaimed Solveig, at once fingering the violet-and-grey stone hanging round her neck. 'Oh! Wait until you see his workshop.'

A bulky figure cast his shadow over Solveig and her father, and they both looked up.

'Ah!' said Halfdan. 'Edwin.'

'May I?' asked the Englishman, and without waiting for an invitation he flopped down beside them.

'We were talking about home,' Halfdan informed him. 'Going home. Solveig was telling me about the carver in Ladoga.'

'I'll be able to see him again,' enthused Solveig. 'The first time I met Oleg was in his workshop. Then we met in the market. And when we said farewell, he told me, "Those who meet twice meet three times."'

'Very true,' Edwin agreed.

'Edith thought he looked like an elf. Oh!' Solveig clapped her right hand over her mouth.

'What?' asked Edwin.

'Edith!' cried Solveig. 'Will I see her? And her baby?'

'Kata,' Edwin reminded her.

'In Kiev?'

Edwin permitted himself a flicker of a smile. 'Maybe,' he said. 'Who can tell?'

Solveig turned round and looked at him, and the Englishman smiled so broadly she could see all his jackrabbit teeth.

'Time conceals,' he observed. 'Time reveals.'

'All these time sayings,' said Solveig.

'All things have their season,' Halfdan intoned.

'Ah!' exclaimed Edwin. 'Christian words! I'm glad to hear them.'

Halfdan grunted.

'A time for slaying and a time for healing,' Edwin continued. 'A time for weeping and a time for laughing; a time for grieving and a time for dancing. A time for loving and a time for hating.'

Sometimes, thought Solveig, I do both at the same time. I hate Harald for his trickery and cruelty, especially for the way he treated Maria, and yet I think part of me does still love him.

'And a time to arrive!' Edwin added. 'Nico says we'll reach Saint Gregorios the day after tomorrow.'

'Already?' cried Solveig. 'And Sineus will be there?'

'Unless he's hopped away,' Edwin replied.

Solveig lowered her eyes and half smiled. She could see his foot pinioned by a Pecheneg arrow.

'I could help you to get him back to Kiev,' she offered. 'I'll help to look after him.'

'Sineus's left foot turned green.' Edwin told Halfdan. 'The monk-doctor on Saint Gregorios had to saw his leg off at the knee.'

Once Nico had safely steered their ship across the Black Sea to the many mouths of the great river, the Danube, the spirits of everyone aboard rose, and many of the guards began to sing. Songs raucous, boasting, bold, brutal, witty, rude, songs tender, full of hope and longing . . .

Just like they are, thought Solveig. All those things and more, mixed up. Fighting men, they're mongrels!

Then the south-west wind ballooned their maroon sail. The Viking ship swept round the coast, and north into the wide estuary of the River Dnieper.

When Solveig sighted the island of Saint Gregorios late on the next afternoon, one memory after another swarmed through her mind.

Bergdis and her grisly bracelet of bones . . . her ghastly filleting knife . . . Edith about to die . . . Red Ottar's funeral pyre . . . the chanting, the acrid smoke . . .

Solveig realised her hot heart was fluttering. She felt breathless.

On Saint Gregorios, the approaching Viking ship had not gone unnoticed.

The gilded vane on her prow gleamed in the blue hour, and on two sticks a man swung himself down to the scruffy quay. A young woman with pink cheeks accompanied him. Her glistening dark hair was flapping over her face, and she was carrying something.

The woman began to wave, and the man leaned on one stick and pointed the other to Asgard.

Solveig peered through the gathering gloom. 'Sineus,' she said. 'It is!'

Then the boat closed with the quay, and there was a rumpus aboard as some of the oarsmen hauled down the sail, while others guided the boat towards the jetty.

'It can't be!' cried Solveig. 'Oh, it is! It is! It's Edith, and her baby.'

Solveig raised both arms. She reached out across the water.

Then, still half enveloped in the folds and waves of the great sail, she turned round to Edwin, demanding, 'Why didn't you tell me?'

But like a go-between, a man of secrets, an occasional magician, the substantial Englishman had disappeared.

Solveig held Edith in her arms, Edith held Solveig, and the little baby was cradled tight between them.

The two young women sobbed and laughed for joy, they laughed and sobbed again.

'Let me see!' gulped Solveig. 'Let me see. Oh, Kata! Kata! You have Red Ottar's eyes.'

The Vikings rowed towards the roaring cataracts. Between soaring granite cliffs, they dragged their ship through Strok, where the Pecheneg arrow had pierced Red Ottar's windpipe. Slowly they worked their way past the Boiler, past White Wave. Assisted by the same hairy wild men who had helped Red Ottar and his crew only six months before, they portaged their boat on pine rollers around the lashing cataract known as Ever-Fierce, Ever-Raucous, Impassable.

As the oarsmen bent their backs and drove the ship

upstream towards Kiev, Solveig sat beside the mast and, with her baby cocooned and cradled in a wooden box, Edith sat beside her.

'I wanted Kata, once in her life, to come to the place where her father . . . rose,' the young Englishwoman explained.

Then Solveig remembered the solemn words Edith had uttered, standing beside Red Ottar's funeral pyre on Saint Gregorios and placing her hands over her womb: 'Now and in days to come, you're with me, quick and dead.' She recalled the words each of the crew had chanted after singing Red Ottar's praises: 'He rises to you, he rises, and we must remember him.'

After a while, Halfdan joined the two young women. He and Edith watched as Solveig began to incise runes on the blade of bone – eagle-stripped, frost-bleached, the shoulder blade she had found on the battlefield at Stiklestad.

'What are you cutting?' asked Edith.

'Life-runes,' said Solveig, without looking up.

> *Life of life*
> *I hold you*
>
> *I'll shape you*
> *I'll name you*
>
> *Rough and smooth*
> *I'll sing-and-say you*

'Sing-and-say you,' Halfdan repeated. 'Rough and smooth, I'll sing-and-say you. Was that it?'

Solveig nodded.

In her makeshift cradle, Kata began to wail, and her mother lifted her out and rocked her.

'Life and new life,' said Halfdan, looking at them rather fondly.

'Soon she'll be needing the ring you carved for her,' Edith told Solveig. Then she got to her feet and padded along the deck towards the stern.

'She's carrying the word,' Solveig murmured, and she smiled a lingering smile.

The leader of the Vikings was standing on his own in the bows, staring upstream. And Land-Ravager, mounted and unfurled, was yapping and snapping beside him.

Copper and saffron crocus. Little crimson dots and crosses.

Solveig recalled Empress Zoe's words: 'Prayers are sewn into it, spells are stitched into it. For as long as it flies before you, you'll come to no harm in battle.'

Oh, Harald, she thought. Harald. Harald Sigurdsson. So icy. So fiery. So proud. Yes, so grand.

Halfdan reached out and put a hand on Solveig's wrist.

'One day, Solva, one day we'll be fishing.'

'Early spring,' said Solveig, 'when the sun's growing stronger.'

'And the days are growing longer,' added Halfdan. 'Up the fjord.' He squeezed Solveig's left hand, and she dipped her head until her golden hair was brushing his chest.

'Just you and me,' her father said in a gruff voice.

Like our brooch, thought Solveig. Harald's gift. A skiff with an oblong sail. Two people sitting in it. That man in the bows – man or god. And the smaller one in the stern. Arms outstretched.

'It's safe, you know,' she said, and she patted her grubby canvas bag.

Halfdan nodded. 'That gold brooch – it's sailed as far as we have.'

Solveig looked up at her father. 'I've worked something out,' she said.

Her father waited.

'What he would have wanted.'

Halfdan frowned.

'Tamas gave his life for me . . .' Solveig gazed at her father. 'I must always live to the utmost. Each waking day. Less than that, and I dishonour him.'

Halfdan grunted. 'Not so easy.'

'I know,' said Solveig.

'This is what we'll do,' Halfdan told her. 'We'll lash your blade of bone to the mast. There! Above Land-Ravager.'

Solveig pursed her lips.

'A bone-banner. It casts no spells. It makes no promises. No, it's a wing – a wing of memory – and it's an undertaking to live to the utmost. It is life's song itself.'

'Father!' cried Solveig, and she leaned right into him.

'Yes, Solva,' her father resumed, 'one day we'll be fishing and the codfish will be rising. And I'll say to you, "Your journey, your great journey, it must seem like a dream."'

'Life of life,' breathed Solveig. Eager. Unblinking.

'Like a dream. Like a story.'

Solveig smiled. 'It is a story,' she said.

Author's Note and Acknowledgements

When I was young, I walked alone
and so I soon lost my way.
But when I found friends I felt rich.
Each of us needs and delights in others.

So says the author of the collection of Viking proverbs known as *Hávamál*, or 'Words of the High One', and so say I!

The writing of a novel is always a matter of teamwork, and I'm lucky and grateful to be surrounded by a force field, if that's the term, of friends and peers who have supported me with their interest, and the sheer warmth of their response to *Bracelet of Bones*: Kate Agnew, Marilyn Brocklehurst, Gabrielle Cliff-Hodges, Paul Dowswell, Judith Elliott, Geoffrey Findlay, Catherine Fisher, Cherry Gilchrist, Sandra Glover, Tricia Henry, the 28 History Girls, Judith Jesch, Roy Mitchell, Ian Mortimer, the Munday family, Philip Pullman, Philip Reeve, Robert Rickett, the Ring family, Rachel Rivett, Lawrence Sail, Francesca Simon, Ray Speakman, Mary Steele, Morag Styles, Fiona Waters, Sian Williams.

But of course some people have given more specific help. Hemesh Alles has drawn the splendid map, and this is the sixth time we have worked together. Richard Barber has lent me precious books on Byzantium, and Helen Barber presented me with the superb cloth-bound publisher's dummies in which I have been writing these Viking Sagas, by hand as always, with my old Waterman pen. Gary Breeze brought here to Chalk Hill his exquisite model of a Viking trading boat; Lynda Edwardes-Evans and I discussed Solveig's character and she introduced me to the fiction of Paul Watkins; Will Wareing's enthusiasm has sustained me, and he alerted me to Tim Severin's Viking adventures. And at Quercus, I've been fully supported by Roisin Heycock, Sarah Lilly, Niamh Mulvey, Alice Hill, Margot Weale, Margaret Histed and my exceedingly sharp-eyed copy editor, Talya Baker.

This leaves me with my utterly crucial 'home team'. As before, Twiggy Bigwood – the only person in the world fully able to read my handwriting – has typed and retyped many versions of this novel, offered judicious editorial advice and regularly researched matters and issues such as horse-whispering, boat construction and Viking insults. My wife, Linda, meanwhile, has once again engaged with successive drafts at every level – character, interaction, situation, tension, language – and has been unfailing in her belief and support.

In much the same way as my novel *Gatty's Tale* was ignited by Gatty's blithe assumption that Jerusalem was just up the road, and that she could walk there instead of going to Ludlow Fair, the driving force of *Scramasax* is Solveig's expectation that she can easily fit into the hard-bitten, masculine world of a Viking army.

What was it actually like, I asked myself, to live the life of a young woman aboard ship, under canvas, laying siege to Saracen hill towns? This question, of course, soon precipitated many more. What excites Solveig? And must she simply accept what appals her? Is she wrong to ask difficult questions? Is her father the man she thought he was? Why do people fight? What is it to be a leader, and what is power?

Can you love and hate at the same time? 'Is there no room in our ranks for pity,' Solveig asks herself, 'or for grief? Is a man less of a man if he allows himself such feelings?'

How, then, is Solveig to remember all those who have died – Vikings, Byzantines and Saracens alike? And how is she to honour the one who died for her?

Chalk Hill, Burnham Market
May 2012

Word List

abaya   (Arabic) a black cloak-like dress, covering the whole body, worn by Muslim women

Allah   (Arabic) the chief Muslim name for God, who has three thousand names

aurochs   an extinct species of wild ox

Byzantine   (adjective) of Byzantium or Constantinople

coble   a rowing boat or sea-fishing boat with a flat bottom and square stern

dhimmis   (Arabic) Jews and Christians (also known as *People of the Book*). Islamic law decreed tolerance for them

dromon   a very large ship used both in war and commerce

elver   a young eel

etesian   a north-west Mediterranean wind that blows in July and the first half of August

fjord   a long, narrow sleeve of the sea reaching inland, often between banks or cliffs

geyser   a hot spring

hijab   (Arabic) scarf or veil worn by Muslim
               women

karv   a ship used for trading and war with
               between 13 and 16 pairs of oars

knarr   a merchant ship about fifty feet (sixteen
               metres) long

lateen sail a triangular sail suspended at 45° to the
               mast

Miklagard   the Old Norse word for Constantinople
               or Byzantium

Morning Star the planet Venus, which can be seen just
               west of the sun before sunrise. In the
               northern world, it was also known as
               Aurvandil

nomisma   (Greek) a 24-carat gold coin, the standard
               currency in the Byzantine Empire. (It was
               first minted by Constantine and called in
               Latin the *solidus*)

ousiai   a warship with a crew of about 110,
               including 50 or more fighting men

pyx   a small box for consecrated bread

shrithing   moving in a sinuous way (a word derived
               by the author from the Anglo-Saxon
               scriþan)

skute   a small, light merchant ship

stringers	longitudinal pieces of wood used to reinforce a boat's hull, to lock the thwarts and strengthen the gunwale
tamarisk	an evergreen shrub with slender feathery branches and scaly leaves
Varangian	a Viking mercenary in the service of the Emperors of Byzantium